S P ROWELL

Woodrush Towers

First published by Rowell Publishing in 2018

First Edition

ISBN: 978-1-9996641-1-4

This book was professionally typeset on Reedsy.
Find out more at reedsy.com

Contents

Chapter 1

Danial quickstepped it past Booze and News as he saw the two-legged arse-hanger-outers banging on the inch-thick divide between shopkeeper and customer. Head down; he'd made it back without his nightly brain blocker.

Legs crossed, his right foot twitched to the harmony of foreign voices reverberating through the thin dividing wall between flats.

A mixture of tiredness and speed of standing had stars dancing across emulsion painted walls. Trapped as the people he worked with, he took two paces to the sink and pulled out the whiskey bottle. It sloshed below the label. Should be enough to slow the cogs from turning.

Filling the mug halfway with tea, he topped up the rest with cheap spirit and flopped back in the single sofa chair to play the *guess who shouts next* game with his neighbours. He'd counted at least three children and two adult voices inside the two-bedroom flat. From what he could make of the bellowing male voice, they were a Latvian family. The police carted off the last tenants two weeks prior, and the conveyer belt of unsavoury neighbours continued.

Vibrating, distorted laughter through the dividing wall had him guessing which channel his neighbours were watching. His mind drifted between the crazies he worked with, whether he'd be alone forever, and his next shift. Clasping his hands together, index fingers on both, pointed at the wall, he fired two shots before blowing his nails. He'd always dreamed of being a secret agent, smart and mysterious, women hanging on like groupies at a pop concert. Instead, he would carry on being the lanky streak of piss they said he was.

His flat was the smartest shithole anyone could wish to own. At least he owned it, unlike the rest of the building, which housed every drug dealer and drunk in the neighbourhood.

The estate agent had performed verbal miracles in assuring him that it would be quiet. The floor only had two flats and a shared landing. Danial maintained it after the maintenance company ended their contract due to the amount of abuse the staff had suffered, along with regular equipment theft.

Folding his uniform, ready for the graveyard shift, he thought about staying up, as he knew sleep wasn't going to come easy today. Bumbling his way to the bedroom, he sat on the edge of the bed. Sandwiched book spines on the shelf across the room looked smooth to the eye; just how he liked it.

Rubbing his fingers counterclockwise around his temples, Danial felt his head lighten. He tried to stand, but fell back onto the bed. The row of books blurred into one as his head trembled. Everything was shaking; for a moment, he thought he was levitating, as the bed lifted from the ground, forcing his long legs to stretch further, allowing his feet to touch the floor. He scrambled to the centre of the bed and bounced, hoping his weight would bring it down; his mind not comprehending what was going on, visions of an earthquake, the building collapsing, the neighbours being terrorists and setting a bomb off next door, but the room was silent. The thudding in his head and his rapid heartbeat against his chest rang through him like the one-man band guy he sometimes saw on the high street. The ceiling was fast approaching. Eyes scrunched tight; he spread himself flat. The tip of his nose touched plaster. He looked through his eyelashes at the flat, smooth ceiling. A rasping intake of breath and thoughts of being crushed widened his eyes. Like a fairground thrill ride reaching its highest point, the bed dropped, propelling him off the mattress and onto the floor, missing the bedside unit as he fell into a half-roll. Dazed, he stumbled to his feet and walked over to the window. The blackout blinds snapped open as he pulled the plastic cord. Although not visible, the sun was setting, casting a shadow on the two multi-storey flats facing his. The old drunk sat out on his section of wall next to the vandalised phone box. Everything seemed normal.

The wooden frame of his favourite canvas picture cracked as he stepped back, sending a sharp pain through the sole of his foot. The whole room was a mess. Lounge was the same. He was a minimalist, after all, but the few possessions he had were now lying on the carpet, broken and out of place. The upturned settee hid what had once been a nest of tables. The TV had moved, cable stretched to the snapping point with the plug still fixed to the socket. Pots, pans, and two plates had left their place under the sink, now spread across the tiled floor.

He paced the floor, rubbing his eyes, hoping what he was seeing was a figment of his imagination; a chemical reaction from whiskey-infused tea.

Something rubbed against his ankles. He looked down, blinking in disbelief.

"Smoke!" He ran back to the bedroom, then to the bathroom and back to the lounge. "What the hell's going on?" He flung a cushion aside; flameless smoke drifted from the sofa. Fearing the building was on fire, he went for the door, but fell as his feet remained grounded. Trying in vain to release his feet from the grip of the yellow, fog-like substance that now covered his hands and his rear, he sat powerless against its grip. Like a thousand tongues, it licked at his flesh as it crawled over his legs, arms, and waist. He screamed until the scream was only the sound of air being forced from tired lungs. With laboured breath, he shouted, "Help me!" As he did, the yellowish fog released its sticky hold and disappeared under the bedroom door.

Eyes fixed on the closed door, he backed away until his heel hit the upturned TV. Speckles of sweat joined together above his brow. Squinting as the salted pool found his right eye, he blinked to the rhythm of a pounding fist. He froze. The thuds fired in quick sets of three. Without moving, he shouted, "Who is it?!" Three pounding thuds struck. He swung the door open, half-expecting to see a fireman. A man, half-naked, gut hanging over a pair of union jack boxer shorts, scowled.

"Why are you making so much noise? I have child asleep," he said in broken English.

"Er, sorry for that, must've been the earthquake. Did you see the smoke?"

His neighbour's face grew redder with every word, "No earthquake, only you make too much noise." Danial shook his head. The man mumbled something upon entering his flat. The moment passed, and with it, the opportunity to confront his neighbour about the noise that had kept him awake from the time they'd arrived. He closed the door and looked around the room at the mess that lay before him.

The overturned coffee table had three legs fixed to the base; the bookshelf lay face-down, its contents scattered with broken spines, and the kettle was missing.

Stilted glances, eyes darting, he said, "Where the hell is the kettle?"

He fell into the TV chair. Head in hands, Danial's eyes flitted between the bedroom door and the wall clock. The second hand completed a full circuit. Every tick shouted for him to open it. He needed to open it and get dressed. He was on the graveyard shift tonight. That's what his workmate Jim had called it, not because they worked in a graveyard, but because it was quieter when they were all sleeping, and those who attempted suicide chose the dead of night after the lockdown.

Taking a deep breath, he counted to three, then lunged at the door with the full intention of swinging it open, but stopped short. His hand refused to grip the door handle. Stepping back again, this time raising his right leg, he brought his foot down on the handle and pushed. Hopping back, he stumbled and fell onto the coffee table, breaking the three remaining legs.

The foggy substance had vanished, but the mess remained. Danial cursed for acting like a wimp. The words *lanky streak of piss* rang through his mind. Not in *his* voice, but the voice of Cane Fisher, and the countless kids that'd rag dolled him through the playground and later, the people he worked with, who would mutter those same words behind his back. He tried thinking through the craziness of what'd happened. He found the missing kettle that'd become wedged between the fridge and the side of the worktop and placed it back on its base. The mess disturbed him. The TV was flat on its broken face. There was no time to check the news for earthquakes, or even to take a shower. Snatching his clothes out of the bedroom with unsteady hands, he dressed in record time.

Danial dreaded firsts. Always had. Today, he'd had a year's quota from the walk past the off-licence to the events in his flat.

He closed the door with a click, trying not to disturb the fat man next door, even though he felt like slamming it as hard as he could. With his nerves still shattered, he figured that he would have his revenge later, knowing full well that if he saw him again, he would more than likely give him a polite wave to avoid any confrontation.

There was a scrunched-up sleeping bag in the lobby area, and warm air emitting from the heater above the automatic doors made it move, as if a disjointed person was inside. Maybe there was; he'd learned over the years not to look or pay undue attention to anything that didn't concern him, as there were always repercussions.

The wino who sat next to the phone box was friendly enough; always seemed happy, but he couldn't recall a time when he hadn't been sitting in that same spot. Night or day. Must sleep somewhere; must have to leave to buy his wine. His mind was racing, the state of his flat causing as much anxiety as the event itself. He'd get to the bottom of it. Had to, he thought, as he walked around the corner.

Looking at his wrist, he noted the time. Not due in for an hour and three-quarters. The pub across the road was filling fast; the evening rabble going in as the day-drinkers stumbled out. He'd never been inside, but he could imagine that the smell of alcohol and vomit and the bravado of the regulars wouldn't be his cup of tea.

After years of continual damage to his car, he now parked it away from the flats, but this meant a walk, and not a pleasant one. Better to walk than face a repair bill, though.

Danial circled his car under the brightness of the only reliable street lamp. No damage, nothing was broken. A purple streak of bird dropping on the back window was added during the night. A lucky omen? Still shaking, he got in, locked the doors, fastened the seatbelt, and sighed at the thought of returning home after the long shift ahead of him.

Arriving with plenty of time to spare, he was torn between entering and having his first cup of tea or staying outside in the hopes that clarity would bless his tired mind. Danial decided to delay the tea, calm down, and compose himself... or risk being reprimanded by the management team for not being fit for service.

The only stretch of grass ran around the perimeter of the car-park, so that would have to do. Counting the anorexic-looking silver birches, all five of his foot lengths apart, he stopped halfway around and took a deep breath. Telling himself to think, self-talk not working, his temples throbbed, half-due to not having any sleep and half-due to what had happened back at the flat.

Dragging his legs and shaking each foot before placing it in front of the other, trying to motivate them, he arrived back where he'd started, facing the double green security gates that would hold him captive until the next day. There were two to get through. The first he had keys for, the second required him and the century on duty to open it alongside.

The giant clock face stood centre to the two large turrets like a medieval castle. He sometimes fantasised that he was of that era; returning from battle, bloody and battered, but victorious. The truth is that by entering the building, he was entering a battle of a different kind.

Chapter 2

Security cameras mounted atop tall metal poles covered all angles inside and outside the grounds. A glint of moonlight on the left tower cast a stretched shadow over barbed fencing. Menacing charcoal clouds hovering overhead gave a haunted appearance to Woodrush Towers; a building already clouded in mystery. First built as a lunatic asylum for the criminally insane, the building was now a part of the NHS.

Danial was a good half hour early. Having made the same journey now for over twenty years, he'd always looked up at the same clock upon arrival, and he was always a half hour early, so he wasn't surprised, but took pleasure that his record of being on time remained intact.

Reaching into his jacket pocket, he pulled out the plastic security pass, placed it on the wall-mounted reader, and waited for the green light to appear, showing a successful scan. He'd never flown, but had seen programs showing airport security, and this looked no different. He slid off his jacket, placed his personals in the plastic tray, and watched as they glided down the pointless three-foot long runway on metal runners, through a scanner, and onto a steel table on the other side. After a padding-down by one of the security guards, he scooped up his belongings.

Walking the corridor of the damned was always an experience.

Danial Morris had named it that after the riot five years ago. It was as fresh in his mind today as it had been on that stormy night. A chill rattled his bones every time he walked the corridor. Thoughts of a zombie apocalypse disturbed his mind, and he was the sane one.

It was almost five years to the day when the inmates ran riot. Staff became overpowered by over fifty patients. He'd not had a full night's sleep since, always thinking of what he could have done. Could he have saved Jim Osbourne from his attacker? He'd been one of six in a six-person unlock; routine when dealing with one of the more dangerous inmates. They always followed protocol and asked the inmate to sit on his bed before unlocking the door. The patient only wanted a drink. Sedated, he showed little risk of displaying violence, but even for the most routine requests from a high-security inmate, they administered precautionary measures. Jim had been a big man and had the job of leaning into the room and placing the cold milk on the floor. The patient must have flown at him with the speed of a train, as he could only recall seeing Jim doing a forward roll into the room and the rain of punches that followed. Jim's bulk stopped the remaining five from being able to get a hold of the inmate.

Whenever Danial got close to that cell, he could still hear the squealing sound — the hiss of escaping air as the sharpened plastic spoon entered Jim's throat. He never told his colleagues about the noises he heard, fearing they'd send him home on medical grounds and consider him unfit for duty. Instead, he carried on, suppressing any thoughts to the far reaches of his mind.

After the attack, the remaining inmates on the assertive rehab ward who had the freedom to roam reacted. Security guards ran to offer help, and by doing so, panicked over twenty inmates awaiting their evening medication. Within minutes, anyone who wasn't locked down attacked guards, nurses, and each other, reaching for anything moveable. A snooker ball hit the large fish tank within the recreational area, releasing gallons of water, adding to the chaos as fish flapped around, gasping for air. Jim, on the upper wing, was also gasping for air, and losing consciousness. They overpowered the inmate; a little late, as Jim died before the paramedics arrived.

Ronny, the inmate, was still in the hospital. Danial Morris, the only remaining witness to the murder in this godforsaken place, still arrived a half hour early, and that's during an earthquake and on no sleep. The thought of this made him feel as mighty as if he had just returned from battle.

Since the riot, things had tightened up. Danial, along with his colleges and management, went on an eight-week training course. Everyone took a lengthy mental examination and trauma evaluation.

Inmates could turn on you as quick as look at you, with no more reason than a biscuit had fallen into a cup of tea or the toilet roll needed changing. Resisting the urge to befriend individual patients after working with them for so long could be difficult. Len was different in more ways than one, but not dangerous. He always made Danial laugh, and was a gentleman at heart. Len always cooperated with him, and at the time of the riot, he had helped two staff members escape before being overpowered by his fellow patients.

He knew he shouldn't engage with inmates of any description on a personal level, but he had a strange respect for Len; not only because he had helped with the control of the other inmates during the riot and saved his life, but because he was very likeable and witty. No matter what mood he was in, he could rely on the few minutes they spent together to bring a smile to his face. Len would either tell him a joke or say something thought-provoking, which always seemed to fit the way he felt. It was as if he knew just by looking what to say for the few seconds they were together.

The hospital was like a game of snakes and ladders, with inmates moving wards depending on their state of mind and the effectiveness of their rehabilitation program. When Len arrived five years ago, he remained on the high-dependency ward for three of them before being moved straight to the rehabilitation ward, where he was allowed to roam free within its confines. Danial had thought this strange, as he'd never seen an inmate move to the free man's ward, where inmates could walk around while under constant supervision. Two weeks later, without reason, he was back on high-dependence. In all his years of service, he'd never seen a patient moved back without first inflicting harm on a member of staff or themselves.

The inmate's crimes were as diverse as their personalities, ranging from arson to torture, and including rape and murder. Unlike a prison sentence, the individual had no release date and little to look forward to. Why Len was there when his medical records showed no sign of mental incompetence or criminal charges, God only knew. Well, not God, but *someone* knew, and Danial'd spent the last year trying to find out but had always ended up drawing a blank or being guided down a dead end by anyone he approached.

The suits only visited two inmates; Len was one of them. They tested them. Danial had only come to this conclusion after overhearing one of them say that the tests on this subject were going nowhere.

Insisting they be alone with Len without the aid of guards or nurses aroused his suspicions. When he questioned their motives and the reason for the cameras and intercom being turned off, his superiors said the order came from the highest ranks, and not to ask questions. Never had there been so much interest and secrecy surrounding an inmate.

Wanting to know why turned into a need to know how they could get away with bypassing every rule in the book. Reaching dead ends, never being told the truth, Danial approached the most senior governor he could find. With an underlying hidden threat, the governor asked if he wanted to remain a valued employee. And if so, then he should stop asking questions. Everything was a need-to-know.

Who were these people?

He was sure they were not the police and weren't trained to deal with mental health issues. From his years of training, that much he knew.

After booking in, he checked the medicine distribution charts and patient's comments for who he was in charge of that night. Flicking through notes attached to the plastic clipboard, he saw Len on his watch list. On the one hand, he had H wing, which held the most severe cases within the prison. These he had never gotten used to, even after his years of service. But on the other, he had Len on the wing, who had a knack for making all those around him calm. *Should be interesting,* he thought, packing his belt with unnecessary weaponry. Unnecessary because they were all on lockdown, and if left alone in a room with one of them, he knew he wouldn't stand a chance without backup.

A few guards would use the baton to intimidate, running it along walls or banging it on the door of a disruptive inmate. Not that that ever worked, but it made the guard feel in control of

12

the situation until the team turned up with sedatives.

Jacket on, he looked at his watch and noticed he still had time for a cuppa and a catch-up with anyone still in the staff room.

Bill sat alone with a copy of yesterday's newspaper stretched out on the table. Danial wanted – no, *needed* to tell someone about the events leading up to him getting to work. Knowing the story would fly around the prison, he bit his lip and made his way to the sink.

"Your friend has been asking after you. Keeps asking whether you made it into work and if you're okay because of what happened to you before you left the flat."

Danial's nostrils flared as he drew breath. He delayed looking around to where Bill sat. Stroking his tightening throat, he shivered like a bucket of ice was being poured over his head. Numbness rendered him unable to speak or move from the sink.

Laughing, Bill told him that Len, his only friend, was inquiring about his well-being. Danial wanted to punch him in the nose but knew it would do no good. He'd get him sacked – or worse, arrested. That'd make his day. Only, Danial was wise to his attempts at sarcasm, and didn't play his game. Instead, he sat on a plastic, director-style chair positioned in the far corner.

Bill's comment had spooked him. How could Len know what had happened? Flicking through the rota, Len was the third person on his call list. Forcing a smile that dampened into a frown, he looked down the page to the section saying who shared his shift. After all that had happened tonight, Bill was the last person he wanted as a partner. He had to see Len, alone. Len would never tell him how he knew about tonight's events with Bill, the walking ego, by his side.

What was he thinking? How could he know what had

happened at the flat? Well, he *was* in the loony bin, as Bill would point out every time he'd defended him as a regular person. Could be a guess, or just Bill misinterpreting Len's kindness in asking after him. Throwing the last few dregs into the sink, Danial arranged the mugs on the stand to show the most used at the top, down to the least used. The chipped ones he hurled into the swing bin.

Avoiding conversation with Bill while walking the corridors wasn't difficult. Bill always did the talking, with Danial acknowledging him from time to time so as not to appear rude. An occasional nod of his head, followed by an, "Um, yeah," seemed to do the trick, and had gotten him through many a night.

How he'd love to put him in his place and tell him what he thought. In his mind, he'd spat words so fierce, they'd pinned him to the smooth grey walls many times, but the words never surfaced and transpired into speech. He told himself that one day, he would pluck up the courage to let loose on him, and after, he would see that girl. There was always one hanging off the arm of the arrogant sod who didn't deserve to be with the women who were only a trophy to him.

Flicking through the patient rota, Bill saw that Len was next on the list of nightly visits. Danial was counting down the rooms and knew this already but hadn't gotten rid of Bill. Shouldn't have been difficult, with him being a senior staff member, but he also knew of the two-staff-per-floor rule that had been enforced in the last meeting. A silly rule, when the patients were locked away and couldn't leave their rooms even if they wanted to.

He suggested continuing on his own. Bill raised his eyebrows. "Not like you to break the rules."

Sweating as he approached Len's room, he turned to Bill and served him a dish of sarcasm by suggesting that if the doors were to fly open, he would be sure to radio it in to him. Bill's glare unnerved Danial, but there was no way of retracting the comment. With little more than a shrug of his thick shoulders, Bill walked off, but couldn't resist hitting back as he looked down at his clipboard. "I see— a palm reading. Should have just said."

Smiling through gritted teeth, Danial watched as the last bit of his bulk disappeared around the corner. He looked down at his watch and knew why Bill was so obliging. He let out a long sigh. 10:55 PM, only five minutes before the evening meeting. He'd forgotten all about it, and that wasn't like him. He was always the first in and the last out, so tonight would prove to be another first.

Chapter 3

The eye-level door flap squeaked open. Pressed up against it, Len's wide eyes startled him. Flinching, Danial jolted his head back.

"BOO!"

Unamused by his dry sense of humour, Danial didn't smile back.

"Len, I need to talk to you, but I haven't much time."

Tilting his head, Len spoke in a voice that was deeper than usual.

"You want to know what happened."

Danial nodded in agreement. His right eye twitched. It always twitched when he was nervous.

Len's penetrating gaze made him feel giddy and relaxed, as if under hypnosis.

"I fear you're not ready for the truth. The phenomena you saw takes more than a few minutes to explain. But unlike the rest who have taken retirement, left due to stress-related issues, and never returned, I know you will cope. He's testing you. Playing games with your mind. Stay strong."

With his back arched, looking through the hatch, he watched Len walk over to his bed and sit cross-legged facing the wall.

"Who's testing me, what's going on, and how do you know?"

"You're late for the meeting. How do I know? Because you

always attend the evening meeting, and don't worry, staying positive is like a knife in his gut."

The silent ward confirmed his lateness to the meeting. He'd gained nothing from Len.

On his way down the spiral staircase, his inner voice questioned him, questioning Len's ability to know anything useful. *Bill could've mentioned something. Len could have twisted Bill's words. It's unlike Len to play games. He always tells truths; considers others' feelings. A genuinely nice guy. For a nut case. Christ, I sound like Bill.*

His heart banged, and his face felt molten. Standing at the closed office door, Danial felt liberated for being late for the first time in his career. His hand knocked thin air, missing the door by a hair. Len's words rang through his head: *Stay positive.* He was the longest-serving member of staff, he'd never been late before, and was always early to meetings. He repeated the words before entering without knocking, half-thinking he'd already done so. Focusing on the shine from his toe-capped shoes, he shuffled past an entourage of dark trousers. He'd worn the same style of shoe since leaving school. Having joined the high dependency hospital as an office assistant-cum-mobile drinks machine, in business terms, he'd climbed the ranks. His awkwardness towards others had stayed with him the whole time.

Sitting in the second row from the back, next to a newbie with the looks of a centrefold, he slid her red handbag toward her and continued to look at his shoes.

"Ah, Mr Morris. Glad you found your way here," said the new manager.

Looking up, Danial gave a little smile in response and wondered just how long this one would last. Since the riot, he had lost count of how many managers had stood in that exact place, in front of the same Formica folding table.

"Where's your floor buddy?" he asked, avoiding Danial as he looked around the room. "We all know to check the corridors in pairs." His voice juddered with laughter and was peppered with self-importance.

A tut of disapproval came from the woman next to him, and he was sure that she was tutting at the git in front, and not at him. He glanced at her before returning his gaze down to his shoelaces without responding to comments about lost partners.

"Or was Len Happy convincing you that unicorns are real again?"

His snide voice joined laughter from everyone in the room apart from the person sitting on his left. Lucy Day.

He spent the rest of the meeting trying to understand why a woman with the looks of a model and the grace of a princess would choose to work alongside a load of hairy blokes and butch women. He'd overheard Bill and his cronies talking about her, saying how her file stated single female. He almost butted in when one of them said she must be a lesbian. Almost.

"So, I hope you all agree with the new plans, and will follow them for the benefit of the team," was the only thing that'd sunk in as they all stood.

Bill bumbled over to Danial and raised his eyebrows at Lucy as she bent.

"So, what do you think of him, then?" Bill asked, including Lucy in the question as she turned to face them.

"Think of?" Danial looked at him, blank-faced.

"You'd be better off sitting with me in the next meeting," Bill said.

Danial edged his way past plastic chairs over to the sink. The array of crusty, biscuit-filled cups wouldn't clean themselves. He didn't have to, but he couldn't continue his shift knowing they were laying in the sink, festering.

The room had cleared; all but Lucy, whom he hadn't noticed standing behind him.

"What did you think about the new changes?" she asked. "What's your name again?"

"Danial," he said, wiping bony fingers down the side of his shirt as if he was going to shake hands, then settling instead for putting them on his hips. Shocked that she was speaking to him, and not knowing how to answer, having taken nothing in at the meeting, he stuttered.

"W-W-What do you think?"

"Not been here long enough to know any different, but he seems to know what's best. I'm on the open ward tonight."

"That's good," he said, turning back to the pots in the sink.

"See you later, then."

The door clicked shut. If the coffee cup could talk, it would say, *Danial's just blown away a chance to talk to her for the rest of the night.*

Flinging the tea towel down, he pushed through the door, intent on catching up to her, but ran into Bill coming in instead.

"Finished playing housemaid yet? There's work to do."

Hesitating, he snatched the tea towel and hung it on the rail before turning back to Bill. He stood a good foot taller than Bill. A good foot taller than *most* people, always looking down or seeing them stretch their necks to look up at him. If only he'd agreed to that management position. Then it would be him telling Bill where to go. Not that he was a lower rank, but due to his years of service, he should demand more respect.

"You even listening?" Bill asked, arching his neck back.

"Er, yes, let's see." Danial flicked through the paper on the clipboard.

"We're on ward fifteen," Bill said, before Danial found the right page. "You all right? You're weirder than normal."

Rubbing his eyes, Danial said, "Got little sleep, that's all."

"That's because you need to move out of the ghetto, mate. That's why you're not sleeping," Bill said. "You're not worried about doing ward fifteen, are you? If—"

"I'm fine with it."

Although Bill showed genuine concern for him, he never knew when the next wisecrack was coming. Could tonight get any better? Ward fifteen. Ronny's ward. Separated from others, he was given a ward after the riot; only a select few were allowed to enter it. Danial was one of the select few, and he'd had first-hand experience with Ronny, who had been deemed too dangerous to be next to other inmates, even with a steel door separating him from the rest of them. Anyone put on that ward ended up committing suicide. Patients hanging themselves or self-harming to the point of bleeding to death wasn't a major event, and was put down to their illnesses, but never had they had so many on the same ward end their own lives rather than be within earshot of Ronny. A ward that had been intended to house nineteen high-dependent inmates now housed only one: Ronny.

Two teams of five would visit him tonight. Due to the workforce required for each visit, they had to get as much done as possible. Danial could object to seeing him, since he'd worked the night of the riot five years ago, but as anyone working that fateful night had now left on medical grounds or had received an NHS golden handshake, he felt obligated. Do it or face ridicule from the staff, as well as endless whispering that always ended just before he had the chance to make out the full sentence.

Two teams joined to make an eight-man, two-woman team. Lucy wasn't allowed to work the high-dependency wards, and only six of the ten had permission to see Ronny. Being the front man of a five-person entrance team, Danial waited for the other two pairs to position themselves. The two female guards stood at the entrance of the ward, and the other three stood in the middle of his team and the entrance team. Danial would administer the patient's medication with two guards who would restrain Ronny if he was unwilling to cooperate. Hatred had turned to pity for the thing sitting on its bed behind the steel door. Although he often saw the good in people no matter what their crime, Danial saw none in Ronny, not even a glimmer. He'd convinced himself that he was an animal; not human in any way.

Filling his lungs, Danial spoke with authority. "Turn around and walk to the far wall. Face the wall, hands behind back, palms open."

Danial watched as Ronny performed this without objection. Then, using a well-rehearsed hand signal and counting down from five, he entered the room with two other guards pressed to either side. Two more guards stood on either side of the open door, with extended batons out of view.

Danial knew his team would pile in at a moment's notice, like the ones protecting Jim—not that it had stopped Ronny from taking his life.

With the firmest voice, he reassured Ronny that he was there to help, and handcuffed his hands behind his back with a plastic tie.

"Now, sit back on the bed with your legs outstretched, feet pointing to the far wall."

He was glad that his repulsion for the man outweighed his fear of him. Hairless and scared, he looked less like a human and more like an egg. He calmed his nerves by thinking of him as a new-born baby, and then as Humpty Dumpty, which would explain the long scar that ran down his cheek. Anything to help him not think of this man for what he was—a monster.

Ronny sat without uttering a word, taking his medication without the need for restraint. Ten minutes later, with all tasks finished, Danial backed out. Ronny looked into his eyes, and for a split second, he thought he was ready to pounce on him, just as he had on Jim.

"Do you think I look like Humpty Dumpty?" he asked, in a low, deep voice that seemed to vibrate through Danial's every bone.

"Er, what-what did you say?" Danial's voice squeaked out the reply, his throat turning sandpaper-dry.

"You said it yourself, but you must know Humpty Dumpty wasn't an egg."

Pain spread across Danial's chest; the guards pulled at his arms. Dazed by Ronny's comments, he walked the long corridor with a blank mind until he reached the metal stairs that led to the lower dependency ward. Distracted by seeing Lucy helping a patient into his room, he almost missed a step. Turning, he saw the other nine following him down; Lucy looked up at the man who'd lead the ten-person operation and smiled.

As he reached the last few steps, Lucy walked up to him, blocking his route to the staff room.

"Mr Morris, what's he like? The man who never speaks?"

"Please, call me Danial."

"So, what's he like, Dan?"

"Well, like any other patient, only with higher dependency."

"They tell me he never speaks. Must be difficult dealing with such a man."

He braved a smile. She smiled back with a twinkle in her eye. The two female entrance guards slapped his back as they walked by, congratulating him on a job well done.

With Ronny's comments not registering as real—that he'd heard him speak for the first time—all faded into insignificance upon seeing Lucy.

Old Spice wafting across his shoulder, coupled with the clapping of chewing gum, eroded his newfound confidence.

"You can cancel Len's midnight sleep check tonight; he's got visitors coming."

Danial looked down as Bill forced a smile. "Visitors." He checked his notes. "I know not of any visitors. Who's seeing him?"

"It is the spirits of the night."

"The suits?"

"Da headless horseman, it is."

Danial checked his watch. 11:11 PM. He double-checked the rota—no visitors scheduled for tonight. No one, not even the governor himself, would visit a patient without an appointment.

He called out to Bill, who was heading into the gents. "Who's the visitor?"

"Came from the top, so no questions asked, I guess."

"Why the hell aren't we asking questions?!" Danial shouted back.

"Above our pay grade. Need a piss." The toilet door hissed before clicking shut.

Walking through the rehabilitation ward, Danial made his way to Len's room. Without knocking, he opened the hatch, but there was no Len. Bed made, the place looked tidy.

In a sudden swift motion, Len popped up from beneath the hatch.

"You're early!"

"God damn it, Len, you scared the shit out of me."

"Knock. Knock."

Not in any mood for games, Danial shook his head in dismay, but knew full well he needed to play along. The words came out as a sigh, more of a yawn than words.

"Who's there?"

"Question."

"Question who?"

"Me, of course. That's why you're here, so stop wasting time with all this, fire away, and I'll try to help you with the things you need to know."

Remaining silent, a dull throbbing started in Danial's temples.

"What's wrong, my friend?"

Danial scanned the corridor. A two-way male conversation came from inside the rec-room. He was alone and out of sight. The staff would be clock-watching until the midnight shift arrived, and the patients, including the ones on the rehabilitation ward, were locked down until six tomorrow. The high-dependency ward had scheduled accompanied breaks, while ward fifteen remained locked.

"Len, you have visitors. I don't know who. It could be the men in suits. They're coming at midnight, but no one will say why. So, we have little time."

Len combed his chin. "They might let me into your open prison," he said, with a smile that hit both of his earlobes.

"Sorry, what? What open prison?"

"Your open prison. The big, outside prison you call freedom." He twitched his nose and continued. "Like a cow roaming in the open moors. It feels free. The farmer standing out of sight eating his cold pasty knows it's just a cow let out to graze."

Danial knew the real reason he had broken the rules to be with Len; he felt compelled to find out more about these mysterious men.

"I checked your file. Your offence page is missing, and I don't have access to the computer files. I know it's wrong for me to ask, but what were you charged with, and who are the men who visit you and Ronny?"

Len frowned. "I helped them, and now I'm here, where they try to dissect my mind."

Wishing he hadn't asked, he checked his watch. 11:33.

"Len, what did you mean when you asked if I'd arrived to work when you spoke to Bill—I mean, Guard Pickman?"

He'd just broken another rule, albeit an unwritten one. Telling patients your first name was frowned upon, as it diminished the Guard's authority.

He waited for Len's response and watched as he combed his smooth, beardless chin.

"I felt something leave here and reach you. I feared for your safety; I know not what has happened to you, my friend."

"Who left here? What reached me?" He spoke fast; steel-toe-capped shoes drew nearer to where he stood.

"Vetala, an evil spirit who has taken the form of one of your inmates. He is playing with you, as he has so many others. He intends to use you for information or escape."

"Who is—?"

But they were interrupted by a voice echoing through the corridor.

"Danial, you should be on ward nine. We have a patient checking into room three, and we have a staff member missing."

Flummoxed, Danial called back, "Er, who's missing?"

"You are, you idiot!"

Bill came into view, shaking his head, then turned and walked away in the same direction.

Danial peered through the hatch, half-expecting Len to pop up from below, before seeing him perched on the foot of his single bed. He asked again what he meant by a spirit leaving the hospital, and what the suits wanted from him.

Sitting deep in thought, Len looked at bare plaster as if it was a portrait of a lost love. Danial waited, but every second felt like a minute. Conversing with an inmate on a ward he had no business being on was against the rules.

Len's neck cracked. Squinting, he turned to the hatch, as if seeing Danial for the first time. "The ones you call suits also know about Vetala and his abilities to feed on negativity. He's weak around me but grows stronger by the day. I've felt his presence ever since arriving here."

Danial knew he was hearing the ramblings of a madman. Maybe his dislike for Bill had blinded him from the truth. Was he walking the sanity tightrope between working and becoming a resident himself?

Footsteps echoed through the corridor.

"Len, I'll check on you later."

Placing a finger between the hatch, Danial slid it out, stifling the squeak of metal. Two suited men halted their conversation upon seeing him and stood to one side, waiting for Danial to pass. He shouldn't have been there, and they knew it.

Danial nodded. "All right?"

Stony faces watched as he walked past them. No hello or greeting came from either. Three hours to freedom. Freedom now had a different meaning after listening to Len.

Chapter 4

"Another attempted suicide." Arms flailing, Bill's hand hit the wall. "Why can't they ever get it right?"

Danial didn't answer. His mind whirled as he studied the ticking dial on his wrist. *Only another twenty minutes. See Len. This time, he can spill the beans on the suits and tell me—*

"Are you listening?"

"Er, yeah. Someone tried to top themselves again."

Bill rolled his eyes and left the canteen.

Danial had checked in the new patient; the so-called attempted suicide. Another transfer from a mainstream upcountry prison. This one tended to cut himself. Most sought attention, some wanted a transfer, and others were safer and better off under Danial's supervision. This one wanted a transfer. A futile suicide attempt had swung it with his mental health team. Danial had no respect for this kind of inmate and spent as little time as possible settling him into his room before returning to the staff room.

Alone, he made a mental list of questions—in less than ten minutes, he'd hit Len with them. Having tried the subtle approach, it was time for a more direct stance, knowing that Len would understand his desperation.

The kettle seemed to take longer than normal to boil. Looking up at the clock, Danial placed the tea bag into his glass mug; a mug that had been with him longer than any member of staff here at Woodrush Towers.

The door swung open. It was the senior manager. Danial had forgotten his name but recognised him as the man who stood behind the Formica table.

"You can get yourself off home now. Your midnight call's cancelled. And you don't look well. In fact, you look like shit."

"Shit!" Danial cried, as boiling water missed glass and sloshed across his hand. Scalding pain reached his elbow. His flinching hand knocked the mug, smashing it into hundreds of little glass bricks across the tiled floor.

"Wow, steady on, Danial." He reached for Danial's hand. Danial pulled away before returning it to the cold tap.

"I'll have to write a report in the medical book now."

Danial pulled his hand back from under the tap and held it out with his fingers spread.

"No, you don't, I'm fine. What do you mean—cancelled?"

"Two officials came with the paperwork a few minutes ago. It's legit. Authorised by the head office. Made the call myself."

Danial didn't intend to knock the manager into the door frame as he pushed through the gap. Not turning to apologise, he muttered the word, "Sorry," under his breath as he hurried over to Len's room. Could be another wind-up; Bill egging on the manager. He had seen no visitors, but with the new inmate arriving unannounced, they could have turned up early and slipped past unnoticed.

He took long strides toward the room. The heavy door stood open. Still not believing he'd gone, he rushed in and looked around the eight by six room. Gone! Danial looked through the yellow-painted window bars. He glimpsed Len getting into a black Range Rover. Two men, taller than Len, manhandled him into the backseat. He followed round taillights leaving the car park, heading toward the motorway. Now out of sight, Danial thought about taking the registration details, but didn't recall seeing the number plate; the red circled lights had been the only visible hint as to the car's make.

The door creaked behind him; he spun around at the sound. Bill filled the gap, loosening his stance upon seeing Danial's knotted expression. "Hey buddy, management wants me to tell you to go see them."

"Three days paid leave. That's what I get for being concerned about one of my patients," Danial said, searching for his lunch box.

"Looking for this?" Bill dangled the blue plastic lunch box from his index finger, pulling it away before handing it over.

"They give you time off, then? I'd say it's a good thing. You take time off and relax. If you don't, you might end up in here. If you get my drift."

Danial got his *drift* all right. And maybe the break would do him good. He'd worked nine days straight, and the three days would only add an extra day to the two he was already due.

Turning the corner into Brampton Road, he looked up at the grey building he'd called home for the past six years. The aftermath of the earthquake was waiting for him—if it *was* an earthquake. He hadn't investigated further than asking Len. A pulse of anger quivered his top lip upon thinking about the fat man in boxers accusing him of making the noise.

Stepping over a filled sleeping bag, tufts of matted hair sticking out of the side of the zip-hole, a strong smell of whiskey and piss hit his nostrils as he sped up two flights of stairs. The Yucca stood proudly in the corner next to his front door. He nodded at it as he opened the door, half-expecting the place to be as pristine as he always kept it, and for yesterday's events to have resulted from a lucid dream—he was wrong. The flat looked burgled. Not stopping to take his coat off, he ploughed straight into cleaning the flat; throwing away broken plates, sweeping up broken shards of glass, and vacuuming the remaining unseen splinters. There was a knock at the door. Danial placed the chain and opened it the allowed inch. The same man stood in the same spot, with the same look on his face.

"What you make too much noise for? Stop it, we sleeping now."

Danial assured him that he'd finished, and apologised, clicking the door shut before it escalated. Letting his body flop into his TV chair, he looked up at the clock that hung too much to the left. Three-thirty in the morning. No wonder his new Latvian neighbour was angry. He would have been too, if it was them vacuuming at this hour. Not being able to relax with the clock not straight, he stood up and re-angled it into its rightful position.

Glad to be back in a routine, he had a shower and a cup of tea before retiring to bed. Flicking through an F. Paul Wilson classic, he couldn't remember what page he'd got to before the bookmark vanished. The words on the page blurred. He'd read the same sentence three times. Eyes closing, head dropping, he was asleep without giving whiskey a thought.

Awakened by rumbling and cracking that seemed to come from the heavens, Danial rolled out of bed, fed his arms into his velvet smoking jacket, and went into the lounge. A blinding flash lit the small gap around the blackout blind. Through a yawn, he said, *thunderstorm,* audible only within his head. He looked toward the door, half-expecting someone to knock. Confident it wouldn't, as even the fat man would know that the whole building must be awake with a storm as strong as this. Opening his curtains, then the blinds, he sat dazed, blinking long and slow blinks. Danial loved a good storm, but the timing couldn't have been worse. Having had two hours' sleep, he would stand witness to one of mother nature's tantrums, as there was little point tossing and turning in bed, waiting for the storm to pass. The last good one was four years back, when he took his ringside seat with a full glass of fine malt. He hadn't prepared for this one, and with his TV now upright, broken, and facing the wall, he hadn't seen tonight's weather report, which was something he did every night before watching reruns of Red Dwarf.

The storm was the best he'd ever experienced, displaying sheet lightning followed by cracks of thunder. Windows rattled with every clap and having no rooms above his own; he knew the storm cloud hovered overhead.

A tapping came from outside the window. The wind unleashing its wrath on the window's ageing frame, perhaps? *Tap, tap, tap.* He couldn't see anything outside from where he sat, so he rationalised that it must have been tree branches—the tree canopy was lower than his flat. Could have been flying twigs, or a loose sill under the shaking glass. The guessing game went on for a few minutes before he stood and walked over to the window. His tired eyes stared back, making him look as old as he felt. He reached over to the light switch and turned the dimmer to the off position.

Tap. Tap. Tap. Even with the lights off, Danial couldn't see what was tapping on the glass. The next flash of lightning took him by surprise, leaving floating doughnuts when he blinked. Rubbing his eyes, he gained focus and looked again.

Stepping back without explanation, Danial felt the urge to pee; the rain heightening the sensation between his legs. Without thought, he went to place a hand on his crotch, but didn't reach it. Tugged backwards, his feet moved, but his body stayed still. Head close to the ceiling, toes pointing down, scraping carpet, he struggled to control his upper body, flapping like a bird trapped in a thermal wind. Running in place like a crazed cartoon character, thrashing out to find an anchor point, a faint voice vibrated, echoing deep within his skull.

"Humpty Dumpty had a great..."

Danial flew back into the mahogany bookcase. The voice changed. A small child, his voice not yet broken, cried out, "Lanky streak of piss—you've pissed yourself, you lanky streak of piss!" The voice faded as Danial pushed the loaded bookshelf over, releasing a volume of books onto his bruised body. He stumbled and turned, switching the dimmer to full light. Without looking out, he grabbed one curtain, pulling it flat across the width of the window. Through laboured breath, he heard his heart pumping blood. Legs like half-cooked pasta, arms jellied and weak, he opened the kitchen drawer. The cutlery tray jangled as he willed his fingers to pick up the meat knife. Pushed into the corner carousel with the knife held between trembling hands, he shouted, "Who's there?! I have a knife!"

There was no reply.

No thunder.

No lightning.

Silence.

Heavy-footed, he went from room to room, switching on every light he could find. Relieved that gravity was working again, he listened to his hot breath. Swallowing metallic, rust-filled spittle from a cut lip he hadn't yet seen, he walked to the window. Knife held between whitened fingers, he slid the curtain back.

The night was turning to day; a watery yellow haze lit the

sky, casting a distorted reflection across the soaked road. The storm had passed, leaving the flat resembling a crime scene once more, and Danial had confirmed that he wasn't dreaming. Not this time. Was it haunted? He believed there was an answer for everything, and if one wasn't clear, then it was only a matter of time before science came up with a solution or explanation. It was the best answer to explain the strange occurrences. Or he was insane, that'd crossed his mind. Maybe Bill had been right. He shook his head, and with it, shook the thought away.

Sitting on the edge of the chair, hugging trembling legs, he repeated, "It's over. It's over."

Tap. Tap. Tap.

His manhood resembled that of a small child as Danial covered his ears, not yet aware that the sound came from the door.

Adrenaline pumped through shaking limbs. The burning impression of his overweight neighbour turned fear into anger as he stood with clenched fists.

Tap... The door smashed against the wall. The door handle wedged itself into the partition.

"What do you want?"

The Yucca didn't answer. He looked down the hallway to no avail. It was empty and silent. Danial stepped back as his neighbour's door flew open.

"What you mean? What you want, you fucking crazy man?"

Danial gave him a seething stare. "Why are you knocking my door? It was the storm."

The man came from behind his door semi-naked, wearing the same boxer shorts Danial had seen him in yesterday. Matted chest hair ran down to his large gut. Matching Danial's stare with one finger circling his temple in a spiral motion, the other prodding Danial's arm, he said, "You crazy man, no storm! The

33

only problem is you."

Danial unclenched his fists as the door slammed shut and pulled away plasterboard the size of dinner plate.

Pacing the flat to clear his head, the welcoming sound of traffic and kids yelling lightened his mood. Sun seeping through a break in the curtains lit the open pages of the strangest book within his collection. Thin metal pages gleamed and flickered, as if asking to be touched.

Tap. Tap. Tap.

This time, Danial fastened the security chain, expecting a mat of hair and a pointing finger to be on the other side.

"Len!"

He flicked the chain off its clasp. "How'd you know where I live? Who let you out?"

Taken aback by the quick-fired questions, Len asked if Danial was alone.

"Why are you here?"

Len smiled. "You've been visited again. I felt it; came as soon as I could."

"Sorry about the mess—come in."

Len took up two cushions on the three-seat settee, gut spilling over the belt holding his grey pinstripes in place, red braces holding the rest in place.

"You look different," Danial said, eyes shifting to where he'd left the knife. His body shivered at the thought of having to use it.

"You, too—dressed in your pyjamas."

Len looked toward the window. "You don't need the knife—unless it comforts you. If so, it's on the sill behind the curtain."

"How did you know I was looking for a knife?"

Len had a habit of laugh-talking, making light of even the most

34

serious situations. He told Danial that it was written all over his face... and he'd assumed, due to the shape of the left curtain, pulled tight over a centre bulge.

By the time the kettle boiled, Danial had dressed, but remained unshaven. He sat facing Len and asked what had happened a few hours ago, and who allowed his departure from Woodrush Towers. Len answered his question with another.

"Tell me what happened to you, Danial. Why is your furniture broken?"

Danial went to speak. Stuttering, he gulped and took in a breath. If he tried to explain the events to anyone other than Len, he was sure that the men in white coats would come knocking, and a room would be prepared at Woodrush, awaiting his arrival. He wouldn't be wearing a staff badge, and Bill would be the one checking him in—or worse, Lucy. He'd tell Len, as there were too many unanswered questions, and he was sure he knew something. Whether he did or didn't, getting it off his chest might spark some sense in a nonsensical situation.

Len remained silent throughout. Danial missed no details, from passing the off-licence to the moment Len had arrived. He'd never seen Len so serious. As he recalled the events, he looked worried, lapping up what sounded as fanciful to him as it must have to someone who'd not experienced the crazy events of late. Running fingers through his hair, Danial tried to rationalise each event, from a loose windowsill to having drunk too much, to stress-related hallucinations.

Holding up both palms, Len said, "You'll be glad to know you're not going mad. The dreams and contact you had were real. Based on what you've said, we haven't got long before he escapes. He's getting stronger by the day."

Danial nodded. He'd listen to Len's explanation, if only

because he didn't have a firm one himself and having someone in the flat—albeit an old patient—would help if anything happened again.

"Vetala is evil. Pure evil," Len continued. "Do you believe in the power of good and evil?" "Not in a biblical sense. There's good and bad people. Extraordinary events require extraordinary evidence." Danial quoted a scientist he'd seen on the Discovery Channel, and wondered when he would use it, but never thought he'd be the one searching for evidence of the extraordinary events in his own life.

Len slurped his tea. "A troubled, powerful spirit visited you. An old soul, trapped within this limited reality. *Your* reality, Danial. The spirit lives within the one called Ronny. A man born out of rape, handed over to a biker gang; shame took the mother's lifeblood. Or so the story goes. He remained the gang's mascot until taken into care. The doctors paid more attention to his mind than his body. After the fifth care home burnt to the ground, he was labelled a freak. Carers died after making contact with him. After killing two of his peers, they gave him a new identity, shipped him off to Italy. Or so the story goes."

Danial's patience ran thin listening to stories. He waved his hand in a circular motion, spurring him onward. Len leaned forward for his cup, noticed Danial's eagerness for him to continue, and retracted.

"After I informed the authorities of his whereabouts, police surrounded the area. They closed in for the kill, but he'd fled. He's been tracking me ever since. Wherever I go, a trail of destruction follows me."

Danial scoped the room and felt a presence; rampant paranoia running amok within his numb, yet alert, mind. He watched as Len went for the cup with hesitation, as if seeking permission.

Danial moved it closer.

"They've let me out because they could no longer hide me in full view without producing paperwork and proof for containment. Too many questions asked. I think your doggedness helped. They had to make a move and released me. But as I said when you visited last, I'm but a grassing cow. The Shepherd is watching."

Danial rocked from side to side, his fingers pressed upon his temples to ease a perpetual drumbeat. "Who's the Shepherd, Len? Who are the suits?"

"Your secret service—MI5, although they would refute that. Not a large organisation, as I've only met two—the same two you walked by in the hall, Danial."

"Why you? What do they want with you and Ronny? I need to know what this has to do with me."

"They called it 'employment'. Their way of saying 'arrested without charge'. Experimenting, trying to find their number one suspect. After containing him, they continued to exploit my ability to predict the future. I complied, mostly, but couldn't make them understand that one man's good intentions are folly to the next. Changing events that would otherwise go unchanged can unbalance necessary outcomes. I think your visits and the games he plays will subside, unless you're the worrier he fears. No offence, but my guess is you've become dragged into this as a means of escape." Slurping the last dregs from his cup, Len wiggled his brows.

Danial didn't laugh. "No offence taken. How can I take offence when what you're telling me is—no offence—not real?"

"What part isn't true? What is real? Is real your rationalisation for the things you cannot comprehend? Am I here, Danial, or am I a figment of your limited senses?"

"How did you find me?"

Len smiled. "The phone book in a pub called The Lost Sheep."

Len's tittering laughter made Danial question his ability to ask a sensible question.

"How could he visit me when he's locked up?"

"Unlike other sentient beings living a human experience, ignorant and unaware, Vetala can transport his mind out of his form to anywhere he wishes. He can project himself, and by what you said happened here, he can now use telekinesis. The people you call 'suits' study him. Like you, they think material thoughts, and are unable to understand the true evil of the spirit that lives within him. He clouds my thoughts and suppresses my abilities, as I do his. That's why I came to help you, and it's also why I'm not sure of his interest in you, Danial. Escape is inevitable. He needs to fulfil his goal, so it may be best to let him leave. He won't stop until he does."

Danial edged forward on the chair. "His goal?"

"To find the thing capable of destroying him. I believe it to be a thin blade used for countless centuries. A person of purity—an awakened soul—will challenge him. Do you think you are that person, Danial?"

"Yeah right, well maybe, makes about as much sense as the things you're telling me." He went to stand. Instead, he nestled further back into the chair. "Sorry Len, but I can't let myself think the way you do or believe the unbelievable. Next, you'll be telling me the devil himself is after me. I mean, it's not that I'm even that interesting."

"I understand your limitations, Danial. And you could be correct in assuming that you or someone associated with you will not bestow the grandeur of battle. It's one or the other."

"Or it could be none. I've not been well of late. I'm under

stress, and the lack of sleep is getting the better of me. People do strange things when they're stressed."

"And you know not of a dagger or spearhead?" Len asked. "It may take a different shape. Anything metal, gold in colour but not gold. A spearhead or a knife."

Danial laughed a nervous cackle; the strained, high-pitched jittering would have matched Len's, only Len didn't join in his hysteria. Instead, he glared. Len's wild eyebrows pointed down to his widespread nose and puffed lips. He spoke in a deep voice that filled the room. "Danial, snap out of your illusion or be a part of his. It's your choice. He wants something you have; he needs you—I feel it—you are in danger, Danial." Len lunged forward. Danial pulled his arm back, tearing his sleeve.

"Len, you're acting crazy. Stop it and calm down."

"Wake up, Danial. If you don't have what he seeks, then let him out. If you don't, then he'll go after Lucy. He'll stop at nothing to find and destroy the one who is able to banish him from this earthly realm. Protect her, Danial; I feel his intentions toward her."

Edging forward, Len sat on the edge of the sofa and said, "I can only protect what needs protecting. Think, Danial; you are a part of this jigsaw, whether you want to be or not. You stand no chance of defeating him on your own."

Danial's top lip raised as he frowned at Len, "Defeat—jigsaw—how do you know about Lucy?" Danial stood and looked down at Len's bulk. "You better start making sense, or I swear I'll—"

Len slid off the soft fabric of the chair. Danial held out his arm, helping him stand.

"I'd have fallen like Humpty Dumpty. Watch your back. I'm none too light on my feet."

"Get out!"

Danial marched over to the door. Swinging it open, he stood like a statue made of bronze, finger pointing toward the yucca plant.

Len pinched his braces, huffing as he walked toward the door.

"I'm sorry, Danial. I have failed you. Negative desperation is for the weak-minded; my mind has become weakened. Please forgive me."

Remaining silent, Danial watched him walk down the stairs before shutting the door. Sliding his back down its frame, eyes shut, he drew his knees up under his chin before opening them to a glint of gold from the pages of the strangest book. Using the door handle to stand, he walked over to the window. Kicking the book into a pile of other, less attractive ones, he held up the blind and saw heads below turn toward a Range Rover not fitting to the area. It rounded the corner before he could see the number plate, but he was sure it was the same one he'd seen leaving Woodrush.

Chapter 5

Palms rubbed the chair's soft leather arms. James McMilan sat at his desk, knees knocking together with every half-turn of the chair. He watched Roger park the Range Rover. The headman of a six-person covert operation looked through the glass walls of his office, down into the games room. Code breaking, algorithmic surveillance, and observational data analysis kept the boys occupied, while James and Roger dealt with the unexplained; those case files gathering dust, given up on, black-shelved for eternity. He and Roger had the job of working through them and reporting back to Mr Green.

After processing, blood samples and scan results got sent to a location north of the games room, and the data got sent back to his team to decipher. James saw his team as delinquent sons, although he would admit—albeit only to himself—that they were on the top of their game, and had an important role to play in the overall operation.

Roger was older and wiser than the youths that worked with him. Years of active service had lead MI5 to offer him the position. He jumped at the chance for a more exciting role. James was both delighted and worried about being in charge of a man whom he had always seen as his senior at work and a best friend out of it. Keeping information locked tight between working partners was paramount. Holding back details from the boys was one thing, but holding them back from a friend was another. Having shared everything with him since being a novice, Roger took him under his wing in the recon division. James would trust the life of his family in his hands and hold back on nothing, apart from the need-to-know work matters.

Roger, a seasoned agent, had forgotten more than most have ever taught. He was an all-around top man who wasn't privy to the hidden agenda. James liked to forget that there was one; after all, the subjects were intriguing enough, and how this linked to war games was beyond even his pay grade. But he knew all the same. And knowledge, without purpose, could be your worst enemy. Could eat you up if you let it. Roger's words, not his, but he'd never forgotten them. In a world of "trust no one", they trusted each other.

The inner control panel flashed green. Roger was already in the building. The four sitting in front of him would have tracked his progress from the perimeter fence, and knew he was arriving. A steel door opened, and Roger walked in, throwing a file into the hands of Mike. Stover, Paul, and Steve lowered their heads, fingers tapping away. They didn't respond to Mike's glasses flying off his face while catching the file. Roger looked into what he called the fish tank. James stood up and walked to the side of the desk. The tapping of his watch met Roger's middle finger, extended skyward.

The glass door opened as he approached. Roger entered.

"Ever thought of knocking?" James asked, returning to his chair.

"Why knock when the All-Seeing Eye knows I'm coming?"

After shaking hands, Roger fell back into the egg-shaped chair facing him.

"Late flight?" James asked.

Roger frowned. "Bloody waste of time and government money. The witness reports were nothing you couldn't find in a book or on YouTube, and the room I stayed in stunk of piss. So yeah, great trip. Thanks."

Roger looked like he hadn't slept a wink.

"They questioned my ID. I spent three hours in an Italian police cell waiting for confirmation that I was a reporter working on the latest edition of *Mysterious Times* magazine—you could have sent me in as a government official. Anything other than a reporter of a nonexistent magazine, for Christ's sake."

"I needed someone not connected. The locals have had their fair share of insurance companies, detectives, and official reporter types."

"So, you sent me as a small-time comic reporter. A tourist would have been easier to explain than an unknown conspiracy mag."

James knew the turning point of Roger's hard-nosed banter, and it was turning right now. Remaining calm, he turned to the coffee percolator and offered him a drink. He declined.

"Did you complete the questionnaires and talk to the head of the church?" James asked, turning back to his desk.

Roger stood up and swiped his jacket off the chair's curved headrest. "Yeah, and he's got a good memory, since whatever happened was over twelve fucking years ago. He laughed when he heard I was reporting on something that had been headline news over a decade ago. *Laughed*, Jim. Thought I was a nut job."

James went to ask another question. Stopping at the door, Roger turned and said, "We have a snoop in Woodrush. Name of Danial Morris. I followed him in and saw one of our vehicles in the car park. Sure you didn't send me to Canneto di Caronia as a decoy? A wild goose chase?"

James dropped his coffee cup onto the saucer. "You went back to Woodrush on whose authority?"

"Did an hour of real work. After my week's holiday, it was the least I could do."

No other words exchanged as the door hissed shut behind him.

"Goodbye, geeks. Have a shit weekend."

James closed his laptop, "Shit—how could I forget it's Friday?" Looking at the team below, they glanced up in unison before returning their attention to the screens.

James couldn't remember stopping at lights or giving way at a junction on his journey home; he couldn't fathom how he'd managed it. He put it down to subconscious programming wired into the solemn depths of his mind. He was comforted by the sight of his dressing gown-clad wife holding her head. Her bloodshot eyes said all there was to say. The perfect excuse not to join Roger for the Friday night game.

"I need an early night. Can you send my apologies to Kath and let her know I'll call tomorrow?" she asked, walking up the stairs before James closed the door. She spoke in a raspy, broken voice. "Wake me up at your own risk."

"I'm not…"

"I'm not kidding, Jim. You always do when you're drunk."

"Was thinking of skipping the game tonight, had a hard week!" he shouted up at her. The flow of bathwater, coupled with Jackie's cold, suggested wasted words.

The second hand ticked on the small carriage clock. A wedding present from Jackie's Auntie Margarete.

7:45. Even if he left now, he would be late.

7:51. James stared at the home phone.

"Bye, babes. See you later."

"Enjoy yourself," she said, coughing her reply. "Try not to wake me up if you're drinking."

James thought about that last comment. What difference would it make if he woke her sober or drunk? Either way, she'd be awake.

James squinted. A security light flooded the gravel-filled drive. Roger stood in the doorway of his three-bed Victorian semi. James got out and crunched his way over to Roger. With a face not dissimilar to the stone statue standing to his left, Roger had his arms folded. Swishing his hand outward, he drew it in before tapping his watch.

Sucking through his teeth, James looked up to a crimson patchwork after the rain. In no mood for an argument, he thought about turning back and heading off without speaking. The thought vanished as Roger stomped up in his slippers.

"Time do you call this?" Still tapping his watch. "Didn't think you were coming."

James raised an eyebrow upon seeing him trying to disguise a grin. Embracing him in a bear hug, Roger walked him to the door.

"Jackie not with you?"

"Got a cold or something. Told me to let Kath know."

Two packs of playing cards lay spread on either side of two full glasses of whiskey. The half-empty bottle sat centre, next to an ashtray filled with mixed nuts. A running joke was that James always refused to eat from an ashtray, calling it council estate monkey food, but always scooped up a few handfuls following a good drinking session. He sensed that this was one of those nights but didn't want it to be. He needed to keep a clear mind for the week ahead.

Kath walked by as they sat. "Poor Jackie. I hope you do not

wake her when you get home. I've said I'll drop you off tonight. I will be up most of the night with this assignment."

James huffed and nodded. "Why ask me to let Kath know if she's going to call her?" He asked under his breath, reaching for the cards.

Three hands in, and he was three games up on Roger, who was remaining professional by not bringing up work matters. Maybe tonight would be easier than he'd expected.

Roger poured another double.

"Steady on, mate, getting me drunk won't turn this game."

Roger was more interested in turning James around over the game. He needed to know the reason behind the wild goose chase.

Eight games in, with James keeping the pace, both with the cards and the drink.

"So, mate did you look at the file I flung at the geeks?"

"I wish you wouldn't call them geeks, Rog; they are people, you know." The words echoed in James' raised glass.

"I know you're hiding something, Jim. I looked like a nut job listening to bigger nut jobs talking shit about the supernatural, UFOs, and the fucking Virgin Mary, for Christ's sake. Throw me a bone, bud."

James didn't answer, but knew this was coming. Choosing to shuffle the cards, he smiled at Roger, but before he could speak, Roger continued. His speech became agitated.

"And why look into stuff a decade old? Going over old ground? Stuff's already in the public domain. There was no internet, Jim; I looked a right fool, not knowing the history of it."

"Is that why you brought me here? To rip into me about things I've not got clearance to talk about?" James asked, looking down at the hand of cards.

"You brought yourself, mate. I didn't call you," Roger said, opening a new twelve-year-old malt.

"Well, who else would drink from the filled glass placed next to my seat?"

"*Your* seat, is it?"

They both laughed. James knew Roger was fishing for more. And why the hell shouldn't he? It was ridiculous to expect him to run the show, not divulging parts of the study that didn't hinder the project's aim. He could see no harm in explaining the reason for his trip to Italy with a questionnaire and a mission to find a preacher man amongst a list of other locals. The thought of Roger getting him drunk so that he sang like a canary entered his mind, but their friendship ran too deep to accuse him. He swallowed the words and said, "So, tell me how it went and what you found out. Heard those Italian girls are tasty."

"Kath's in the next room."

Guilty of nothing, but knowing Kath hadn't been keen on him going, he gave James the evil eye before saying, "Told you. A load of fruitcakes, talking about the supernatural. The preacher man must have had a tight grip on the locals, I'd say."

James nodded and said, "Well, go on! What do you know?"

Leaning back in the chair, Roger stretched his legs under the table and placed both of his hands behind his head. "You want to go through my findings now? Tonight? I thought there were rules about talking work within social surroundings."

"You started the bloody thing. I'll divulge what I can. So, what happened when you were over there? Leave out any sordid details with the native girls."

Roger lowered his eyes and rubbed his chin. Maybe the scotch did the trick. He poured another.

"I doubt there's anything new. Guess you saw it online."

James sipped at the crystal cut glass. "Try me."

"Just about every expert has paid a visit. I'm talking *everyone*. Geologists, physicists, volcanologists, the electric suppliers. Everyone. They shut down the supply of electric, but still, the fires happened. Spontaneous combustion of mattresses, beds, cars, fridges, even turned-off mobiles. A resident told me how her vacuum cleaner burst into flames and both neighbours' houses burnt down, but she only lost the vacuum. Then things got crazy."

James raised an eyebrow. "Crazy?"

"Yeah, crazy. Said they saw a UFO."

"Already ruled out. No radar or air traffic," James said, reaching over the table for the bottle.

Roger raised his hands, palms up, as if to say, *I know*. "I dug deeper. There were claims of a demon. Others said a stranger was roaming the streets."

"Description?"

"Who?"

"The Demon."

"Funny, they all gave a similar description. They're all delusional. The preacher went missing the night the fires started. Said he had to hide the book. Left his whole congregation. The locals said the devil took him. When I pressed them on the book, they looked freighted, U-turned, and denied there was one. It's a golden book, that's all I got. Absolute bullshit if you ask me. I reckon he had something to do with the fires, but for the life of me, I can't work out how he set a water main's pipe alight. I think he absconded with the charity pot—and the book, if it was valuable—and fled with one of the women you keep mentioning. Anyhow, no one saw him again. Out-of-character, they said."

"So, what did he look like?"

"Black robe and white dog collar, I suppose."

"The Demon, Rog. The stranger."

"Some said he had glowing eyes. You know, the usual when describing something out of a movie. But they all said he was tall, bold, gaunt, and naked. Like our subject one—wait, you don't think…"

"I'll read your report Mor day and have a chat when my head isn't buzzing. This is good scotch."

"Hold on a minute. I told you what happened; now I want answers. Why was I sent to Freak Town, and what the hell does it have to do with any of the work we're doing?"

He wasn't privileged to all the details himself, but he knew about a connection between Subject One and the fires that took place in Italy.

James held his hands out. "Hold your horses, Rog! They only give me snippets. Green said Subject One might have killed the preacher and started the fires. And I suppose if we pin that on him, then it would give us better insight into his abilities."

"Ronny caused the fires?"

"I don't know." He laughed as he felt his head slope to one side. The whiskey had taken effect. He'd said enough for one night while under the influence of the finest damn whiskey he'd had in a long time. And there was the talk of a book going missing. Could the preacher have hidden it before being killed? If Ronny had killed him, then the body wasn't found. The world's media hadn't reported a murder or a suspect.

"So, tell me, Rog, who's this Morris feller?"

"Need-to-know only, mate," Roger said.

Kate walked in, asking if James needed a lift before she ran a bath and settled for the evening. Agreeing, he said his goodbyes to Roger and stumbled to the car. The fresh air gave new meaning to light-headedness.

Chapter 6

A dim amber glow from solar path lights was Lucy's guide to the steel steps that led to her flat. Stopping on the second of six steps, she waved her arms. The security light should have pinged on by now. Installed by the previous owners, she couldn't reach the moss-covered plastic if the bulb blew. There was little room to place a step ladder, and she wouldn't be able to lean out that far. She fumbled with the keyhole cover that did a three-sixty every time she tried to place the key in its hole. Smoky was on the other side of the door, crying.

Smoky, an American grey, had taken up residence with her over a year ago. He was more than just a cat to Lucy; he was her companion, her best friend. Left devastated and frightened after David's arrest, she sought solace in the cat. Unlike Dave, Smokey was non-judgmental and listened to her. Self-aware of her withdrawal from people, she spent more time tending her garden alone with Smoky than building friendships. Her plants needed her to grow and prosper, and Smoky needed her as a companion, and right now, that was enough.

Things were looking up after she'd landed a new job working with the mentally ill. Never would she have imagined ending up working in a high-dependency hospital, and although she vowed never to get close to a man again, in her short time working at Woodrush, she liked a man who worked in a senior position. He was the total opposite of any man she had ever met. Kind and considerate, thoughtful and honest, all the things she wished Dave could have been. For all the hurt and humiliation that she'd endured, it had given her a better understanding of the people she handled. Woodrush had its fair share of Daves, but now she could close the door and turn the key on them.

Snagging a nail, she pulled back the plastic film cover on a meal-for-one; Smoky watched and purred as she pressed the go button on the microwave.

"I bet you're hungry," she said, looking down at the cat, who was winding his tail around her leg.

"Would you like biscuits? I promise I'll buy tuna tomorrow."

Smoky went from purring to a screaming meow; he leapt onto the windowsill, knocking the TV remote off the arm of the sofa.

"What is it, Smoky? Am I not fast enough for you?"

The microwave pinged. Her fish and chips dinner was ready. She plopped the fish onto the plate and saw Smoky scratching at the curtains.

"Smoky, stop that. What's the matter?"

The cat became more erratic, pawing the window as if to get out. Burning her fingers trying to hook the chips from their plastic compartment, Lucy raised her voice toward him.

"You know how to leave. Use the flap in the door, not the window."

Placing the ready meal on the largest of a nest of three tables, she looked for the TV remote, then leaned over the sofa and scooped Smoky under her arm.

"Now, that's enough of that; you can stay outside tonight."

He sprang out of her hands, a blur between fading solar lights. The hedge rustled as he passed under it. She looked up; the sky was darker than normal, moonlight obscured by low hanging clouds. Faint radiance given by street lights and an alien blue glow from Mrs Baker's sunbed were visible. If a gym-going bronze pensioner turned her on, then she'd be in her element as the curtains—if there even were any—were always open in the room across the road. Squinting, trying to fathom where Smoky had gone, a pot smashed under the steps. There was no telling which one.

"Smoky, is that you?" she called out.

Lucy looked back through the open door. Steam rose from the fish and chip dinner. She called him again before closing the door.

Picking the remote off the floor, she sat down, letting a long breath flow between closed lips. "Me and a frozen meal."

Fork in hand, she flicked through the TV menu. An engine outside juddered to a stop, sounding like a van. Living in a small cul-de-sac afforded her the ability to know the sound of every car, even down to how the door sounded when it slammed shut. This one wasn't familiar. Not giving it a second thought, she tucked into the meal and settled for a repeat of a survival documentary she'd seen only two nights ago.

The book was where she had left it, on the bedside cabinet, alongside last night's half-glass of water. She looked out the bedroom window, hoping to see Smoky. The solar lights had faded to a pinprick glow. She thought about calling him, but upon seeing no lights coming from any of the windows, she took a chance on being woken up. It wouldn't be long before he remembered he hadn't eaten.

The endless chapter had ended. Not wanting to start another, she closed her eyes, thinking of Danial and the way he took charge of the team.

Awakened by the sound of laughter, she reached for the radio alarm clock. Stretching, she yawned, expecting Smoky to run in and pounce on her bed.

"Even the cat has a social life," she said as she filled the kettle. Lucy could never function without a strong cup of tea after waking up. She had her routine, something that Dave had never let develop, always demanding that she cooked his breakfast before anything else.

Due into work at five, she had at least six hours to herself. The tea caddy was empty, with four left in the box. Looking into an empty cupboard, she thought about going food shopping. The thought soon faded. Weeds ran rampant after the rain. Tending the garden wasn't a priority, but she found it therapeutic.

"Shopping can wait," she told the old green garden chair from the window. She'd bought it last week from a charity shop on the high street. The little oasis took her the better part of a year to clear out. Rubbish and rubble left by the previous owner, most of it buried or disguised as rock features, had become a progressive mini-paradise.

Wearing an old pair of grey tracksuit bottoms, a baggy top, and a pair of pink trainers, she thought about the next project after weed pulling. Having done everything she could to the small ten-by-twelve garden, she now read countless gardening magazines and tuned into the Sunday afternoon gardening programs to perfect the art of turning what was once a muddy, weed-filled garden into a growing creation.

Meow!

"Smoky—use the cat flap," she said, rummaging in the kitchen drawer for her gardening gloves. She opened the door and saw a ginger tabby looking up at her.

"Do you know where my Smoky is?"

Her eyes flicked to the garden below, back to the tabby, and down to the garden again… but this wasn't her treasured oasis.

The cat clawed at her leg as she ran down the steps. A solar light crunched and splintered underfoot after she jumped the last two.

"What—how—who did this?"

Her neighbour drove past, waving from his open window. Suppressing the urge to run up to the car, she stood with her fists clenched. Her creation had turned to hell. Twisted stems of plants were pulled out, and bushes were soaked in brown liquid. A mixed aroma of paint and nail varnish stung her nose as she assessed the overall damage. This wasn't nature's doing; neither was it foxes, cats, or anything other than mindless vandalism. Someone had even gone to the trouble of cutting the base of the hedgerow. Still upright, it would perish with its lifeline cut. Her nose wrinkled up to the size of a button creating a dell, letting her tears flow free.

Using the back of her wrist, she wiped her eyes and looked for anything salvageable. Every plant and scrub uprooted the little green chair—the only thing still intact. She'd gone from vexed to helpless as energy drained through her pink trainers. Musing, she sat on the chair under the steel steps. Eyes closed tight, head hung low, her long blonde hair covered a visual despair that she had not felt since her time with David.

Time had passed; how much, she wasn't aware, but enough for her to no longer feel any sensation in the lower part of her body. Her buttocks were numb, and both feet tingled. Solemnness gave rise to slight amusement as she tried to stand. She wiggled her toes and eased herself from the chair. Thoughts of her Gran being riddled with arthritis, deteriorating before she passed away, ran alongside whether she should call the police.

Giving a backward glance in the hopes that Smoky was

following, she entered the flat and dropped onto the sofa. Snatching a cushion as she fell, she held it to her chest, wrapped her arms around it, and squeezed.

"To hell with this. I'll re-plan it. Better this time. I'll install a camera."

She flicked through the latest copy of *Home and Garden* to find the earmarked page that had struck her interest.

"Time to get it together, girl. First things first, call the police and report the crime." Lucy reached for the phone. Its display read 3:59 PM.

She slid the magazine back under the table. The police would have to wait until tomorrow; there wouldn't be enough time to wait for them to arrive—if they even arrived at all for such a strange act of vandalism.

Lucy closed the door to her Mini Cooper and looked out for Smoky. She'd read something about how cats strayed within the mating season; he could be sowing his royal oats. Slowing, she looked up and down roads. He might be hurt. Suppressing any thoughts by hitting the stereo's plus button in rapid succession, the late David Bowie wailed "Space Oddity" through the car's speakers.

Chapter 7

Thirst woke him after six hours of undisturbed sleep. Popping, cracking, and snapping emitted from otherwise never-thought-of joints. Oxygen, nitrogen, and carbon dioxide released from tightened tendons as they found their rightful position after a night scrunched up on the chair. Stretching, he stood up and wiped bristles on his chin with the back of his hand.

Gulping down a glass of water, he pondered over Len's visit and his comments about Lucy, the girl of his dreams—and now, his nightmares. He'd never obsessed over a woman before, especially someone who wouldn't give him a second thought.

He looked under the sink at a space where the whiskey should have been next to the cornflakes. Remembering he'd binned the empty bottle, he questioned his sanity. Cogs in his head turned like metal left in the rain to rust.

How can I help Len stop Ronny, and help a girl that doesn't think she needs help? How do I explain this to her without her thinking I'm a loon?

He looked up at the wall where the square wooden wall clock should be, then to the floor. 4:55 PM.

After showering, he dressed in his work attire, making it to the clip-on tie before remembering that he wasn't due to work. Flinging the tie at the radiator, he snatched it before it had the chance to fall on wet tiles. Lifting his neck, he clipped it in place.

Pacing, he stopped to check himself in the bedroom mirror every time he passed.

Need to get to work.

Got to see Ronny.

He knew he'd be in serious trouble, but had to confront him. Tell him he wasn't afraid. Tell him he knew about his antics and show him that it didn't bother him.

Straightening furniture that had been moved in the night, he picked up broken glass, and a razor-sharp shard pierced his palm. He threw it at the wall. Two thumps from his neighbours on the other side of the wall spurred him into snatching the kettle, not letting it follow the path that the glass had taken. Instead, he placed it back on the worktop.

Stuffing bin liners with clothes, books, toiletries, and anything else he thought he might need for a few days, he left the flat. With a bounce in his step, he scaled the stairs. Anger grew with every step. Slapping his hand on the rail as he descended, he mumbled, "Warn Lucy. I don't care if she thinks I'm mad. She needs to know. First see that fucker, then tell Lucy."

Slowing as he approached the gates leading to the staff parking area, he waved to the guard. The guard waved back and opened the gate. Anger had turned to a boyish nervousness for the actions he was taking. Having been sent home, he had to avoid the manager who'd sanctioned it. He wasn't worried about the others. He'd been there long enough to know that no one knew who was on and who was off at any given time. The norm was to bring people in on short notice.

Routine security checks completed, he made his way to the office where the keys would be. He would need to grab, run, and replace them before anyone noticed them missing.

Face flushed, his heart pounded. Adrenaline rushed through

his body, causing blood flow to slow in his legs, directed instead to his heart and rapid thoughts. His legs wobbled like half-boiled spaghetti.

The keys were missing. A team must already be up there.

"Shit!"

Thinking of reasons for being somewhere he shouldn't, he walked up the stairs to the corridor that led to ward fifteen—Ronny's ward. The ward in which Vetala resided. Bill pushed past him, one hand raised, shouting into his radio. He stopped, turned to Danial, and shouted, "Raise the alarm! Go to ward fifteen!"

He knew this wasn't a prank before he could ask why the alarm sounded. Blue lights flashed above every room. Danial froze, jelly legs now set in stone, unable to move, unable to talk. Thoughts of Jim raced through his mind.

"Not again, please not again."

What he saw was all too familiar. Being the only person having any experience of what was happening—the last one left standing from the riot half a decade ago—he stood, watching as his colleagues manhandled inmates into rooms. Inexperienced new starters created panic, shouting at inmates, intensifying their unstable minds into a frenzied, manic state.

A plant was hurled across the communal area and struck the side of his head. He ducked to avoid the second object; a TV remote. Two inmates based on the rehabilitation ward kicked and punched their way to locked exit doors. Guards now in full riot gear stood their ground; bloody knuckle-marks streaked the shields they held.

With over half the staff on ward fifteen and the rest struggling on the rehabilitation ward, Danial stood between the two.

Pushing inmates into any room with an open door, Danial

pointed new staff toward wondering patients. Those he told, did it. Others gathered, looking for further instructions.

"Fire!"

Danial turned and saw Mary unlatching the extinguisher. Fire raced up the wall, turning as it hit the ceiling, moving across in a straight line. With no time to process the unnatural movement of the flames, Danial snatched an extinguisher and aimed straight at them. He looked for its origin, a bin, anything flammable. The building was designed not to burn. Floors were concave into walls, and the ceilings were featureless. All were coated with fire-retardant paint, and the furnishings were likewise designed with that in mind. Still, they burned. Looking beneath the fire, he expected to see a smouldering blanket or a box full of paper, but there was nothing.

Panic from patients and guards intensified. Fights were breaking out among the few remaining inmates. Attempts to restrain the fire only increased its intensity. Others from the upper floors joined him; none found the fire's starting point. There wasn't one.

"Where the hell's the fire brigade?!" Danial shouted. "Evacuate the building! Two per inmate! To the courtyard!"

His attention focused on the sound of screams coming from ward two. Carl, one of the milder inmates, was ablaze, his clothes burnt to ashes, his skin on fire, smouldering flesh where hair used to be. Every effort to douse the flames met a spontaneous defiance as they rose from his already-burnt flesh. The sound of sirens gave assurance that it was only a matter of time before they gained control.

The first fire in the communal room had now taken hold of furniture; thick smoke engulfed the room. Through the fire, Danial saw that the door to the staff room was open. A red handbag hung on the back of a plastic chair.

"Lucy!"

Asking anyone he saw. Again, he shouted, "Lucy! Where's Lucy?!"

Making his way through the wards, he saw small fires, some no bigger than a smouldering ashtray. He watched flames self-ignite. Without reason, pockets of flames appeared on walls, floors, everywhere. An inmate had his back against the door. Danial looked past him as the window bars raged, flames licking metal with no clear cause.

Dashing through empty rooms, he saw no sign of her. He ran to the next empty room and wiped condensation from the barred window. An army of fire engines, police riot vans, and ambulances lit the car park and the outer perimeter. A portly figure entered, shouting, "Out! Out! Everyone, this way!"

Danial ran toward the stairs. An arm swung around his chest. Slipping, he steadied himself with help from two fire officers. Shouts sounded muffled under alien-looking breathing apparatuses. "Follow these." They pointed to staff and guards, retreating to exit points.

"What about the patients?" Danial asked.

Both pointed to the exit with a firm arm. "Most are out. We need to clear the building. Out, this way!"

A guard bolted down the stairs, his bulk not allowing him to stop as he ran head-on into the two men. Without hesitation, he followed the waving finger, joining the others who were filtering their way through the fire exit. Danial shouted, "Bill, where's Lucy?!" He screamed the words with enough force to break through the creaking, cracking, and popping around him. The guard, not dissimilar in size to Bill, swung around. "Ward fifteen, I tried—" Two firemen dragged him to the exit.

Climbing two flights, three steps at a time, he looked back at an inferno. Forces, staff, and inmates had evacuated. Smoke thickened, his eyes watered, mouth dry like chewing burnt rubber. Danial dodged and zigzagged his way through dripping flames, checking each room.

"Lucy!" Again. "Lucy Day—" Like a father calling for his young sibling, he continued to shout until stopping short of ward fifteen's entrance. Painful cries echoed through the corridor.

"Help, Danial!"

"Where are you?" Darting into empty rooms, the voice called out to him again. "Lucy, which room?"

Her voice came from every room he entered, but she wasn't in any of them.

"Lucy, where are you?"

The heat on the ward was unbearable. He continued down the corridor. Glancing back, he saw the stairs ablaze. The non-flammable surface came to life as flames licked the bannister like a serpent twisting around its prey.

Fast approaching the last room, the calls for help faded. Whimpering came through an open door.

He heard a voice. Not Lucy's. Feminine, like a small child, "Please help me—I'm scared."

"Lucy."

Danial swung open the door and stood on the threshold. Hunched under the window, Lucy had her hands tied. Her chin was low to her chest. Foam bubbled from a closed mouth. She spoke with a wheeze. "Danial, I'm dying."

A burning orb appeared between him and Lucy. He tried to dodge it, but it moved with him before exploding, sending him back through the door. Intense heat scorched his skin; the blinding flash left a silhouette of Lucy in flames, trapped inside a burning coffin.

With smoke-filled lungs, he staggered toward her painful cries. His vision cleared enough to see Lucy raise her featureless head. Shaking, Danial stepped back as the body rose from the ground. It stood before him ablaze, laughing, legs together, arms stretched out to either side.

The room vanished under a blanket of powder. Pulled out the room, Danial collapsed in the corridor. In shock, he looked up into the eyes of Len Happy. He tried to speak; his head felt as if it was floating. He followed a calming bright light. There was no pain, no thoughts, just blankness.

Chapter 8

Roger ran down the street, compelled to lift the receiver that was vibrating inside the old-style phone booth.

"Hello."

"Rog, it's me. You awake?"

"Who? What?" His eyes snapped open. The screen on his landline flashed as he held the receiver.

"We have a situation. See you in twenty."

Roger dropped the phone back onto its cradle. Kath turned and muttered something incomprehensible. Roger sat on the edge of the bed, taking in his surroundings.

"Bloody time you call this?" he asked, yawning.

He got showered and dressed within ten minutes—a record time, considering he'd been awakened midway through a lucid dream of being in hot pursuit of someone who had done something. Exactly who and what though, had vanished when James called.

Roger peered through the darkened room. Kath was sleep-talking. He thought about waking her to explain. But how could he explain when he had no explanation? Instead, he wrote a note telling her he had to go to work early and would call later. Finishing it with several Xs, he slid it under Kath's glass of water and tiptoed past the bed and out the door.

Roger pulled up into his space opposite James and switched

off his headlights. They met in the middle of the two cars. About to ask what was going on, he thought better of it. Possible spies were doubtful, as they were on surveillance cameras since leaving the main road. Paranoia was a friend they both shared.

Following James through the steel door, they made their way down two flights of stairs, past several signs repeating the message that the building housed toxic waste, others reading, *Government-protected. Trespassers shot on sight.* Entering a password-protected lift, the retina reader confirmed their identity.

Roger was surprised to see the geeks already on their computers. Each one looked up as they entered. Mike lowered his head when Roger looked at him, fingers on his glasses, holding them in place.

Before entering the office, James turned to Stover and said, "I'll be taking control of the cameras for a while. You're allowed to take full control if you see Subject One or need to record evidence. I'll be recording all my views."

No one noticed Roger shrug his shoulders. Unable to disguise his curiosity any longer, he watched the glass walls of the office dim.

"Enough of the James Bond shit. What's going on, mate?" Adding the word *mate*, as James hated it when he called him Bond. Fearing this was no time for jokes, he sat down in anticipation of an answer.

No words were forthcoming as James tapped on his keyboard. Dark glass walls turned to bright screens displaying what looked like a movie. But this wasn't a movie. It was Woodrush.

Roger watched an estimated ninety-strong team comprising all emergency services working to put out the fire and bring back order. Ambulances lined up along the outer perimeter.

Police vans with riot shields for window screens blocked the entrance. Staff formed a line between corridors of the first-response medical teams. Some rushed over to a makeshift meeting point. Others were being carried on stretchers into the open doors of ambulances.

"What's happening, James?"

The screen changed pictures, showing the full extent of the chaos. The inner grounds were a mass of walking wounded, and the unconscious few had medical teams surrounding them.

"Something big. Look!"

The screen switched once more. Roger gasped upon seeing streams of water firing at the burning building. Vapour clouds gave way to rolls of black smoke. Flames appeared the moment a hose moved in a direction more deserving.

The intercom flashed. "T.O., Boss!"

Roger didn't know which geek was shouting *take over*, but the screens were rewinding, flicking between inner and outer shots. The thought of it being a movie ran through Roger's mind; too unreal and well-documented to be true.

"What's that about?" Roger asked.

"My boys have taken over. They're onto something."

"Who? The geeks?"

"Yes, Rog. The geeks."

Roger watched the car park clear out. Fire engines, ambulances, and riot vans backed out, and flames flew back into the building only to start over again.

Zooming into an individual making his way through the crowds, the video stopped.

The intercom flashed once more.

"Boss, we have Subject Two entering the building," Steve said over the loudspeaker.

"Who?" Roger stood. "Hold on a fucking minute." Hands on hips, he said, "Stop talking 'subjects' and talk English. How's Len Happy breaking into a high-security prison, when he's already in there? You telling me he started the fire, broke out, then went back in again to finish?"

"Len was released. I knew after the event."

"If you didn't allow it, then who the fuck did?"

"I got a call, Rog. From Mr Green. You going to question his motives?"

"Damn right I will. The big cheese of MI5 murdering innocent people trapped inside a big oven?"

"Rog, stop."

"He'll be on every newspaper's front page. *Boss of MI5 aids in the arson attack on innocent staff and puts an end to patients' misery by way of burning them alive.*"

"Rog… Stop! I need your help right now. And if you're right, I'll be by your side. But right now, we need to know what's happening without jumping to conclusions."

"Okay. But you promise not to keep anything from me. The need-to-know bullshit stops right here."

Placing his hand on Roger's shoulder, James looked up at the screen. Roger followed his eyes with his own. They were back inside the building.

The intercom flashed. It was Stover. "Only three cameras are working inside. Building's cleared. All counted and present."

Roger swung open the door. "How do you know everyone's accounted for?"

"The staff rota. Eleven walking wounded heading for the infirmary. Two serious burn victims heading for The Royal Hospital, and twelve treated at the scene."

Roger looked at James, then back to the geeks.

"That's what they do, Rog. They find things out," James said, closing the door.

Roger opened it before it had time to close. "What about Len? Where's he now?"

Mike looked up. His right eye twitched, and his top lip followed, "Er... He left."

"What do you mean, 'left'? It's a high-security prison surrounded by police. How could he leave?"

"He was last spotted dragging a body out of the building, then joined the rest of the walking wounded at the assembly point. Then he was out of camera sight and hasn't shown up on the person count."

It was Roger's turn to shut the door. This time, with as much strength as he could muster; the force of his swing restrained by the soft-closing hinges.

James flicked through paperwork—a strange sight to see in a paperless office.

"We think Subject—Ronny and Len are connected in some way. As you're already aware, Ronny is mute, or at least chooses not to communicate."

"Yeah, go on."

"Ronny gave off gamma rays; one reason we cleared the ward of inmates. Len subdued the energy he expelled. After being transferred to another ward, they increased."

"Ah, right. Len's release would allow Ronny to access his full potential and burn people alive. Makes perfect sense when you put it like that," Roger said.

"Not me, Rog. You're barking up the wrong tree. Told you I had no idea until last night."

The phone rang. A red light flashed with every ring. James put his finger to his lips, signalling to be quiet, before taking the call.

Roger left the room and walked over to the geeks. "Do you have any way of finding Len Happy?"

They all spoke at once. Three backed down, leaving Stover to continue. "Yes, we have a lock on his location right now."

"A lock?"

"Yeah, we have him bugged up like a sweet that's dropped into an ants' nest."

The others snorted their approval, stopping when they saw the look on Roger's face.

"How did you manage to bug him if you didn't know he was being released?"

"Roger," James called, waving his arm as a prompt to enter the office. "We need to attend the incident. Our brief is to take overall control of the situation until we locate both subjects."

"Why not ask the four fuckheads out there where Len is? They know."

"What?"

"They told me Len's bugged. So, either you're lying about not knowing about his release, or you're clueless as to the events unfolding in your building. Which one is it, James?"

James felt lightheaded. He fell back into the egg-shaped chair.

"You okay? You've turned white."

"I'm all right. Got a pain in my chest."

Before Roger could reach for the phone, James stood up. The colour in his face returned.

"Well?" Roger persisted.

"I had no idea, Rog, so yeah, I guess I'm out the loop."

Filling his lungs with air, James released a stilted breath before pacing over to the geeks. Roger followed.

"Do you have a fix on Len?" James asked.

"Yeah, he's on foot heading southwest onto Holden Hill. All five tracks are operational, and the dish places him on Moor Road."

"Dish?" Roger said.

"Satellite navigation system. Like what you have in the car," Stover replied, with condemnation for Roger's inability to understand his terminology.

"So, how do you boys know Len had been bugged?" Roger said.

"Asked head office a question and got the answer," Stover replied.

Roger gritted his teeth; certain they were mocking him. James sensed his friend's anger and pulled him back. The others didn't notice, but Roger was aware.

James addressed the team. "We're leaving now. Keep me posted on Len's location, and I'll be in touch. Send no messages. Ask no questions. Ask me before checking elsewhere. Understand?"

"Okay boss, but what if we get a request from head office?" Stover asked.

"Then you fucking call us before acting on it, shithead," Roger snapped. James raised his eyebrows but did nothing to reinforce his statement.

"Send anything and everything to Big Black, guys," James said, before leaving with Roger.

Big Black was the name that had been given to the Range Rover. Painted black, with blackout windows, a black leather interior, and a dashboard to make a Boeing 747 jealous, it was bulletproof, but otherwise looked like any other executive vehicle.

Roger tried to contain his excitement. "Never thought I'd be driving that beast."

"Who said you would be?" James said, approaching the driver's side.

"I'll do the return trip," Roger said.

Not answering, James pressed the ignition button. Roger's mouth dropped upon hearing it come to life. The dashboard was an array of lights. A twelve-inch computer, central to the dash, showed every angle of the garage.

"You'd have thought they'd make a garage door that doesn't take a fortnight to open," Roger said, resisting the temptation to press the multitude of buttons sprawled out in front of him.

They saw smoke rising in the distance as a convoy of ambulances, police vans, and prisoner transport vehicles flew by on the opposite side of the A38.

"Think we're late for the party, mate. What use are we taking over if they're already on the move?" Roger asked.

James glanced over at him. "We're not. Just need to confirm Ronny's whereabouts."

"So, what about the fire? Don't we need to confirm who started it and assume command?"

"No," came the curt reply.

A roadblock stood between them and the lane leading to the Woodrush Towers High-Dependency Hospital. Plastic police fencing filled gaps between police cars. Three police officers stood behind them. Roger saw them spring into action upon spotting Big Black.

"Bet they think they have their first catch of the day," Roger said, lowering his window.

They waited for their ID to be checked and verified. Two of the three cleared a space in the road.

"Yeah, move out the way, bitches!" Roger said through the closed window.

"Is *everything* a game to you, Rog?"

"You don't tell me enough for me to be any more dedicated than I am mucker."

"Holy shit!" Roger cried, looking at two large buses parked bumper-to-bumper. Police formed a funnel around guards, who had escaped the effects of the fire, and guided patients. Like the walking dead, they shook and staggered forward. Others laughed, while one was pulled out of the line, chanting that they were going to the gas chambers. Three officers tried to pin him to the ground; his strength demanded help, as two more joined them.

"New plan, Rog. You can stay with this lot, seeing's you're so keen on taking control of the situation."

"Yeah, fuck you. I want out of here as soon as we locate the subject," Roger replied.

"Subject, Rog? Thought you—"

"Bloody Ronny, the nut job. You know what I mean."

They pulled up alongside a police car; two suits walked over to them.

"Who might they be?" Roger asked.

"Could be insurance. They're quick off the mark in emergencies."

James recognised one of them. Couldn't place a name, but knew he was secret service. What the hell were they doing here? Something fishy was going on, and he felt less in control of this operation by the minute.

They both smiled, and the one James recognised went to shake Roger's hand. Roger didn't offer his.

"Agent White." He raised his eyes toward Roger, expecting a name.

"Agent Nun."

James knew Roger's follow-up line... *none of your fucking business.*

"Roger. And I'm James. What are you boys doing here?"

"Mr Green wanted us to take a look around, make sure the register was in order. It is, so we're going."

"Is he alive?"

"Who?" asked the tall, dark figure with a strong Nigerian accent.

"Never mind. Bye."

James pushed past them both. Roger followed.

The temporary administration was set up on the far side of the car park underneath a large white marquee—the sort that would be more fitting for a grand wedding than a building fire. Luck sent the smoke that was still billowing from the remaining structure in the opposite direction. Fire crews had doused the flames and had the situation under control. The structure remained, but the roof had fallen in, creating clouds of dust. James and Roger looked at the two thin face masks that had been handed to them by one of the fire crew; the sort you might wear if you were painting a wall or spray painting a car.

A man dressed in civilian clothing stood behind a fold-out table at the far end of the tent. Piles of files and books stood unorganised by his side. James asked to see the register and was met with a disapproving tut. "You lot have just asked me all I can tell. Unless you have anything else to ask, I don't see the point in wasting time. All hell is breaking loose. Better things to do than entertain you lot, and before you say it, I know you're FBI or secret-something, and I don't care."

"I need to know the whereabouts of a patient housed on ward fifteen."

"Like I told your friends. He's gone."

"Escaped?"

"No, dead. Fried to the bone, found handcuffed in his room. Could even be a murder case if the guard who secured his fate is still alive."

"How many still not accounted for?" Roger asked.

"According to the rota, everyone is, but if you ask me, whoever killed that poor bastard needs charging after the embers settle. He might have been a criminal, but no one deserves to die with no chance of escape."

After thanking him, James and Roger headed back to Big Black. Roger wanted to ask what the hell that was all about, but James paced on in front; it could wait until they were back in the car.

Much to Roger's delight, James climbed into the passenger side. Much to his dismay, his partner and best friend looked deflated. Like he'd had the wind knocked right out of him.

"James, you don't look right."

"Just drive, Rog."

Roger drove behind a grey bus and followed it out of the compound. A joke about why the bus's windows were so clean entered his mind, but he thought better of it. James pressed the screen in the centre of the dash. Mike's face appeared.

"Mike, have you had any other communication from head office?"

"Er, no sir."

"Location status update on Len, please."

"Len, Subject Two?"

Roger bit his lip.

"Subject Two's location. Let me see. Ah, yes."

Roger bit his lip harder.

"Send it to my phone, please. No information is to leave your desk, not even to the chief himself. Nothing."

74

"Er, okay, what about sending the info directly to the car?"

James shook his head, looking more ashen than he had before.

"Do as the man told you, you four-eyed fucktard!" Roger said, pressing any button he could see to end the call. James pressed the right one. Mike's face disappeared. Roger took a deep breath, aware he'd be in bad books with James.

"Thanks, Rog. You took the words out of my mouth."

James asked Roger to pull over in the lay-by just before hitting the A38. As he did, James' phone dinged. Mike's name appeared on the screen.

Chapter 9

Danial opened his eyes, gasped, and swiped the restraint from his face. A soft hand stroked his cheek, then covered his nose and mouth with an oxygen mask. He raised his hand again, unsure of his surroundings. The nurse guided it down by his side. Danial caught sight of someone standing beside her; a male doctor of East Asian descent. He spoke in a low, reassuring voice, telling him that he must stay still, or he'd dislodge the tube connected to the back of his hand. The doctor asked him his name, then asked question after question until Danial stopped him mid-flow.

"Did anyone make it out alive?" His eyes welled at visions of Lucy on fire; the sound of her pitiful cries still ringing in his ears.

"I saw her die, Doctor. In front of me."

The doctor looked into his eyes and said, "Who died? No women have died. Please, Mr Morris, you must stay calm, you have inhaled smoke. Slow, deep breaths. All you need to think about is yourself. Every person in the fire will be cared for by myself and other doctors."

Danial took a deep breath and coughed it out; a crushing feeling in his chest made his eyes bulge.

"No, you don't understand, I saw her on fire. For God's sake, you must know that." He turned to the nurse beside him, then to a bag hanging on a stand next to the bed, attached to a tube that ran into the back of his left hand. The pain in his chest subsided as the nurse gave him a sedative. Her explanation for what she was doing trailed off into a void somewhere between sleep and blissfulness.

"Doctor, we need your help, we have a female in the burns unit," said an overexcited male trainee nurse. Leaving Danial with the nurse, Dr Lu hurried over to the burns unit. Dr Cape, the on-duty surgeon, was midway through fitting a catheter to the female in question.

"I need a little help to clean this one, if you would be so kind," the surgeon said matter-of-factly. Like Dr Lu, his calm persona came from years of desensitisation, having worked on and lost more patients than most had ever seen.

The doctor listened to the surgeon's instructions; his patient looked in a critical state.

"Mr Cape, have we identified her? Shall I arrange for a nurse to contact relatives?"

At first, the surgeon ignored him and asked him to hold open a wound while he pulled out debris.

"Female member of staff. Another burn victim from Woodrush. Guess she wasn't expecting this after a long shift." His slow speech sounded almost sinister as he pulled out what looked like a piece of glass from beneath a patch of skin.

"Have we had any female fatalities, do you know?"

The surgeon raised an eyebrow. "No, but we've lost two males—one staff, one inmate. There was nothing I could do; both suffered fourth-degree burns, lost consciousness before I got to them. Shame, if they'd arrived sooner, I might have stood a chance. Why do you ask?"

"My last patient told me of a female who burned alive and died

77

in front of him, by the name of Lucy."

"Well, she's not dead, and she's not going to be. She'll recover." Dr Cape handed Dr Lu the scalpel. "After my work has finished and healing time has run its course, she will be beautiful again, but never the same. I'm good, but nothing ever fully returns. This is Lucy, Doctor; the first of many. I'll say one thing; she's a strong one. That fighting spirit will aid her recovery. The fire crew said a colleague rescued her. Said they'd liked to thank him, but he ran back into the building. Told me he was a goner; anyone crazy enough to run into an inferno wasn't coming back out again. Not alive, anyway. In a body bag, maybe."

Following Dr Cape's orders, Dr Lu wiped around a fold of skin and said, "May I tell her friend of her condition?"

"If that brave but stupid colleague of hers hadn't rescued her, she wouldn't be here. Bloody heroes always take it too far. She'll recover. She's responding well to treatment; airways are working fine. Early doors, Doctor, but I'd say it's short of a miracle. Please, hold this now. No more talking."

Dr Lu was ending a double shift; he had to retire for the evening or risk not only his patients, but himself, as fatigue had come, gone, and was returning with a vengeance. Before finishing, he called in to see Danial.

"Excuse me, Nurse, excuse me. Please, where has Mr Morris gone?"

After checking the bed records, she confirmed he'd moved to the recovery ward and should be able to go home tomorrow.

Long blinks and a jaw with a mind of its own, locking into yawns he couldn't control, Dr Lu considered the time it'd take to walk to the recovery ward. The ward was the furthest from the staff car park. If he didn't tell Danial the news, then who would?

Avoiding eye contact with fellow doctors, support nurses, and caretakers, he paced over to the ward. Danial had his back to the pillow, sitting up in his bed, trying to drink tea. A nurse steadied his shaking hand.

"Mr Morris, sir, I have information about your female friend."

Danial dropped the cup and contents on the bed table.

"Please, Doctor, Mr Morris has been through enough for one day. He needs to rest," the nurse said, mopping tea from the tray.

"I understand. I'll be one minute." He drew the bed curtain around himself and Danial. As he pulled a chair under the screen, he heard her complain to the senior duty nurse. Holding up both hands in a submissive gesture, he sat beside the bed.

"Mr Morris, sir, I have information on the lady called Lucy. She is not dead; she is very much alive. I saw her myself."

"Impossible, she—" the doctor questioned his good deed as Danial wheezed. "She crumbled like ash, her eyes... Doctor, her eyes fell out. She couldn't have made it out. I saw her die."

They heard two voices from outside the curtain before it was slapped back on its tracks. "Please listen, we have a positive ID on a Miss Lucy Day. She is recovering. She is in one piece; a man carried her out. I thought you would want to know this information. I need to go now."

Disbelief gave way to hope. "Er, thanks," Danial said.

The nurses reassured him, taking turns glancing back at the doctor. Danial questioned what the doctor had said. Nothing made sense. He watched her burn; unable to save her. He shuddered as her cries for help rang through his head.

"She laughed."

"Mr Morris, how are you feeling?

"It wasn't her; Lucy wouldn't do that."

"Can I get you anything?" asked the duty nurse for that evening,

"Is Lucy a relative?"

"I need to see her; she's here." Danial reached for the bed rail. It collapsed, sending him rolling to the edge.

Already briefed, the nurse knew of Dr Lu's unconventional visit to the patient. Word spread fast when a senior nurse hit above her station. A complaint against him had already been logged.

Her smile was both warm and understanding. Emphasising his short recovery time, she told Danial that he was being observed, and advised that the effects of smoke inhalation demanded rest at this stage, before assuring him that it wouldn't be long before the doctor gave him the all-clear to leave.

"How long?" Danial asked, perking up at the news.

"Only a few days. A doctor will check up on you in the morning. I'm sure your friend is doing fine. She's in the best place."

Danial sighed, his chest still tender. The nurse held his fingers and offered him something to help him sleep. He declined.

"Please try to rest. Otherwise, you'll be here a lot longer. I'll come back in a while to check on you. I've got a full ward tonight, ah… Forgot to give you your bag. It's behind the desk; I'll go get it."

"Bag?"

"Feels like books. Your uncle dropped it off while you were asleep."

"Uncle?"

The nurse told the patient in the bed across from Danial that she would be with him in one minute. Another cried when she told him the same.

By the time the nurse finished her round, forgetting she hadn't given patient Morris the bag brought in by his uncle, she walked over to his bed. Danial was asleep, sedated for the night. She tucked it into the cupboard beside a large bottle of water left by a previous bed dweller.

Lights out, few sounds remained. An occasional cough, low-level ringing from the reception area, and grunts of pain from a bed furthest from Danial. Asleep now for over an hour, Danial's hand raised before slamming back down onto the side rail. The tube attached to his hand pulled free from the bandage. Danial woke, fright gripping him as he scrambled for the tube. He was floating. Toes curled upward, the bottom rail being his only anchor.

He screamed. No one came.

"Help!"

He could see two evening staff in conversation, but neither looked.

"Put me down."

A force pushed him down into the bed. Pressure hit his chest. A tightening in his throat, as if gripped; held down against his will. He kicked and snatched at the invisible hand around his neck. His head shook as a voice whispered, "Humpty Dumpty had a great fall." The words trailed off before rising into hysterical laughter.

Danial sat upright and bellowed, "I know who you are, Ronny! Or should I call you Vetala? Your games don't frighten me anymore."

The response, one of tortured surprise: "I have ended the life of your tormentor."

The bed moved again, raising heads as patients gawked. The bed flew past stationary beds; the sides rose on either side of his own. Wheeled around the reception desk, Danial glimpsed two green double doors fly past as they banged on the bed rails.

He woke within unfamiliar surroundings. Looking around, he was the only person in the pastel blue room. The door knocked three times; he swung himself off the bed. A blonde nurse entered, young, with radiant, blemish-free skin. She held a blood pressure monitor; a stethoscope hung from her neck.

"Good morning, Mr Morris. Your notes say you had quite a night last night. I'm Lora; I'll be doing a few preliminaries before your visit from the doctor."

Frowning, Danial stretched the green throwaway gown across his thigh. "What do the notes say, Nurse? Er, Lora. Is that why I have my own room?"

"Better the doctor explains. Now, please hold out your arm."

"No, I need to know if you saw him."

"Sorry, I don't understand. Who?"

"Never mind. I meant to ask what happened last night."

The nurse focused on a clipboard hooked on the bed frame. "Let me see... you had a nightmare, woke other patients," she continued reading. "You must have fallen out of bed and knocked over the IV stand."

Pondering, Danial asked, "Are there any cameras on the ward, Lora?"

"Mm, I don't know, Mr Morris. Now, this may feel a little tight around your arm. It'll only last a few seconds. You'll be able to see the pressure changing on the monitor."

As she spoke, Dr Lu entered.

"Hello again, Mr Morris. How are you feeling today? Did you have a good night's sleep?" Danial watched the nurse unhook and pass him the plastic clipboard. "Doctor, you may want to read these. Mr Morris had a little discomfort during the night."

Danial snapped at the nurse, "A little discomfort? The bloody bed was flying, I tell you! Just check the cameras and see for yourself."

"Dreams can seem real," Lora said.

Dr Lu waved her out. "Danial, hello again. May I ask what all that was about with you wanting to see the camera?"

Danial liked Dr Lu. He muddled his words a little but showed genuine interest in him.

"Doctor, would it be possible to check the ward's cameras to find out what happened last night."

"You are suffering trauma, Mr Morris. I'd be having nightmares if I went through what you have."

Having no way of explaining the unexplained without the doctor concluding that he was unstable, he agreed, then asked if he could see Lucy. The doctor explained her condition and offered to pass on a message instead. Abashed, he searched his mind between throbs. What message could he give?

"If you can tell her I'm thinking of her, Doctor."

"I'll pass on your regards."

"Who died in front of me on ward fifteen, Doctor?"

Lowering his head with a look of regret, Dr Lu confirmed that the person was William Hatfield.

"Bill... No, that couldn't be. You're mistaken. He left the building. He told me Lucy was up there. It had to be Ronny."

After explaining that they'd identified the victim, and relatives were informed, Danial dropped his head back on the pillow. Tears fell down his cheek.

"Do you have anyone I can call to look after you and take you home, Mr Morris?"

Danial wanted to say, *call my wife, my girlfriend, my sister or brother.* He had no one.

"No, it's fine. I'll get a taxi. Will it be today?"

"We're waiting on results. All being well, you can go home

after lunch."

Danial neither wanted to go back to the flat or extend his stay in the hospital. Nothing was out of reach of the thing that Len had called Vetala.

On his way to the Urology department to see a patient suffering from kidney stones, Dr Lu detoured to the critical care ward. Glad to see that Dr Cape wasn't with a patient, he asked about Lucy Day, as he wanted to pass on Danial's message.

Dr Cape looked ashen, as if slapped hard in the face by someone incapable of the act.

"You haven't heard?" Dr Cape waved Dr Lu into a storeroom. "She's recovering at a rapid rate. As crazy as it sounds, she's repairing herself."

Dr Lu lowered his head, raised his shoulders, and said, "Well, that's a good thing, isn't it?"

Dr Cape shook his head, "Come; I'll take you to her. She's down the corridor, room on the right. Don't act too surprised; I know you will be."

The transformation verged on magical. Sitting up, Lucy smiled as he studied her exposed limbs. No visible scarring. The skin tissue had but a mere scalding. Pinkish red patches remained on the lower legs, but the open wounds had healed. Not improved; *healed*. As if they were never there.

Questioning his years of expertise, Dr Cape looked to Dr Lu for confirmation of what lay before them. He followed Dr Cape into a storeroom housing a variety of cleaning stuff.

"We are men of science. This defies logic," Dr Cape said. "She has relatives arriving soon. I may need you to confirm her condition—her earlier condition. Her uncle saw her in the state you did. He'll have trouble understanding the dramatic change."

"They would be pleased," Dr Lu said. "Almost forgot, I need to pass on another patient's regards."

Dr Lu passed on Danial's message, then asked if her uncle would come back. Baffled, she squinted, telling him she hadn't any uncles, as far as she was aware. Only parents and a younger sister; a small family. No grandparents, uncles, or aunts. Excusing himself, he walked toward Dr Cape. It was his turn to follow Dr Lu into the cleaning cupboard.

"She said she has no such uncle."

"I'll check with reception," Dr Cape said, distracted by the older version of Lucy peering through the glass panel of the double doors—her mother. The family was here.

Chapter 10

Danial, having been given the all-clear, wanted to see Lucy, so he asked to see her. After checking, the nurse said she had visitors, and after-hours visitation applied only to close family. He wasn't family, nor her partner, nor a close friend, and saying he was a sad, borderline obsessive wouldn't go down well.

Peering into a plastic bag; dirty underwear, magazine, a crushed can, and chocolate wrappers summed up the entirety of his possessions. Another bag, which he thought he'd left in the back of his car, had a few books, some clothes, and toiletries; things he would've used before leaving. He shoved it into the other. Thanking the nurse, he left the ward and headed for the main reception. There was a wall-mounted phone, the sign above selling the services of a local taxi firm. Several threes and two zeros. *Call free now.*

He sat facing the double glass-fronted entrance doors, awaiting the arrival of the taxi, his focus drifting between an overflowing bin and a vending machine. Thoughts turned to the flat and what had happened. He needed to clean again. For what reason? Another thrashing from a ghost that was a man... or a man that was a ghost.

A solitary life filled with routine had left him with no real friends or people whom he knew may offer to let him stay a night or two. If he had relatives, he questioned whether he'd put them at risk from his nightly visitor.

A bald, brutish guy walked through the double doors and over to the reception area. Looking out, Danial saw a taxi. He hadn't been in one for over twenty years. He had thoughts of a uniformed driver, or at least one who didn't have armpit hair sticking out from under a stained t-shirt.

"You Morris?" he asked.

Walking past him, he boarded the yellow Hackney-style taxi before Danial could respond. Danial stood, his teeth gritted. He'd been through too much to cower under this sweaty excuse for a human being. "Give me one excuse. Just one," he said to himself, under his breath. As he walked over to the taxi, he noticed a black Range Rover parked in front of a sign that read *NO PARKING, Ambulance turning point.*

The driver, already in his seat, set the metre. Glad to see a screen dividing them, Danial nestled back into the seat when the back door flew open.

"May I ride with you?"

Something inside Danial snapped. He glared, flushed face, anger rippling through him.

"Len, what are you doing here?"

Len didn't answer and climbed into the backseat.

"You all right, boss? You know this bloke?"

Confirming he did, the taxi moved. The Range Rover blocked its path.

"Bloody idiot, move your fucking wagon!" shouted the driver.

Len told the driver to go around them. "Mount the side verge if you have to—just go."

With a continued press of the horn, the taxi got around the Land Rover; the driver gave the bird in protest, then continued to rant as he pulled out of the main entrance and onto a side road.

Danial slid the dividing centre panel closed, more to block out the driver's twaddle than to give them any privacy.

"You heard about the fire?" Danial asked.

Len looked over his shoulder at the Range Rover pulling out from the turning point. It was following them.

"Trouble?"

"No. Since my release, they've followed me."

"Who's following you?"

"The same people who let me out. Where are you heading, Danial?"

Danial told him about his stay in the hospital, leaving out most of the details, including the disturbing night before.

"They gave me the all-clear. Heading back to the flat and my bed."

"No, you can't. He's escaped. Get as far away as you can; as far away from me as possible,"

Len noticed that Danial had turned a wash of grey. "Are you all right?"

"No, I'm far away from bloody all right... What the hell is going on? The news said all inmates were recaptured. I've had about enough of his visits. Last night, I confronted him. Told him what I thought of him. And he knows that I know who he is. His cover's blown."

Len fell silent. Danial knew spurting out a few words in the effort to convince himself he was in control would not impress him.

"Energy can neither be reasoned with, nor destroyed. Transferred, maybe, but that requires the warrior sent to destroy him. Like a negative charge is to a battery, he's a necessary evil. Balance is what I seek. Imbalance is his only goal. I need to keep moving until such a time as the warrior—the one who is pure consciousness—presents itself, or I find out who or what…"

The privacy screen opened. The driver's arm entered the rear of the taxi. A zigzag tattoo faced them. Thick fingers spread out on the screen provided stability as he turned his head to face them.

"Shall I cut through to Highlands and risk getting stuck in traffic on the one-way system, or do you want me to take the loop road, mate?"

Len asked if he could get out on the high street; a busy road with no parking available. The driver grunted his disapproval.

"You'll have to jump out at the lights; I'm not risking a ticket."

Glancing back, Danial saw the Range Rover trailing three cars behind. Len grasped Danial's hand, unnerving him.

"He'll lose interest when he knows I am no longer in any contact with you. Gather clothes and things you may need and leave tonight. Go to a hotel or a friend's house; anywhere other than the flat. It will take time for him to find you; time needed for him to realise you play no part in this."

"So, I go to the Holiday Inn and hope he doesn't find me? Is that what you are saying?"

Len looked him straight in the eyes and said, "Anywhere I am unaware of, so no, not the Holiday Inn. Tell no one. Just turn up, and don't call before getting to your destination. Just go."

The driver slowed as the traffic lights turned red.

"The stowaway can get out here. You two splitting the fare, or what?"

"No, I'm paying," Danial replied. "Were you the uncle who brought my bag of books?"

"Amongst them, you have a book more valuable than diamonds. Be careful with it, and view it only with a pure heart."

Len opened the door. Danial tugged at his shirt. "How did you get the bag out of my car? What book? What are you saying?"

"The one you bought from Harden Antiques. It can only talk to the chosen one. The one who will capture Vetala. The one I need to protect. When the book is ready to move on, it will, but it wants to stay with you. For what reason, I don't know."

"You broke into my car?" Danial shuffled along the seat. Len stood outside, peering through the gap in the open door. "How do you know where I bought it? And what do you mean, it chooses to stay with me?"

"I sold it to you, not because you wanted it, but because it chose you. I think you're a pawn in the race to find the chosen one. The book will leave you when it's ready."

"Or until I throw it away..."

The privacy screen slid open. "Got to go. Either get out or close the door." The driver snapped the screen shut and rolled the car forward.

From the window, Danial saw Len run into Hill Moor Shopping Centre. The Range Rover pulled into the space the taxi had left, leaving its rear sticking out, blocking passing traffic. The sound of car horns firing and disapproving faces shouting through rolled-down windows must have unnerved them. A man dressed in a black suit got out, saw Danial looking at him, edged toward the shopping centre, and then got back in again.

The taxi was nearing the Highland Estate. Tilting his mirror to get a better look at the commotion, the driver said, "Look at that fool with his hazards on. Lucky he didn't get jacked. It's not a nice area, this."

Danial grinned, saying, "I know, I live here. Take your next right onto Brampton Road, if you will. I live in the largest block of flats."

"Better you than I, mate. I wouldn't live here if you paid me."

About to question the extortionate fare, Danial couldn't find the energy to argue. What good would it do anyway? Having handed the meathead taxi driver a twenty, he waited for his fifty pence change. The taxi driver drove off, finding the need to roll down his window and shout, "Thanks for the tip, shithead!"

Danial approached the stone steps leading to the apartment block. He had only been away for two days, but things seemed different. Neighbours he'd never seen before had their doors open and were talking. Even the resident drunk was engaging in conversation.

Feet fast and head low, he climbed the stairs. Noticing black shoes half-coved by black trousers, he stopped, looked up, and saw several uniformed police officers taping off the floor where he lived. A man dressed from head to toe in white, carrying a black, oversized briefcase brushed past him. One of the uniformed officers asked, "Where do you think you're going?"

Danial was shocked, not by the police presence—that was nothing unusual—but by the tape stretched across the hallway, blocking access to his flat. He assumed they'd arrested his neighbour. Ducking under the tape, two officers blocked his path.

"You can't go past this point." The officer tapped the tape. "Go back down the stairs."

"I need things from my flat," Danial said.

One leaned his head on his shoulder and spoke into his radio. The other held him by the arm.

"Let go!"

"Your name and flat number, please?"

"What's happened?"

Shrugging his arm away from the officer, he craned his neck

for a better look. The door to his flat was open. Plasterboard littered the hallway. He blinked hard when he saw a large open space inside. The wall separating his flat from that of his neighbours was missing.

"What the hell has happened?"

"We need you to come to the station, sir. Answer a few questions."

Danial shook. Cold had struck, sending his skin to pimples. Adrenaline threatened to take over. "Are you arresting me?"

"No, sir. It's not the place to discuss getting your belongings. Please follow Officer Patterson."

Why they had to keep his things at reception and why he had to attend a police interview to gain entry into a property he owned, Danial couldn't grasp. He was led into an interview room. It was smaller than he imagined, having only a desk and three chairs. He sat. Two officers—one he recognised from the flat and one other—sat closest to the door opposite him. He declined their strong advice to appoint a solicitor and had to confirm this, along with his full name, into a recording device before they began. He'd done nothing wrong, and whatever the police thought, he had an alibi.

After ten minutes of answering the same questions with the same answers—"I don't know. I was in the hospital."—he was alone in the room while they went to make further inquiries. Before leaving, they leaned forward and spoke into the recording device, telling it who they were and that they were leaving the room. This was too formal for a simple break-in or an immigration issue. Every time he asked what had happened, they ignored his question and asked one of their own.

Sitting alone, he questioned whether they thought he'd committed a crime. The way they kept asking the same question over and over with squinting, accusing eyes... He sat in silence, hands pressed between his thighs, looking at the smoke-stained yellow walls and the scratches on the desk; more than he could count.

Why his flat? It had to have something to do with the fat man next door. A raid, maybe. Or the neighbour could have burgled his flat, knowing he was away. Revenge for making too much noise? His mind raced.

Claustrophobic, hot, and faint, Danial stood. With no room to pace, he moved the chair under the desk, aligning it into a mirror image of the other. About to open the door, two people entered; the officer from the flat and a replacement for the other officer. The replacement wore a blue pinstriped suit. Not off the rack. It looked tailored and was complemented by a crisp white shirt with gold cufflinks. The strange, suited man looked at him, gave no introduction, and sat beside the officer. The silence continued until Danial spoke.

"Are you going to tell me what's going on and when I can collect my things from the flat?"

The officer switched on the recording device. "Time is 6:32 PM, interview room two. We have Officer Paul Mitchell and Mr McMilan present. Beginning the interview with..." Officer Mitchel flicked through his notebook. "Mr Danial Morris of Apartment 23, Brampton Road, Highlands Estate. Picking up from where we left off, you said you were in the hospital. After being discharged, you travelled by taxi to the site of the incident, is that correct?"

Rolling his eyes, Danial said, "Yes, you know this already. I've answered your questions, but you're not answering mine."

The officer told Danial he had to ask standard questions and assured him that he would have the opportunity to ask questions after he'd finished.

"Do you know anyone with a grudge against you or your neighbour, Mr Morris?"

With growing contempt, Danial told them he didn't. What else could he say? That evil spirits visited him, and he hated his neighbour? That they had a magic book behind the police check-in desk? The suited man held his hand up to the officer, who took it as a prompt to wrap the interview up with a simple, "Thank you for answering our questions. The time is now 8:14 PM, and all parties within interview room two are leaving."

James McMilan switched the recorder off, and Officer Mitchel stood. Danial followed his lead, only to have James ask him if he would like coffee. Danial declined and walked around the desk. Seeing the officer out, the suited man calling himself McMillen closed the door.

"Please excuse the police asking so many questions, Danial. Take a seat. We shouldn't be much longer."

Danial didn't need a map to find his breaking point. He'd found it, sat in a shit-stained, tiny room. He raised his voice; something he was getting used to of late.

"I have done nothing wrong. I know not what is going on. I have rights. What you are doing is illegal." He blurted something else through gritted teeth; something he didn't understand himself. Breathless ranting; a new, unwanted trait.

"Tell me about Ronny," James said, in a tone that would be more apt if a friend was asking.

Banging his knee on the desk as he stood, Danial bit his lip, determined to leave. James spoke faster. "Ronny escaped the night of the fire; the night you went into the hospital. We believe he broke into your flat after slaughtering the family next door. He wrote something on your wall and used their blood as paint—Mr. Morris, please take a seat."

Danial held his neck; it was expanding. Lunging forward, a torrent of vomit splattered the silver paper bin next to James. The smell of vomit hit James as he reached for the door. Officer Mitchell rushed in, asking, "What did you do to him? If this gets out, my career is on the line." They helped Danial to his feet and led him to an accessible toilet, telling him they'd be outside. Their tone was now one of caring concern.

Nausea had passed, leaving him weaker than before he heard the news. He sat on a brown leather office chair in a larger room that had undergone a recent refurbishment. Lingering odours of paint and new carpet threatened to ignite settling stomach acid.

He moved back for a tray of biscuits and tea, brought in by a cleaner or someone not within the police force. Cradling the cup, he sipped and waited.

The door opened. McMilan entered.

"I'm here to help. You said you have nowhere to stay; I've arranged a hotel room. I'll send two of my best to guard the room. Tomorrow, I'll arrange something more permanent. We're not arresting you, but we must protect you."

Danial looked around the new room; sparse, but more welcoming than the last. He swivelled on the chair behind a desk where someone of importance would sit. He placed the cup on a leather-like coaster. With tiredness dampening any emotional reaction, he agreed.

Like a recovering alcoholic, his hands trembled upon seeing the same Range Rover that'd followed the taxi.

"Please climb aboard. Watch your step."

Fight-or-flight. Should he turn and run or get into the Range Rover? A strobe light of questions flicked through his mind.

Why were the same people who wanted to capture Ronny following Len Happy? Why was Len helping—or was he? He knew better than to ask one of the two guys sitting up front, or the beefcakes sitting on either side of him. James introduced a pissed-off-looking fellow as Roger. Roger gave James a disapproving look.

"These two will be with you all night. No one will get anywhere near you without them knowing. Well, introduce yourselves," he said to the men sitting on either side of him. The one to his right—whom Danial thought could do with discovering deodorant—introduced himself as Mac, and the other said his name was Max. James smiled through the rearview mirror and said, "You can call me James."

Danial had his theories of why the men next to him had only three letters in their names. His instincts told him that the names they went by were not their own. For the rest of the journey, he considered more suitable names. He'd got a half dozen before they arrived.

Light pollution tainted the stars with a shield of haze. Danial followed Mac out of the car. Max and James followed. The pissed-off-looking fellow remained in the passenger seat. Approaching the main entrance, a sign above the door read, *Welcome to the Holiday Inn*. Danial stopped. Turning to Max and James, he said, "I can't stay at this hotel. It's not safe."

James tried to ease any concern by looking at the two heavies on loan to him.

"This was the only hotel willing to accommodate our needs on such short notice. You're in safe hands, Danial. It's only for tonight."

Remembering what Len said in the taxi, he wanted to object, but how would he explain that the person they'd followed had advised not to come here? That because he'd mentioned the hotel to Len, Vetala would find out? It sounded crazy to him, so it would sound even stranger to them.

Having never stayed at a hotel, Danial had no expectations. The room had a rich, royal blue carpet, a fitted wardrobe with a desk attached, and a large double bed with crisp new sheets tucked under the mattress. It was as if they knew he dressed his bed that way. One thing was clear; he'd never see his bed or set foot in that place again.

The need to collapse upon the welcoming mattress didn't fit his routine. After taking a shower, he made a cup of tea and sat channel-flicking. A man selling a piece of elastic, a thigh band for stronger curves. A woman selling gardening gloves. An American game show, and the weather. Danial fingered the bag of books and pulled out the one he'd bought from Harden Antiques. It looked the business, which had been one reason for the purchase. The pages contained, at first glance, old-style writing and pictures that looked etched onto gold pages. A beautiful book with little content. He recalled turning to a random page and seeing what looked like his block of flats; the other reason he'd parted with the cash. The block of flats was a sure sign that the book wasn't old, and over half of the pages were blank. What did Len say? It chose him. Flicking through, he could no longer see the block of flats. His eyes were instead drawn to a picture of a building with a clock on its tower and swirls coming from the roof and windows, as if the artist had been angry with the tool he'd used. Violent scribbles leapt from the main design, spoiling an otherwise fine drawing. Stick trees were spaced equally below. A sick man holding another across his chest and half a stick man vanishing off the page. He fumbled back through the book and found the picture he'd seen prior. This time, he looked closer and saw things that he hadn't before. A figure sitting on a wall between what could be a road and the building. Another looking out of a top window, and one floating mid-air with SATANA etched over it. He couldn't recall seeing anything written on the page, but remembered slapping it shut when he saw that half the book was blank.

He knew the men were outside the heavy teak door, but that didn't bring comfort, as he knew Vetala would appear when he least expected it.

Setting his phone to record, Danial balanced it next to the empty teacup, laid back, pulled the sheets up to his chin, and entered sleep in the knowledge that his protectors were standing guard.

* * *

Roger flinched when James opened the driver's door.

"Tired, mate?"

Stretching his hands, the flats of his palms touched the roof. "This seat is comfier than my bed."

"I've made a call, and we can borrow the shed tomorrow."

Searching his memory, Roger remembered the shed. "You mean the interrogation floor on Downs Road? That's harsh, even if he started the fire. I can remember it being full of spiders and shit."

"Not now, Rog. They've built a witness protection suite. Mod cons an' all."

As Big Black left the car park, Roger arranged a morning lift with James, leaving his car back at the office. No point in swapping cars and making the night longer than it already had been.

"So, what's Len's interest in Morris, then?"

James switched the heater on and watched the condensation dissipate.

"My guess is Len has talked Danial into helping him find the ghost he reports will destroy humanity. He's gutless; there's no way he started the fire."

"Len?"

"No, Danial. Len could have, but I don't think so. I think Ronny started the fire to escape."

"That doesn't explain why two people who are free wanted to break into a high-security establishment, and lo and behold, a fire breaks out."

"Look, Sherlock, there's more to this than meets the eye."

"Well, Bond, it doesn't take an MI5 agent to work out they went to great lengths to get in, and then it burned to the ground."

"It's Watson, Rog. Not Bond."

Roger looked out his window. Long blinks followed a yawn that sounded like a strangled cat; his head flopped back onto the headrest.

"This magical being that Len and Ronny both seek... I can only assume it's for different reasons."

"And your point is?"

Eyes still closed, Roger continued. "What's the reason?" Blinking, as if waking from a nap he was unaware of having, he added, "I mean, the *real* reason. Not the reason Len has given us. What's the *real* reason, James? Find that, and shit will flow."

James looked sideways to Roger; he'd closed his eyes once more. "As we're not buying into the notion that a prophet or warrior will come to kill Ronny, we can rule out Ronny being let out on a trace."

"Can we?"

"He escaped, Rog. Even if he didn't start the fire, he used it to escape. Green's playing his cards close to his chest. He enforced a strict need-to-know, limiting my enquiries into the subjects."

Roger yawned and said, "I'm more interested in why they let a study subject out halfway through our program. Not to mention everyone knowing about the rota not allowing for our man Morris, who wasn't supposed to be on that day. The news that Ronny had escaped took its time in coming. Even the boys back at the office thought I must have known."

The centre screen flashed as if they were making a call. For a split-second, a sound not dissimilar to a dial tone broke the silence.

"James, do you remember what I told you before you became my boss, back when you were a snot-nosed recruit? That time when you laughed so hard, it made your cheeks sore? You had so many questions. Question after question, you asked. Remember?" Roger looked at him, then to the dashboard.

James remembered. "Tell you what, I'll pick you up in my car tomorrow. No need polluting the planet with this big bugger."

"Good idea."

They remained silent for the rest of the journey. Not even a goodbye. Just a wave and a wink.

Chapter 11

Three consecutive bangs. Danial went from sleep to alert. He reached for his mobile phone. His fingers fumbled on the screen; the battery had drained.

Muffled voices came from outside the room. "Mr Morris, are you awake, sir?"

Sweat speckled his brow. Wiping it, he looked down at his watch. 11:11 AM.

"Yes, I'm just getting up now. Won't be long," he called back.

Danial put on the complimentary dressing gown and opened the door. The same two had been there all night.

"You guys look tired."

Max huffed through his nose. Mac said, "Well, yes, we both are. We were instructed to leave you until after nine. It's gone eleven."

"Er, yes, sorry about that."

"No, it's fine, you've been through a lot. Did you get a good night's sleep?"

"Best night's sleep for a long time. Uneventful and undisturbed."

As Danial showered, he thought about his recurring dream. The brunette with Lucy's face. How she made him feel. As always, he woke up before making the final connection. An emotion-fuelled dream that he wished was a reality.

James and Roger took over for the loaned thugs. Both waited for Danial to get dressed. Unaware of the switch, Danial heard the base tone of the beefcakes turn into those of James and Roger. He pressed his wet ear up against the door, hoping to catch them in conversation. If they were talking, then he couldn't hear anything audible through the thickness of the wooden door.

Taking a deep breath, he opened the door. Roger seemed different than James; less formal, more normal than his sidekick or boss. Could be just an act, as he'd already experienced the good cop-bad cop routine.

"So, are you guys going to tell me what's going on?" he asked.

"Yes. Not now. There's a safe house not too far from here. I think we can learn a lot from each other," James said. "We'll both be able to rest when we find the person who broke into your flat and dismembered your neighbours."

"Dismembered?!" Danial felt a tightening in his neck.

"Please, not here. Follow me."

Roger waited for him to pass. Danial walked centre, as if following a well-planned routine.

Few words were exchanged on the way to the safe house. Only lighthearted chitchat, which Danial didn't acknowledge as he tried to block out images of the horror that had taken place in what he used to call home.

With no idea of what a safe house would look like, he started to imagine a house in the middle of nowhere, surrounded by woodland, far down the only lane that served as its entrance and exit. Instead, they entered a car park of a single office block.

James swiped a card through a reader and looked into a camera mounted on a door frame of an exit, or the tradesman's entrance.

"I thought we were going to a safe house. I'm having second thoughts."

"You're free to go whenever you want. You're not under arrest. Going back to the flat is out of the question. Not until we wrap this thing up and forensics have dusted," Roger said.

"Welcome to the safest building this side of the water, Danial. Everyone here is vetted, and they all work for me," James added. Roger frowned at that point.

They boarded a lift like no other. Old pull-chains ran down either side; grinding workings squealed as it rose through floors. It stopped with a jolt on what must have been the top floor. Roger muttered, "Refurbished?" James either didn't hear or ignored him.

They entered a large space with wooden blocked flooring resembling a school hall. Unlike the school hall Danial remembered as a child, it had a new plastic smell and had been painted no longer than a few weeks ago. Danial followed James to the only other door. A space laid out like a self-contained hotel room, it had a kitchenette, shower room, and mod-cons, not dissimilar to his flat.

"You're welcome to stay here until he's apprehended."

"Er, no. No thanks. I've come..." Danial remembered a movie where two CIA agents tied a man to a chair in a room similar to this one. He shuddered. Chairs pulled across the room by the man calling himself Roger threatened to spur him into running back to the elevator.

"Sorry for not having anything more comfortable. We don't normally use this place. Here, have a seat," Roger said, pointing to one of the brown plastic office chairs.

Danial felt a droplet of sweat run down his temple. He wiped it with his sleeve, making it look like he was combing his hair back with his fingers. Not good at starting conversations, Danial took a deep breath and sat facing the two men. "So, what's going on?"

The two suits waited for him to continue. His face turned pale white to a blush red as blood congregated above his shoulders; one reason he never lied. The uncomfortable silence lasted until Roger sighed and James spoke.

"You were lucky to escape the fire. Can you remember who rescued you?"

"No, but when I find out, I'll thank him," Danial said.

"Him?" Roger added. "It was a male, then."

"No… I presume it would've been; I'd take some lifting." Danial sat dumbfounded as a flashback to flames, smoke, being pulled, and collapsing hit him. The bright light, then looking up into the eyes of Len Happy.

"You don't look too good. Have you remembered something that might help?" Roger asked, waiting for a reply that never came. "We're gathering information. We know an escaped inmate violated your flat." Rubbing his chin with his fingertips, James waited for Danial to speak or Roger to continue.

"I know. It was Vetala. I mean, Ronny." Danial added, hoping his slip went unnoticed.

Roger stared at James with open-mouthed concern. Danial looked towards James and saw his eyes dart away from him.

"Vetala?" Roger questioned.

"I meant to say Ronny from Woodrush Towers. The man who escaped." Danial raised his voice. Not out of anger or guilt, but to suppress his nervousness.

Roger was about to ask another question, but Danial got in first.

"Look, I don't know what you want with me or why you've brought me to a movie set. And what are you, agents?" He was fidgeting in the chair. James and Roger were losing his attention.

Roger stood up, walked over to the kitchen area, and looked back. "Brew?"

"No, I'm okay!"

"Suit yourself. I'm having one. Bit chilly in here. And yeah, come to think of it, this place *does* resemble a film set."

Roger vanished into the custom-built studio flat. Danial heard the kettle reaching its climax. He sat face-to-face with James, about ten feet away from the sound of Roger whistling "Show Me the Way to Go Home".

Danial tried to steady his knees. "Is this legal—I mean, shouldn't the police be here?"

Roger popped his head around the door. "Told you he'd rather deal with the cops. Why don't we call 'em?"

Roger disappeared again. The kettle pinged. Danial turned to James.

"What's he mean? I'm the bloody victim here. I've done nothing wrong!"

"You'll have to excuse Roger. He gets ratty when he's tired. But he has a point. The police are aware of the escape." James shrugged. "The fire started after you entered the building." He shrugged again. "After going on stress-related leave, you knew not to come into work; not to mention, they now have proof of a released patient whom you were fond of breaking in and finding you. He bypassed everyone else in need of rescue to save your life."

Touching his forehead as if in thought, Danial closed his eyes. "None of this makes any sense."

"Doesn't have to. My guess is they'll slap you with arson, manslaughter, and –"

"Stop!" Danial shouted.

Roger walked in, holding three mugs of tea.

"I made you one. In case you change your mind." He sat next to James with his legs stretched out, smiling.

Danial licked his drying lips. The tea was still too hot to drink.

"Look, I went there to confront Ronny. To warn him—tell him I know it's him visiting me, playing tricks."

Like a schoolboy who had been told his parents would be called if he didn't tell all, he told them everything he knew. All that happened before the fire, that is. Visits from a ghost-like figure things that Len had told him about Ronny possessed by Vetala, an evil entity which, if killed, would move on to another being, and that the only way of stopping it was containment—how and by whom, he didn't know.

Thoughts of the tea being poisoned were overshadowed by Danial's need to quench his thirst. Reaching down, he picked up the mug and downed it in three gulps. It wasn't sugared; he didn't realise until a bitter, tan taste lingered.

James and Roger remained silent. No written statement was taken. He was about to tell them about Len warning him that Lucy was in danger. The taxi ride to his house with Len, and Roger looking like the man he saw. He wasn't sure it *was* Roger. He wasn't sure about most things. He forced a smile in their direction.

James said, "Do the words Humpty Dumpty mean anything to you?"

Roger lowered his head, aware of the call from forensics.

"How did you know?"

"Know what?"

"Know he spoke when I checked his room. The first time he'd spoken, as far as I'm aware."

James frowned, raising his right eyebrow upon hearing new information, then asked what had happened the night he'd checked the room. Had anyone else heard him speak? Danial didn't know how they knew. He told them about the other guards with him.

"The poor bastards in the flat next to yours—or should I say the same flat, now the walls are missing," Roger sipped on the mug. The only thing required was the family photo album and a yawning dog. "He used the victim's blood. On the walls, floor. Even the fucking ceiling. Ronny is one crazy son of a bitch, and we need your help to stop him."

Danial looked at the lift, thinking about making a run for it.

"Do it. Go. Fine by me, but this fucker has a hard-on for you. For what reason, I don't know. Maybe you pissed him off, and now he wants revenge. Maybe because you're friends with the other sicko, Len Happy."

Danial stood, his heart pounding, and he had those jelly legs again.

"Going somewhere?" Roger asked, standing.

James interrupted, "Danial, we're here to help."

He walked over to the lift with his eyes screwed tightly shut. If they were going to shoot, it would be now. James walked up behind him. Danial turned, opened his eyes, and took the plain white business card from between his fingers. There was nothing on it. He flicked it over and revealed a mobile number scribbled in Biro.

"We brought you, so we will drop you off," Roger said.

"Thanks, but I'll be getting a taxi to my brother's. He lives up country; I'll be safe enough with him."

His face flushed with every word. Hoping they hadn't noticed, he nodded before boarding the lift. The cogs clucked, and the cables screeched. Bent at the knees, Danial pushed the balls of his feet down in a futile attempt to quicken its decent.

The air outside seemed fresher. Like a new-born taking its first breath, he inhaled until his lungs reversed the intake. Arching his back, he placed his hands on his knees. Like a criminal, he glanced up at the building, and started to jog with no destination in mind.

Roger put his hand in front of James, stopping him from pacing the floor for the fourth time.

"More tea, Vicar?"

"Your tea tastes like cat wee, Rog. Do you think he's going up country?"

"I used my flight time to do a little research. He's an only child. No close family to speak of, and little-to-no friends. A sad case."

"Bloody hell, Rog. Why didn't you tell me?"

"When are you going to tell me the reason I had to go to Italy as a writer of a shit magazine?"

Dizziness struck James; he fell into the chair.

"Mate, what's up? You're acting weird. This isn't the first time, either. What's with the heavy breathing? Think you need a holiday."

"It's not that, Rog. You know me better than anyone. I can handle stress; I'm good at keeping secrets, but…"

"Thought I could feel a 'but' coming."

"But I don't know what my role is anymore. Like you, I understand we all have our parts to play, and crossing the line is taboo. I mean, no point in telling someone the full picture if it distracts from their mission, right?"

"Right," Roger agreed.

"But ruining someone's life—someone who has helped us solve cases; a selfless man who only seeks world peace and flies the hippie flag for humanity—well, I take issue with that. And I fear letting him out can only mean one thing, Rog."

Finishing the last dregs of tea, Roger walked over to the kitchen area, rinsed the cups, and looked back over to James. Fearing his friend was going soft, he walked over and punched his arm.

"Listen, things have got out of hand, that I understand. Len Happy could've started the fire and could even be in with Ronny. You were the one who said don't underestimate him," Roger said.

James shrugged his shoulders, "He can find a boat in the middle of the ocean with only a piece of paper and a pen. He gave exact coordinations as to its whereabouts. He's found missing people for us. So yeah, he's smart. Smart enough to not fall for our tricks even when we tried to convince him that the information he gives in our target countries would bring peace. He never fell for it, and he said everything needs balance. Middle road. What's right for one can be wrong for the other."

"Yeah, so he talks shit most of the time," Roger added.

"That's my point. I can't use the son of a bitch anymore, because I agree with him."

"And Ronny? Do you agree with him?" Roger asked, wishing he hadn't.

"What do you think?"

"Sorry, mouth ran away with me. So, what now? We throw in the towel, pack it in after getting this far? I take my orders from you. You take them from Mr Green. Like any job, we do what we're told."

"Even if that means aiding in the murder of an innocent man?"

"Were you told this?" Roger asked.

"Green wants him gone. Gone for good. He knows too much. I tried asking for more time. The next thing I know, Len's free and Ronny has escaped. My bets are with them both being a target now."

Roger rubbed his chin in contemplation of his friend's concern.

"So, we find him first and warn him. Then find the evil fucker and kill him. Come out smelling of roses. Tell Green we wasted them both, and he'll call off the dogs. Len Happy can take his crystal ball and hippie schtick underground. The rest will work itself out. Your conscience is clear."

"No shit, Sherlock."

"No shit, Bond."

"You're supposed to say Watson, Rog. Not Bond."

Chapter 12

"Sixty pounds? Are you sure?" Danial asked the taxi driver. "Sixty?"

"The fare is sixty-twenty-five. I said, call it sixty."

Danial paid. His car, outside of Woodrush Towers' perimeter, wore a coat of soot, having a smell not dissimilar to burnt toast. Glad the building's charred remains were out of sight, he threw his bag on the passenger seat and rounded the car to the boot. No damage. How did Len retrieve the bag? The book—he checked, it was still there. Crossing his fingers on his left hand, he turned the key. It started.

Screams and calls for help mixed with evil laughter tickled the inner workings of his mind while trying to accept that Bill was the person within Ronny's room. The person was thinner; a woman. Lucy. What did Ronny mean when he said he'd ended the life of his tormentor? Did he mean Bill, or was he talking about the neighbour? Danial shuddered and engaged the car in a forward motion. The need to get away was paramount; somewhere he'd never been, where no one knew him. Being homeless and unemployed added to his list of many problems.

Droplets of rain splatted the window. A single tear left his eye, tickling his nose, forcing him to use his sleeve as a tissue. More joined the first, blurring his vision. Years of pent-up longing and isolation sent a torrent rolling down his contorted face. He pulled into a layby. Speeding cars rocked his own. How much of this had been his own doing? Like the patients he'd looked after, comfort-rocking for hours at a time, he didn't know.

A thud as a book slipped from the carrier onto the rubber foot mat. Flipping the bag over, sealing its open end, he looked down at the gold spine of the book; the book that had chosen him. He laughed and banged his forehead with a clenched fist before picking it up.

One blank page. The other was filled with a drawing he'd never seen before. Looking closer, the last page differed from the one he had seen in the hospital. Etched on the page was a building like his own, square, with windows, but smaller. A set of steps at one side, a door, a garden, and a street lamp. That being the focal point, other buildings stood in front and on either side. A row of shops with little stick men going about their business. Artistic in every way. Why? How did it get there? Thinking, he laughed again. He had been in the hospital, slipping in and out of consciousness, tired and confused. Having answered the reason for not noticing the obscure picture, Danial pulled off onto the dual carriageway, with no clearer understanding of where he was going.

Keep moving. He'll lose interest when he knows you're not the warrior. Danial couldn't shake Len's notion of a warrior coming to Earth from the realms of God-knows-where to kill a mortal, capturing his spirit. In what? A glass jar—my God, man, *think.* Danial swerved, missing a pedestrian getting into a parked car. Slowing, he pulled into a delivery bay. A hardware store, chip shop, hairdresser, and Mount News convenience store laid beyond the passenger side. He couldn't recall taking the breath; it left him in a stilted, nervous fashion—"I Want to Break Free" was playing on the radio. He turned it off and opened the gold book. Flicking past what looked like pages of hieroglyphic writing, fighting scenes, and his apartment, to the last page. Relieved it hadn't changed and therefore, had to have been there all along, he looked closer. Why, he didn't know. He should have been looking for somewhere to live; a job. Like a drug addict after the hit, his veins pumped, and his heart raced, so compelled was he to keep looking.

His eyes widened upon seeing a silhouette of a woman standing at a window. He marvelled at its detail. Squinting, he could make out earrings protruding from flowing hair. Her chest rounded, curving in and down past the windowsill. The woman resembled the one from his dreams, although she'd had brown hair. The woman in the etching had golden hair. Gold in gold.

It moved!

No. Impossible. Danial blinked, frightened to open his eyes. He did, and saw the woman move away from the window. Another figure—that of a man—took her place, rose his hand, and lashed at the woman, who fell below the sill, leaving the figure arched as if he was looking down at her. He slammed the book shut and threw it behind him. It bounced off the headrest and onto the backseat. Open—on the same page. As he reached to close it, he saw a lady leave Mount News. Lucy? No... it couldn't be Lucy. He did a double-take as she walked around the side of the store. It couldn't be. She looked different with her hair down; various shades of spine-length blonde hair. He didn't get a good look at her face, but something—call it chemistry—told him that it was her. He had to know. Opening the door, he swung one leg cut, but the other refused. What was he going to do? Run after her in the hopes that it was Lucy? And what if it was? Would he say, "Hi, fancy seeing you here"? No, he'd be branded a stalker if it was—even worse if it wasn't. His deliberation cost him his chance; she'd gone.

A blast of a horn. Danial looked. The driver's cabin wasn't visible. He pulled out to allow the delivery truck access. The lights were red. Three women crossed, two peering over a double buggy. The gitty led to another street. A gang of school kids filtered through, shielding any chance of spotting Lucy. A horn blew again, this time from a small Honda. Waving his apologies, he rolled the car forward, turning at the third set of traffic lights, convinced the rear of the shop must be close. Swishing his head in the hopes of catching her, he'd arrived. She wasn't there.

Bleakness washed over him. The reason he needed to see her failed him. He just did. Ronny's escape, and to warn her of the things Len Happy had told him, were two good reasons. He had to make sure she was all right.

With the engine still ticking, he walked up and down the long road, peering through windows, hoping to see her. Short of standing in the middle of the road and shouting her name, his attempts were fruitless. Lucy was gone. Like everything else. Gone.

Returning to his car, Danial flicked through the book's gold pages to find the last. He followed the gap between the shop and a row of houses. A car stood at the shop's rear. The double buggy, three stick figures, two bent forwards. The lights.

"Fucking hell."

He looked closer. It was a map. Was his mind filling missing gaps? But those things were new on the page…

Following the page up from the shop to where he'd seen the woman in the window, the drawing had changed, and she was no longer there. He looked at the road opposite to where he sat. He walked over to it, a casual stride, whistling, as if out for a stroll. The cul-de-sac had a mix of semis and boxed two-storey flats. Gardens were neat and tidy, with plants arranged in a uniformed, keeping-up-with-the-Joneses way. The only exception was one that stood out from the rest. Smashed pots, plants pulled from their roots. Even the hedge was leaning inward; the base of it cut.

A man's voice bellowed from within the flat. Danial looked up through a gap in the broken hedge. It was coming from the first floor. The netted window didn't afford him a clean view. He stared. A silhouette of a man shouting, his calls of anger echoed from the window. A scream, that of a woman, fired in rapid, desperate bursts.

A strobe of gold pages flicked through his mind, stopping at the image of the figures in the window. He felt Lucy's presence. Without thought, he smashed through the hedge and ran to a set of metal steps. His long legs skipped two at a time until he reached the top. Emotions erupted as he kicked the door open, smashing a glass cabinet that stood on the inside as the door swung inward.

Lucy cried, "He's got a knife!"

The man had Lucy's hair wrapped around his fingers, a kitchen knife gripped in the other hand, held under her chin. He shuffled back toward the kitchen.

Through motionless lips, she murmured, "Dan." The flat end of the knife pressed against her windpipe.

"So, *you're* the new love of her life. You'd rather be with this lanky streak of piss than me?"

Danial had seen the same wide-eyed manic look before, on the face of an inmate. And those same words from Cane Fisher, the person who'd branded him a lanky streak of piss throughout

115

his school life. He wanted to rip the knife from his hands, but knew that whoever this person was, he had no rational thought left in him. The whites around his eyes showed a look of terror mixed with desperation.

Danial raised his hands, palms out to calm the man.

"Look, I don't know who you are. I know Lucy from work. Nothing's going on, so please just put down the knife."

"You'll be able to read about me after I cut off this bitch's head."

Lucy stood firm, not able to move with the knife pressed against her throat. Leave, and he would kill her. Try to get the knife, and he'd risk him cutting her. There was no reasoning with this man. He stood eye-level with Lucy, a good foot shorter than Danial. He wore full combat gear; his shaven head looked to be an attempt to hide a natural bald patch.

Danial stared into his eyes like a snake readying itself before it strikes. He laughed. Half in fear, half for the incongruous way he'd discovered Lucy. He didn't know why or what good it would do, yet he continued. Lucy's face was painful to see.

"What's so funny? I'll do it. Then I'll do you."

Danial smiled at him. "Takes a big man to hold a helpless female hostage with me as an unarmed witness." He continued to mock him by chuckling away to himself. "Things are not looking good for you, are they? You must know you are doing this all wrong."

The man lowered the knife a fraction, allowing Lucy to lower her head.

"How d'you reckon?"

"Well, I reckon," he answered, mimicking the man's voice, "that if you kill her, then you will have to catch me before I run out the door, and my legs are longer. I'm unarmed, so if you went for me first, then the exit's blocked, and you'll have all the time you need to do whatever you want to her. That's what I reckon."

A single shove sent Lucy into the wall. She drooped like a rag doll falling from a top shelf. He lunged the knife toward Danial. Danial jumped back; the knife missed his chest. *This guy's for real.* The thought stayed with him as he moved back until he had nowhere else to go. The door behind him hung on one hinge, covering the exit.

Going against his instinct to run and hide, or to cower in a corner hoping the man would show compassion, he stood his ground, tired of running away from bullies and fed up with feeling like a coward.

"You missed."

He lunged again. Danial raised his arms. The knife nicked him, cutting through his shirtsleeve. He wobbled. Those jelly legs were back.

Lucy rose from her slumped position. "Dan!" she cried out.

Danial snatched a drying towel from a radiator next to the door. Holding it stretched in both hands, he swiped it around the man's neck, pulling back with all his might. Dropping the knife, the man put his hands out to stop himself from falling. Danial jumped on him, pinning his arms down with his knees.

He was fighting his first-ever fight. Bullied as a child, he'd returned to his grandparents' house with black eyes and cut lips. He'd never fought back. He took no pleasure in the final punch, followed up by his long leg kicking the man out the door, sending him sliding back down the metal steps. He fell onto a little green chair, smashing it into pieces.

Danial looked at his bloodstained right hand and watched it grow. Hunched on the floor, Lucy raised her legs up to her chest and buried her head between her knees. An engine revved. They both looked at the open door.

117

Danial was first to the door. Lucy followed. Embracing his back, she peered around his right arm. Danial turned, wishing he hadn't, as Lucy released her grip.

"Er, sorry, I didn't mean to damage the door." Inhaling, he spoke through a stilted release. "I was passing. Are you all right?"

Damage the door. I just happened to be passing. Of course she's not all right.

"Yes, I'm all right." Touching her throat, she looked down at her fingers, "No damage done—apart from the door."

"I'll fix it."

He winced when she wrapped her arms around his waist and pressed her head to his chest. He moved his hand and yelped as a sharp pain ran to his elbow.

"Dan—your hand." Her eyes darted around his person as she examined him. "Your lip's bleeding, too."

Placing a finger on her lips, she flinched and recoiled from the contact. Danial remembered watching a film once where the hero did that same action. Not that he thought himself the hero. Everything was still a blur, but at least they were both safe.

"Sit down, and I'll get a cold towel for the swelling."

Danial tripped on a small silver pet bowl. Lucy was in the kitchen. Another saving grace. How many could he have left? Saying that after what he'd been through, it was time for a change of luck.

Water splashing on cloth dampened Lucy's words as she spoke.

"I should call the police. Dave'll not give up, now he knows where I am."

She entered the lounge and squatted between his legs. "This should cool it down," she said, dabbing his lip before wrapping a wrung-out tea towel around his hand.

She lifted the phone from its cradle and dialled 999. Danial twitched as she explained what had happened to the operator.

He mouthed, "Be back in one minute." Twisting his good hand in pantomime fashion, he added, "Need to switch off my engine."

Lucy nodded at him while confirming her address to the operator.

Being interviewed by the police or the suits wasn't an option. Danial walked over to the car, glancing back at the broken hedge. Could the madman be hiding, watching to see if he left? He'd lied to the agents, telling them he was heading up country to visit a brother. *What if they turned up, followed me here? They think I started the fire. I was at work after being suspended. They let me go. Why? The murder, the neighbours. No, they know it wasn't me, couldn't be, I had an alibi. Now, this. Another lie, I shouldn't be here. They'll know I lied again. How did I get her address? The book – Shit, the book.* He looked through the window at its glimmering mottled cover.

He drove partway into the road. Decision made. Go back and face the music. Excuses were flowing, and although not outwardly expressing them, his face grew hotter with every word. *I could say I was just strolling down the road and heard a commotion, and then I did what I did, nothing wrong with that.* For every excuse came a little mocking voice deep in his head disbelieving his propaganda.

A patrol car paid him no attention as it turned into the cul-de-sac, pulling up two cars in front, three down from Lucy's flat. Danial's hand throbbed. The tea towel had turned warm. He'd driven in first gear using his other hand. He watched as a uniformed female officer got out, followed by a smaller male officer. Walking to the gate leading to Lucy's garden, the male officer turned to Danial. It took Danial two attempts to close his door, riling the female officer as she looked in his direction. The male approached. Danial caught the warm tea towel mid-fall with his good hand. The officer jerked a sealed pouch hanging from his belt.

Calling out from the top of the metal steps, Lucy waved the officer in her direction and must have seen the look on Danial's face as she told them he was a friend. The officer relaxed and smiled. The female narrowed her gaze and gave him the once-over before turning to Lucy.

Danial explained his participation as the male officer took notes. The female sat with Lucy. Danial could tell she suspected him of wrongdoing. He'd avoided mentioning roaming the streets looking for her, the book, and the events leading up to him finding Lucy held hostage by the man she called Dave.

Lucy struggled to compose herself as she gave background information. The female officer asked Lucy if she wanted Danial to leave. Adamant that she wanted him to stay, Lucy continued to fill in the blanks on her ex-boyfriend, Dave.

Danial listened to Lucy's agonising report of the things he'd done to her before his imprisonment three years ago. His new-found anger turned to a longing to hold her close; to protect her. He had come to warn her; to tell her everything he knew about Ronny, and that he believed, to some degree, what Len had said about her being in danger. If he did, it might tip her over the edge, and would serve no purpose other than adding to a troubled mind.

After the police recommended a lock change, Danial called a twenty-four-seven boarding-up company to secure the property as a matter of urgency. After calling four companies—each saying they couldn't attend right away—he called a small advert; the person said they'd attend but wouldn't commit to this evening.

Assuring Lucy that a patrol would circle the area and keep an eye on the property, they departed through the broken door. The female officer, still suspicious of Danial, gave him a wide berth and a look that said: *Your story doesn't add up. I have my eye on you.* If it wasn't for Lucy validating his actions, he knew they'd have arrested him on suspicion of breaking into the flat.

"Would you like me to find somewhere for tonight?" Danial asked.

"I'd love for you to stay, but you have a home to go to. Sorry, I'm selfish."

"No, I meant for me to find you somewhere to stay, away from here, somewhere safe. Not that he'll be back, that is. Maybe I should stay until the door's fixed."

"You should call home." Lucy's nostrils flared, catching two tears. "I don't want to disturb your day any more than I have done."

"I don't, er… I'm single and live…" Words escaped him. "You could have stayed with me, but I don't have a home."

"Silly, where do you live?"

Lucy's smile retracted as she recalled the fire. "This on top of what you've been through. Lucky you weren't at work when the fire broke out. You know about Bill, don't you?"

"I do, I was there."

"No…"

"My flat was broken into when we were in the hospital. I asked after you."

"The Chinese doctor. I remember, but I thought you'd called up, checking on everyone. I didn't realise you were in there, too. Will you stay? I can make up a bed on the sofa, or you can sleep in my bed. Don't think I'll be getting much sleep tonight, and you look tired."

A torch aimed at the door startled Lucy. Danial approached the sound of clanging as the boarding-up man climbed the outside steps. A short, over-friendly man wearing blue overalls introduced himself as Peter. His strong Polish accent had Lucy baffled. Danial understood every word and waited until he'd finished. The door was back on with thick plyboard, screwed both outside and internally.

After paying the tradesman, Danial finished the cuppa that Lucy had brought him halfway through Peter securing the second panel. He smiled at her, more from pain than joy, certain he'd broken his hand. He told her he'd pop around tomorrow with his hand in plaster. Agreeing, she hugged him. The fresh smell of her hair enhanced a sweet, perfumed sweat. He didn't want to leave, but he had to. With all that had happened—was *happening*—he needed time to concoct a plausible way to explain the things he knew without Lucy thinking he was as crazy as the man he'd fought. To stay would be selfish, as the comfort Lucy would feel would turn sour if he tried to explain the unexplainable. That, and he was no good at improvising. Lying wasn't an option. Having met Lucy on a personal level, and hearing her story, he couldn't bring himself to lie or tell the truth. All the more reason to leave before she asked questions. They exchanged numbers. Lucy watched him as he left through a part in the broken hedge. Something he hadn't asked about, but he guessed it had something to do with Dave.

Steering with the same hand, he changed gears, which proved difficult. The slightest pressure on the hand that had thrown the final punch was like a vice tightening. He needed the A&E department but couldn't face further questions.

Premier Inn was a welcoming sight. Checking his mirrors

every other second, making sure that Dave wasn't in pursuit, he questioned what Lucy must think of him, leaving her alone.

Danial parked at the far end of the carpark and walked into the small reception room, where a middle-aged man wearing a name badge welcomed him. Brian looked up, and his smile quivered into a grin as he asked, "Can I help you?"

"Room for one, please."

"Good night, was it?"

Brien must have thought he'd been drinking and got into a fight. Well, he was half-right, and the other half of Danial needed to calm his nerves and gain focus. He'd glanced in the mirror of his car and didn't look too bad. He hadn't given it a thought when he walked into the hotel.

"Yes, thanks—well, a mixed bag of good and bad."

Aware he resembled an escaped convict, he changed the tone of the conversation.

"Do you take credit cards?"

Placing the card reader on the counter, Brian said, "Fifty-nine pounds, please. You'll be in room four, along the corridor."

Danial sat on the bed with a fresh cup of tea, looking at his swollen hand. His bruised body and ribs ached, and his ankle had swelled. Thoughts of two crazed men after Lucy, what she'd been through, and what she might still face raced through his mind. It was doubtful that Dave would come back for a second round, but who could contemplate an obsessed mind? Ronny was his concern, as well as the suits, and the things Len had said. Not to mention having a book that wrote itself, coming to life without warning. Yes, it had warned him. The book could stay in the car. Tonight, his name wasn't Danial. It was Dan. That's what Lucy had called him. He could still feel her embracing him, crushing his tender ribs, the sweet smell emitting from her soft blond locks as pungent as if she was here in his room. An almost exact match to his recurring dream, although in his dream, she was a brunette, and he'd never made contact. With Lucy, he had, and hoped to again.

Chapter 13

Pulling out a blue holdall from under the dressing table, Len unzipped the larger of the two side pockets, unfolded a map, then moved the ruffled quilt to the far corner of the bed. Putting it out with his large hands, he spread it onto the mattress, careful not to tear it. He peered over his pot belly and studied it like a cryptozoologist finding an undiscovered species. Placing the holdall down, he rummaged through the inside, and then the smaller of the two zipped side pockets. He found a neck chain with a crystal attached. There was nothing special about the crystal; it held no supernatural powers, even though Len would argue that all crystals held energy. He'd acquired this one on a stall at the indoor market before arriving at the guest house.

Looping the neck chain around his index finger and the ring finger of his right hand, he created a cradle. In a clockwise motion, he waved the crystal over the map. Eyes closed, he hummed as he exhaled. Lowering the crystal onto the map, it came to rest at an unknown location. Pushing the pendant into the map, marking the spot, he then knelt at the side of the bed in a praying position, removed the pendant, and revealed the place name. *Church Knighton,* a small village on the edge of Dartmoor, Devon.

"A village, of all places. Is the warrior a farmer?"

After making the bed, Len headed to the breakfast room. The

room housed six small tables, all dressed in lace tablecloths. A group of condiments sat centre of each. The owner walked over to him.

"Good morning, Mr Happy. A fry-up, like yesterday?"

"Yes please, Margret, that would be splendid," he replied, pouring fresh orange juice into a tall, thin glass. As she neared the door, Len said, "Tell me how one would go about getting to Church Knighton from here. I'll be on foot."

"Church Knighton? Well, I know the place well. A little village. Gone downhill, if you ask me. You would need to drive there. It's miles away. I'll give you an extra egg to give you enough energy for the trip." Raising her eyebrows, she gave a wink of befuddlement.

Since his arrival, Margret had laughed more than she'd ever done in her sixty-three years. Looking at his funny fat face was enough to turn a manic depressive into a hysterical circus clown. He oozed charisma, and his comedic talent was natural and timed to perfection.

"Back soon, my dear." She wiggled her fingers as she walked out.

The night Len arrived, Margret asked if he was visiting or in town on business. He told her he was there to make her smile; to make her happy again. His response unnerved her. It had been a year to the day when her husband left her for younger women. Lawyers went toe-to-toe, ending up with Margret keeping the guest house. Closed for business for a little over a year, she decided to open it and worry about staff, chefs, and housemaids before the season started. A practice run to get her back into the swing of it. Mr Happy was her first customer. That night, she'd locked and bolted her bedroom door, and had little sleep. Vulnerable without her husband, her first guest being an oddball troubled her.

Yesterday, after eating a full English breakfast, he asked her if she wanted to play a game of cards. At first, she told him she was too busy. He wouldn't take no for an answer. They played all morning and the better part of the afternoon. As if chatting and laughing with a complete stranger wasn't enough, she told him things she hadn't told her best friend. Things about her childhood, her husband, and her fear of running the guest house alone. She asked him about his past, about his partner, and his occupation. He either avoided the question or joked about being tracked by MI5 after his release from a mental institution. He was the funniest man she'd ever met.

Drumming his gut with thick fingers, Len called over to Margret, who was standing behind the reception desk, lost in thought. He was leaving her; she wasn't looking forward to saying goodbye to her new-found friend.

"That was the best breakfast I have ever had, my dear," he called across the dining room.

"Glad you enjoyed it. Are you still planning on that long hike? There's plenty to see around here; I could show you the sights, if you have the time."

"Thank you, but I must set off. I might have work to do when I get there."

"You mean you don't know if you have a job when you arrive?"

"I'm not there yet; logic doesn't play a part in this instinctual game. Can I show you a magic trick before I leave?" A pack of cards materialised before her eyes. "One for the road?"

She couldn't imagine him knowing another, after performing one only yesterday.

"Okay, this one is a trade secret. Please pick a card; any card will do."

She tapped the pack three times, selected a random card, and pulled. Suddenly, she was blinded by a cloud of mist, odourless and thick, twinkles of light popped in and out of the ever-increasing spray.

She giggled like the girl she had once been, amazed by what she saw as real magic. Star-filled fog enveloped her where she stood. She called out, "Mr, Happy... Mr Happy!"

Margret felt a giddy high. She'd never taken an illegal, mind-altering substance, but imagined this being similar. Any resentment for past events drained, sucked from her being, replaced by an awesome, intangible love for life.

The star-spangled show ended as fast as it began, leaving her alone and happy. Hands on hips, she waited for him to reappear or announce his presence. Neither came. She moved from room to room; all were as she'd left them, empty and devoid of life. She trotted to the dining room window, moved aside the curtain, and saw the unmistakable bulk of Len Happy walking down the road. He'd made ground, but she knew it was him. As she mouthed the words, "Bye, Mr Happy," Len turned on his heels to face the window and made a gesture with an imaginary hat. Certain he couldn't have seen her from such a distance, and she would've had to have used a megaphone for him to hear her calling, she felt an overwhelming sense of joy, released from shackles of the past, revitalised and excited about the future. Margret closed the curtain. A stranger walked into her life, and the stranger shared the same name as her new mood - *Happy*.

* * *

Awakened by the sound of his phone vibrating, the name LUCY appeared in capital letters across the screen.

"Hello—Lucy is that you?" The sound of crying snapped him

fully awake.

"Lucy, who's with you?" He feared the worst.

"Dan, tell me you didn't do it. Please tell me you didn't do it." Her raspy voice repeated the statement.

"Do what? Lucy, are you okay?"

No answer came through the earpiece. There was a quaking breath; a wheeze that could only come from someone too upset to form a proper sentence. Some words materialised; the rest were up to interpretation by the listener.

"The police are looking for you, Dan. I need you to tell me what happened."

"Lucy, I don't know what you mean." Thoughts of being accused of starting the fire began to plague him. Had the suits involved the police after all? Jumbled words flittered through his fatigued mind. "What did the police tell you?"

"Did you kill him, Dan?"

Thoughts of starting the fire vanished in a flash. "What? Kill who? What are you saying? Lucy, are you still there?"

The receiver crackled. A forced, nerve-steadying breath tickled his ear. "The police found a body not long after you left. It's Dave; someone murdered him. After what happened, I wouldn't have blamed you if things got out of hand—but not like this, Dan. No one deserves…" She fell silent.

Flinging the duvet aside, Danial stood, one hand on his head, the other gripping the phone to his ear. Nothing she'd said registered.

"I went straight to a hotel. To bed. You woke me. Please believe me; I had nothing to do with it. Are you sure?"

Danial continued pronouncing his innocence. "Lucy, you have to believe me, I came to find you last night. To warn you about Ronny and explain what's happened."

"Dan, the police are asking questions. You're a suspect."

"I can prove it wasn't me. I'll go to the police station now and prove I had nothing to do with it. I need you to leave the flat. Tell no one where you're going. Not even me. Just leave, and I'll explain later."

"You can explain now," Lucy protested.

"I think Ronny is after me. MI5 are watching me, and Len Happy... Lucy, are you there?" She'd hung up.

Closed doors became a blur as Danial darted through the corridor. Four uniformed officers stood within the small reception area; an impenetrable blue wall. A woman covered her daughter's eyes and pulled her into a gap between the drinks machine and a tall plastic plant that had now found a purpose.

Danial jolted to a stop, eyes darting between the crying child, the concerned receptionist, and the officers. His stuttered explanation held no weight. He'd expected them to throw him down, pin him to the reception floor with the force of a knee to his throat. Instead, he was handcuffed, read his rights, and lead out to the waiting van. This was becoming a habit. It would take time to check his side of the story, confirm his innocence, and release him—time he didn't have.

Chapter 14

Roger watched a hand rise, as if pulled by strings. "Sir, I have intel on Danial Morris. He's in custody. The prime suspect in the murder of David Ash, the partner of one of his work colleagues, Miss L. Day."

Roger and James locked eyes. James knew the look Roger gave. *He thinks he's left out of the loop again.*

"What's your interest in Morris? I asked for a fix on Len Happy," James snapped.

"Sir, the dismembered body is within the escape radius of Subject One. I was about to log the event when I received information about Danial Morris."

Steve looked back to his keyboard, as if he had something else to add to the statement. Silence turned to an inaudible hum.

"Hot off the press, he's still in the wagon. Not arrived at the station yet," Stover added, breaking the silence.

James slammed his hand on the desk. "Do I look interested in a domestic between two people who have nothing to do with my subject? Ronny's in the public domain. Every goddamn force is out looking for him. When the blues find him, log the time and place and call me. We need to locate Len Happy."

Roger scrunched his nose at the three pairs of eyes staring back. Having fixed his glasses, one avoided direct eye contact with Roger.

"We're going out. Same spec. No contact with anyone without my prior consent. And I'm still waiting for that fix on Len. We're not using company transport; please send information to my phone."

Like the nodding dogs popular in the eighties, all four agreed before turning their attention back to the computer screens.

"I have a fix on his location," Stover called.

"To my phone." Without turning, James waved his mobile.

James's pocket vibrated. Ignoring it, they remained silent, as they had inside the lift leading to the car park.

Roger started the engine. "You gave them what for."

"No more than usual."

"He's holding back on you, mate. Can see it a mile off."

"Who, Mike?"

"The geek without glasses—slap head."

"Stover?"

"Yeah, he's the ringleader. All that 'yes sir' bullshit doesn't wash with me. Too long in the tooth to be played by that little freak."

"Are you suggesting that I am, Rog?"

Roger thought fast. He didn't want to upset James, all too aware his mouth was running ahead of his brain. But James had to know. Agreeing to continue the chat over breakfast—or as James called it, "brunch" since it was after eleven—they pulled into the service station. A large mobile stand advertised a full English. Roger had decided before reaching the doors.

Looking at the menu, James commented on the lack of healthy options and settled for an omelette. The place was quiet; a few people dotted here and there, with at least two empty tables in-between each seated customer. Settling on a table furthest away from the counter, James pulled out his phone and read the message out to Roger. "Subject Two, last location, 243 Plaza Place. Cornwall. Either a guest house or a motor garage, both next to each other. Last feedback 8:08 AM. No contact after. Transmission failed. Looking into error message 453."

"Cornwall? How'd he get to bloody Cornwall, of all places? I thought he was heading north?"

"He was, Rog. Must have doubled back on himself."

"Well, he's got three choices. Stay in Cornwall, head back through Devon, or swim," Roger said, looking at the growing queue at the counter.

"They're big places, Rog. Without tracking, it'll be like finding a unicorn at a farmer's market."

"Code 453, you say? That's an old admin code. Denial of access. Had that flag up a few times."

"You've used a computer?" James frowned.

"Had office time. Leg in plaster after chasing some scumbag down a dark alley."

"It was daytime, Rog, and I caught him."

"Yeah, forgot. But not before his accomplice ran me over, and you left me for dead."

"You taught me well, Rog. Get the prize, you always said. Anyway, go on."

"Snooped. Wish I hadn't, the bastards demoted me. Got a warning. Big slap on the back of the head, and the screen I was looking at displayed error code 453."

"Thought as much. If my lads haven't seen it before, then it could be a block."

"*Your* lads, or *their* lads, James?" Roger looked out the window. A family estate, the driver black, the passenger a white male. Both suited. He couldn't see any children.

"I'm thinking the same," James said, just before a young girl with a ladder running up her tights wiped their table.

The nonverbal confirmation of their thoughts required no explanation. Between each mouthful, they discussed viewpoints on who was controlling the geeks. Their conclusion ruled out deviousness on their part. They agreed that Green using the boys made more sense. Kids—even those with massive IQs—could be groomed by those at the top; those never spoken about in public, a myth to authorities, feared by public-facing officials, but spoken about in a service station café.

Under any normal circumstance, Roger would have finished his food before James shook the salt. This morning, he chewed every mouthful as he listened to the real reason Len and Ronny wound up in Woodrush. War games involving psychics were still played within the US, USSR, and Germany. The British Secret Service cancelled their psychic reconnaissance program back in the early Eighties, due to funding. The results were average at best, and not justifiable for the long-term. This all changed when Len Happy spoke about an evil entity, reborn into their realm, occupying a little boy.

Roger smiled, catching a piece of egg white as it tried to escape his grin. "We took his word for that crazy nonsense?"

"They stumbled upon him while investigating strange accuracies in Canneto di Caronia. They concluded he was another overexcited member of the public. Suspicions arose regarding his non-Italian descent and no ID. That, and the fact that the fires took place after his arrival. Should have been an open-and-shut case. One for the local police. After being contacted by the Italian Military Intelligence Agency, MI5 sent over an agent."

"You were that agent, right?" Roger asked, forgetting his fork was loaded with a combo of food, hanging in mid-air.

"No—I've never lied to you. I was chosen a week before I

convinced them you were the man for the job."

"Convinced," Roger said, showing the inner workings of his food factory.

James *did* convince Mr Green that Roger was the right agent. They were, after all, the sixth team created to deal with paranormal investigations. This time, they wanted agents with no interest in the subject, to take a more logical approach with the psychics and mystics willing to prove their abilities. Len had no such ambitions, no agenda, and no wish to be famous. His fanciful story about an evil spirit entering an orphan boy was laughed at, until James confirmed his abilities.

"Okay, they thought you were the best man for the job," James said, looking above Roger's head.

"Liar," Roger chuckled. "Well, at least I know why you sent me to Italy, the questionnaire, the church... Yeah, why the focus on the church and the missing book?" Chewing food from a loaded fork, Roger continued. "Give me a straight-up answer, do you believe this crock of shit? Not understanding what's behind a magic trick doesn't turn the trick into magic, Jim."

James ran through half a dozen instances of Len bringing an end to otherwise dead cases. Roger had heard many before, having experienced most of them with James. Concentrating on his plate, Roger remained silent.

"There was no trickery with the rescue cases. The powerless boat adrift in the Indian Ocean that was a no-hoper if ever I've seen one. Last mayday call confirmed no provisions. Injured parties found a week after the power failed." James waited for a nod of agreement, then continued. "Len's coordinates took us to them. He was correct. No tricks involved, Rog, and the missing persons, the girl—"

"Yeah, I hear what you're saying, Jim. It has nothing to do with other realms, spirits, and things that go bump in the night, now does it? So, what about the fires? Do you think he caused them? And why's the Bible relevant?"

"Bible?" James said.

"I assume it's a Bible; it was in a church."

James moved his omelette aside. "When did it happen, Rog?"

"What?"

"You, becoming so cynical."

"That's my role, remember? I'm the Scully in this relationship. You said they wanted a neutral."

"Biased, I'd say. All I'm hearing is negativity for the facts before you. You taught me open-mindedness, Rog. No matter how crazy the mission is, we need to follow leads. That's our job."

"Not so open that your brains fall out," Roger said under his breath. "I'm your employee now, so I'll follow your lead."

"We're partners, Rog. Try to be open to the impossible being possible." Tilting his head, James said, "The title... it bothers you, don't it?"

Rubbing a napkin over his mouth, Roger stared at the nearly finished omelette. "You know what bothers me? You holding back. Yes, I know things are on a need-to-know, but if what you say is true about seeing me as a partner, then fill me in. Spill the beans. Tell me what you know, and we'll work this out together. I'm tired of running around questioning why I have to do this or that. Everything, Jim. I need to know everything."

James nudged the omelette towards Roger. "Want it?"

Roger smiled, said something about Kath and sloppy seconds, then stood up. "I'll get us a brew." Walking toward the counter, he turned to James. "*Everything*, James."

James nodded. It would be more than his job's worth, if he still had one. Torn between the spooks guiding him, the boys being guided without his knowledge, and a soon-to-be-dead Len Happy, what did he have to lose? "I'll have water, Rog."

The queue emptied. People rushed, choosing to grab and run rather than stretch their legs under one of the many empty, smeared tables. The girl with the laddered tights approached, cleared the table, and promised to return. Roger took her place and sat down, awaiting new information. James didn't know a great deal more and swore to stop if Roger took the piss. He should be out looking for Len, not divulging information that could lose him his job.

"Coke for you, tea for me." Roger placed the drinks on the table.

"I asked for water. This is full of sugar."

"Ah, sugar-free, diet. I couldn't ask for water, Jim."

Roger waited as the girl wiped the table. With casual stealth, he viewed his surroundings. Satisfied they were out of earshot, he asked James to elaborate on the reason MI5 wanted Len killed.

"He knows too much." They both drank. "The launch codes to Trident, Rog; he knew them."

"Len? My God, are you telling me he can launch a nuke?"

James knew Roger was playing him; his vocal restraint had an undercurrent of sarcasm. "No, Rog. It takes more than codes, and they change, but that's not the point. If he can recite them at will, then God knows what else he can do. Can you see now why we can't dismiss his stories as nonsensical?"

Roger agreed. James knew that his mannerisms had changed back to the Roger who had employed him; the serious version of many.

"So, are we sticking to the plan? Ronny finds Len, we find both of them, down Ronny, and warn Len of his pending execution. Kill two birds, so-to-speak," Roger said. "Timing will be an issue.

Long-ass stakeout."

Deep in thought, James fingered the salt pot. "*Three* birds, Rog. You're forgetting Mr Morris. Danial Morris is another key on the ring."

"Pencil neck? I don't think he's involved. By association, maybe. You think Ronny's still after him? I think he's long gone, and Ronny's not your normal Joe. They'll arrest him before we get to Len. Every uniform is after him. Let's concentrate on finding Len, and if the stench is still lingering, then we pull the chain."

"You wanted to know everything, Rog; you'll change your mind with what I've got to say." Curling his top lip in, James nibbled the flesh of its partner. "Ronny won't stop until he finds the one person who can kill him. Danial might be that person or knows the one who will. You need to separate Ronny the man from Vetala, who lives within him. Ronny, the man, had a most unfortunate childhood. Raised by bikers; subjected to endless pain and humiliation. Vetala entered him, and things changed. The boy became uncontrollable. Evil, Rog; evil to the core. Killing Ronny will not put an end to the spirit that is Vetala. It will move on to its next victim, becoming more powerful with every incarnation. Len's mission is to find and protect the one with the ability to defeat the evil within Ronny."

Trying not to mock him, Roger said, "The one who can kill Vetala needs Len for protection? Mate, come on. I'm trying to understand, but you're not making it easy."

"If they do assassinate Len, then Ronny will wreak havoc and grow stronger. We have a fix on Len's location, so let's move. We can talk on the way."

Roger glanced out the window. The same car drove past two empty spaces. "James, we might have company. A purple family estate. Noticed them earlier."

James nodded, and didn't question why a family estate would trigger Rogers's suspicions. His partner—his friend—didn't do paranoia.

* * *

Black, tar-like slime seeped through the body's fingers. Evicted from its resting place, sewer water served notice as it ran through the body's spread legs. Eyes had no purpose in the sewer. Black. Everything black, apart from the slime above its head, shimmering with sparkling brilliance. A shoe or boot. The tread thick, new, blocked the light.

It enjoyed the anguish of men working overhead. Their emotions fed its hunger. Made it stronger.

The men above tried not to think of the corpse as human. Desensitised, they'd seen much death, but struggled to work with the mess it had left them.

Could they sense it, looking through small, glass-like domes, staring at them through the road grate?

Two police cars reinforced the blue and white tape spanning the road. Masked forensics popped in and out of the privacy cover, while uniformed officers averted pedestrian curiosity away from their place of work. They hadn't found a weapon or tool for the job. Twisted flesh and bite marks suggested an attack by a large animal—this was the city, and no dog nor pack of them could inflict what they saw. Perplexed, the team continued to catalogue the crime scene, unaware of what lay beneath their feet.

Chapter 15

Car fumes, amplified by damp air, hindered Len's movement. Shortness of breath forced him to slow his pace along the grass bank of the motorway. Thumb out for over an hour, he noticed it turn a shade of milky white.

Rain broke through moist air. Len hummed the old classic, "Raindrops Keep Fallin' On My Head." He thought about skipping along to his out-of-tune vocals but couldn't afford the attention.

A Nissan Micra pulled up a hundred yards in front. As he approached, he noticed a hand forcing the passenger window open. Len walked up to it, arched his back, and saw a fair-haired young man.

"Wanna lift, dude? I can take you to the next service station."

Len smiled. The passenger door squealed as it opened.

"Thank you. The next service station will do just fine." Struggling to fit the seatbelt around his midriff, Len settled for tucking it under his buttock.

"Has your car broke? Didn't pass one."

"No, I am heading to a village called Church Knighton. Was a nice day until the rain came."

Alex laughed. "What are you going there for?" he asked.

"I think there's work waiting, or so I'm told," Len replied, still trying to keep the seatbelt in place. "What brings you down this long stretch of road, my friend?"

"Going to see my girl. We've been together since we were kids at primary school, on and off. Her Dad has never approved. Don't know why. I've even got a job and everything. He says I should wine and dine her, and I'd like to, but I'm always broke two days after payday. Too many bills when you've got your own pad."

"Well, I'm sure you're doing your best. What's your line of work?"

"Computer programmer. Been hacking since forever."

"Hacking?" Len inquired.

"Nothing I can't crack. Nothing illegal, but I have exposed big companies. You know, when they're dodgy. I hack their mainframes, then post what I find. Like a modern Robin Hood."

Pulling into the service station, he thanked Alex for the ride and offered to pay him. Alex refused, saying he was heading this way anyway, so it wouldn't be fair.

Alex stopped outside the main entrance, wished Len good look, and said he was popping in to buy a bottle of water. Len thanked him again and watched him enter the service station.

The rain had stopped. Sun warmed the back of his neck as he bent down to unzip the bag. His hand gripped the rubber handle of a flathead screwdriver. He wedged it under the rubber seal of the passenger window, enough to fit in his fingers.

Len moved his bulk closer to the car as an executive BMW pulled up alongside him. The driver was shouting into his hands, shaking his head at the concealed mobile phone. Pleased to see the driver hadn't noticed him at work on the window, Len threw the screwdriver back in the bag. He walked over to a bin and pulled out a stained envelope, opened it, and shook out a gas bill before returning to the car.

Lifting an old brown leather wallet from his grey pinstriped trousers, Len emptied folded notes into the torn envelope and folded it in half to create a temporary seal. It bounced off the passenger seat onto the floor.

With the Nissan Micra now out of sight, he sat down on a damp metal bench and looked up to the sky. Wispy clouds obscured the sun, making it feel colder than it was moments ago.

Legs stretched out, feet crossed, he said hello to every passer-by. Those choosing to ignore him would share his good wishes with others, creating a positive ripple effect.

Len's gut thumped and growled. His dry tongue, glued to the roof of his mouth, demanded a drink. A woman walked to the bin next to the bench, dropped three fast food bags into it, and gave Len a quick smile.

"Any food left in there, my dear?"

"Oh… well, just leftovers," she said, trotting back to her waiting family.

"Thank you. Have a safe journey." Cementing his thanks with a raised thumb, Len pulled out the bags, shook the fries into one carton, and made a full burger from two separate halves. The oversized Coke would do just fine.

Len closed his eyes, unsure of his calling, having faith in a power greater than himself. His instincts had never let him down before. His vision of the village was clear. The reason for sitting at a service station was not so clear. Like a magnet attracted to a washing machine, his head swished from side to side with the thought of finding the one with pure consciousness; the cure for Earth's degradation; the thing that would send Vetala back to the outer realms. As hard as he tried, he couldn't picture anyone or anything capable of it.

No person possessed it, he was sure. Nothing had obtained

it. It may not yet be in this world. But still, he was led to these places and people. Finding and protecting it, until it brought balance to this unbalanced world, was his purpose; the reason he was here.

His eyes flickered open to the sound of shouting. It was the man from the car park. His voice raised, raging into the phone held out to his mouth, the person on the other end took a barrage of curses.

Len stopped chewing and looked in his direction. The man turned his head, swearing and cussing. A couple gave the bench a wide berth, the woman's hands covering her son's ears.

Len looked again. Trying to get the man's attention, he coughed. "Sir, please... little ones are listening to you."

The man slid the phone into his shirt pocket with impressive accuracy. "Who do you think you're talking to, tramp?"

"A rather rude, angry man."

The man threw a verbal assault; words Len had never heard before, their intended meaning unmistakable. The man's face reddened in response to Len's ever-increasing smile.

"Useless, worthless, dirty tramp," the man said, swinging his hand in an upward motion, catching Len's drink. Its contents spilt over Len's crotch.

Aware that his smile was vexing the man, Len raised his hands. Ice fell from his legs; coldness seeped through his trousers. By the time he looked up, the man had gone.

Slurping dregs from the carton, Len placed it in the bin, then walked into the restaurant and the toilet. The hand dryer wasn't the push-button sort. He'd never seen one like it. Backing away, he observed the way it should work; hands into the gap, move them up and down.

"Ah, so that's how you do it," he said, looking up at the man.

"Not you again. Get out of here. Piss off."

"A little spillage," Len said, trying to angle his crotch over the hand gap. The man cursed more on his way out. Len knew he would not dry his trousers on this contraption.

Searching empty tables, Len filled a cup of orange juice and a carton of fries to see him on his way. Aware he was being watched, he tilted his head toward the counter and saw the same man standing in the queue, tapping his phone.

Covering the phone with one hand, the other active toward a young girl, each shake of his hand exaggerated his tone as he told her she should work somewhere else based on her eating away the profits, that she needed to hurry, that he had better things to do than waiting for a sloth.

Strolling over to him, Len rubbed the crystal beneath his shirt.

"Never enough time to do the things you need, always enough time to change the things you can," Len said.

Too consumed by the sound of his voice, the man snatched a bag of food and coffee off the counter and swaggered over to a high table, burger in one hand, phone in the other, oblivious to anyone within earshot. He stopped mid-sentence upon seeing Len leaning over his table, chewing like a grazing cow. He pulled on the sleeve of a girl, pointed back toward Len. "Get this tramp out of here. Get me your manager!"

Following the line of his finger, she looked around for a homeless person. They didn't get many this far up the motorway.

"I'm sorry, sir?"

"Him, there… Get him out. Do you even know who I am? Letting dirty tramps pick at leftovers."

Len was gone. The girl continued to look around the room. Seeing a smart, yet bedraggled man throw rubbish inside the recycling bin, she asked, "Is that him, sir?"

"What do you think? Does he look like a normal customer to you?"

His derogative tone altered her mood to one of bitterness. She walked over to the bin area.

"Excuse me... excuse me."

Len turned to her.

"We have received a complaint."

Len smiled. The girl relaxed.

"It's okay, my dear; I'm leaving now. My work here has finished. Which way would I go to get to Church Knighton?"

Before she could answer, the man across the table raised his fist. Len smiled once again before leaving.

Scrunching the burger box, sweat pooled into his palms. A drip rolled to the back of his hand. More fell from his forehead as he loosened his tie. He held a fry... or was it two?

"Are you okay, sir? Do you need a seat?" said a uniformed man with five stars over his left pocket, under them a badge bearing the name Stuart.

He wanted to shout, curse, tell Stuart someone poisoned him. "Yes, please," he said, as though his speech was under the control of someone else. "Yes, please," he said.

Stewart beckoned for help from the girl who the man belittled earlier. They helped him over to a low-level chair. Wetness on his shirt was visible. Perspiration dripped from his chin. His eyes stung, head light, drifting. He tried to stand. The room spun as gravity forced him back into the bright orange, faux leather chair.

Like a fox cornered by a pack of hounds, he trembled as he took the plastic cup of water from Stuart, thanking him like a young child would thank his mother.

"What's your name, mate?"

"Er, Cane. Cane Fisher."

"I will call an ambulance. Do you have any medication with you?"

"No, I'm fine now."

"Please don't stand," the girl told him.

Cane stood and wobbled through the restaurant, knocking plastic chairs aside like a homeless drunk. Crazy legs wobbled under his weight. The automatic doors opened. Stumbling, he found a metal bench. He slumped, head lowered, hands between his knees. He was about to topple forward. A hand guided him back.

"Hello."

"It's you. The man. What have you done? What's happening?"

"You are facing your fears, and your ego isn't here to protect you."

"Who are you?"

"My name is Len Happy. I mean you no harm, but I feel I need to protect you from yourself, in order to protect others."

The last thing Cane remembered was seeing a bright light before he fell forward off the bench, the fall cushioned by Len's hands.

He awoke to the faint sound of his name repeated by a man holding a stethoscope, standing next to a woman wearing a tunic-style top over dark blue trousers.

"Mr Fisher. Cane Fisher. Cane, can you tell me where you are?"

He sat up and looked at the blue-curtained enclosure.

"Why am I here?" his voice was subdued.

Cane was neither troubled by his surroundings, nor fazed that he'd just missed meeting the chairman of the company. All he could think about was seeing his wife and daughter. A warm feeling ran through him when he heard little Milly shout, "Daddy!" as she pulled the blue curtain over her head. His wife followed and stood beside the doctor, a troubled look on her face, her right hand stroking hair across a bruise below her right eye. Cane's outstretched arms welcomed her. She looked at the doctor, then approached him, smiling. He couldn't remember the last time he'd seen her smile.

Little Milly climbed onto the bed. He held them both in his arms and reassured them that from now on, things would be different, starting with that family holiday they had never got around to taking.

* * *

Glad to have left the toxins and noise of the dirty dual carriageway, Len plodded along a dirt track. A muddy back lane. *His* sort of dirt, natural in every sense of the word—if you discounted the tractor indents. A lane seldom used by locals, due to its narrowness and uneven surface. Tufts of grass grew centre, showing infrequent use. Faced with another vehicle, one would have to find a break in a hedgerow.

He'd memorised the places leading to the village, but with no compass, and his map only showing a broad view of the country, he relied on instincts and his gut feelings to get him there.

Needing to replenish fluids lost along the journey, he stopped at the entrance to Apple Tree Farm. Leaning on the wooden gate, tied shut with an old faded blue rope, he gazed across the vast expanse of green. Horses ran free. A small herd stood by an old barn. Bleating lambs called out to him through the towering maze of hedgerows, matching the calls from his stomach. Reaching over from where he sat, a hand full of blackberries subdued hunger pangs. Birdsong gave hope that he would reach his destination soon.

Shadowed by the hedge, Len shuddered and rolled up his sleeve. Five past one. The descending sun told him after five. Tapping and winding his watch, it refused to turn; he pulled the back off with a quarter turn, and the innards sprang out onto his lap. Sifting through cogs and gears, he noticed a small plastic square, not belonging to the antique manual watch.

"Let a man go, but don't set him free!" he said aloud. "An invisible leash." He continued chuckling away to himself.

Wiping his face with the back of his hand, he looked up at darkening clouds curling in on themselves, threatening to open into a shower or worse. Lambs stopped singing, and horses gathered next to the old barn. A breeze of fine rain hit the back of his neck as the wooden stile creaked under his weight. One final heave. The ground squelched under his shoes. He smiled at the absurd sound.

He offered a clump of grass from the side of the barn to the horse blocking the entrance. It devoured the handful of grass, along with the small plastic misfit.

"Will you let me in, my friend?"

The barn was dry—ammonia-tinged, but dry. Pinching his nose, Len scoped his surroundings. A bale of hay in the far corner. Above, a nail held a green wax jacket. Below a pair of black rubber wellingtons, green woollen socks hung from each.

Sitting on the bale of hay, he rummaged through a bin liner containing a pair of waterproof trousers, a green shirt, and what would have once been a white t-shirt.

Failing daylight filtered through a hole where a knot once sat. The light was intense, flickering like a drained torch as menacing clouds broke the sun's rays.

Something glistened from behind the hay bale. Len reached

down and pulled up a shotgun, a half-full bottle of water, and an unopened packet of biscuits. Lowering the gun back, he smiled at the welcome find.

"Where there's one, there will be more," he said, taking off his shoes. He peeled back the insoles. At first, they seemed normal enough, but upon closer inspection, he felt a raised area between the tongue and lace hole. Ripping out the tongue, he found it—another one of those little black squares. He continued to undress until he stood naked.

Looking down at the pile of clothes, Len tore open the bin liner. The waterproofs fitted, the elastic stretching around his waist. The t-shirt was a tight fit; the shirt was at least two sizes too small, so he wore it open and rolled the sleeves. And the jacket—albeit small—would offer protection from the elements. Leaving everything, apart from his damp socks, for the clothes he'd taken, he folded the socks into the blue holdall, along with the provisions he'd found.

Sitting on the stack, savouring each stale biscuit, Len closed his eyes and fell into a meditative state.

* * *

James slid his phone back into his jacket.

"What was that about?" Roger asked.

"They lost the trace three miles from the guest house. Walking on the motorway, they said.'

"You believe them?"

"Not sure what to believe anymore, Rog... Green wants us to head back to base for a virtual meeting."

"And are we?"

"I need to find Len, you can—"

"Yeah, I can stay with you. I'll call Jackie and let her know I'll not be home tonight."

James changed the Satnav setting from Elvis to an annoying female who grew angrier when approaching roundabouts.

James clenched his rear at the thought of disobeying an order to return. Roger was in his element; nothing he liked more than living on the edge. He'd always been the rebellious sort. In part, that was why, after Rogers demotion, James took him on as a partner of paranormal investigations.

"You know what, Rog... We should go into business for ourselves. Start a private investigator business. We could call ourselves the Agents of Odd."

"I need to pee," Roger said, rocking back and forth, holding his manhood.

"How old are you?" James asked, trying not to laugh.

"Look, you pee a lot when you're a kid. Then nature regulates you for a while, then when you reach the dark side of forty, retrogression strikes."

James changed lanes. Roger was the first to see the sign for the service station. The truth was, he'd been counting down the miles since the last sign that said twenty miles to the next WC facilities.

The holiday season hadn't fully started. The car park to the service station was quiet. They bought coffee and sandwiches and headed back to the car. It was getting late, and neither of them had eaten since breakfast.

Incoming calls blocked every attempt to contact the guest house. Twelve missed calls and counting. It rang again. This time, it was Mr Green. James felt his chest tighten.

Roger hadn't asked about his health after the last episode of hyperventilation. Recovery was quick, and within minutes, he was himself again. Roger took the phone from James and swiped the screen to the off position.

"I'll call the guest house on the way. Let's eat and run," he said, getting into the driver's seat.

Roger called and reserved two single rooms. The owner said that if they arrived too late, she'd put keys under a stone dog placed inside the rain porch. Rooms three and four were ready for them upon their arrival, and breakfast was between seven and eleven.

Roger glanced over at James. "So, you fancy yourself as a PI, do you...? PI Bond."

They spent the rest of the journey mulling over the idea with no seriousness attached to the conversation. Just lighthearted banter about who James would employ, where Roger would find business, and who—if anyone—left in the agency would support their venture.

Chapter 16

Securing the back doors, Charlie twitched at the repugnant smell wafting through his lorry. The drop was for a Chinese takeaway. He wasn't paid to question what was lingering in the wooden containers. Whatever it was, didn't smell edible. Not that he'd eat such food. More of a pie and mash man, was Charlie. There had been little he hadn't seen in his forty-two years of service, and he told the same story to anyone who would listen. He'd driven long haul up and down the country, never once having had an accident. An unblemished record to date. After the scaling down of the company, he remained loyal and took whatever work he got. Food deliveries, restaurants, convenience stores, and the occasional residential home. Often, he would pick up a hitchhiker. It passed the time, and he'd make a friend for the short time they were with him. He'd never told the firm, and it was only on the odd occasion. Having a good eye for people, he knew the good from the bad, and had never once picked up anyone abusive; just folk down on their luck, run out of petrol, and the occasional number plate holding car transporter.

His last one was strange. Not in a bad way, but peculiar all the same. Kept telling him he was on a mission to find something that, as yet, didn't exist. He did, however, show him some amazing card tricks. Only after dropping him off at a guest house did he realise that he'd done all the talking. A big fellow who listened like no one had ever listened before.

Charlie had been awarded a gold-plated watch and a certificate of loyalty. The framed certificate hung above the mantelpiece, and the watch only ever left his wrist when he bathed.

The engine rumbled to life. No need for a new-fangled directional gadget. Having never been to the restaurant before, he knew to head toward the guest house. The lads at the depot could never work out how he found places. He'd tell them he followed his nose.

* * *

Dark again. Eyes not able to penetrate the blackness. It didn't need eyes. It sensed everything. Dry at last, the body didn't like to be wet for too long. It was learning more each time, and with every passing day.

Need to feed the machine, or it will fail. Need to fill it with fluid so it can pass through the body. So many things learned during its stay at Woodrush. *More difficult now. No one to bring the things the body needs. The fish would provide essential energy, the red ice trickling through the body's fingers would fill the engine with fluid. This tar-stained body would not fit in with others. Need to clean it. It is as frail as any human body, but the best so far. Strong and lean. Its mind was pure and clean when taken. Almost innocent, for such a grown specimen. Much better than the boy.*

The body had no sense of taste, so didn't reject the fish and blood-tainted fluid. The body was resting and eating and would soon have the energy it needed to continue.

The body's original spirit looked to the sky for guidance, curious to learn. People had followed with blind faith. It took pride in stealing the body from a holy man, so wholesome and intelligent. More *inherit* than *steal,* as it had no choice which life it would live. Not yet, anyway. But soon, after it found and destroyed the one with pure consciousness, it would be free to evolve.

Entering the minds of others took vital energy. It could move things and create illusions, but still could not find the cure. It was out there, it was sure. The man Happy knew it, too. He had helped the vicar rid the boy of Vetala. It was glad to inherit the vicar, and not the man Happy. His persistence in trying to find the cure would be his downfall. Vetala could connect with him and would follow him to the one with pure consciousness.

Need to keep this body. If the body dies, a feebler frame full of restrictions and limitations could be the next. Need to care for it. The body has lost teeth from biting down on the last one. Unavoidable, he would have hurt the body. The stench given off by the man called Happy was strong. He was here.

Vetala fought its instincts to make the driver find the one called Happy; to kill him as all humans should be. Humans were the problem. Nature's greatest mistake. A correctable mistake. It was smart. It would wait.

If Vetala kills, they find Vetala. Must not kill. The words repeated as a mantra.

As if in a trance, Charlie continued due west to the coast, semi-aware that he was heading in the wrong direction but compelled to do so all the same. The surroundings looked familiar. He'd travelled this route before.

* * *

Having told them he had no fixed abode, his whereabouts confirmed by the hotelier, Danial left the booze-tainted, stale air of the police station out into the fresh night air.

He'd been there all day, and mostly sat alone waiting for a solicitor to arrive, who insisted that the officers involved should apologise. This caused an unnecessary argument between the investigating officer—who was, after all, just doing his job—and the arresting officer who had detained him at the hotel earlier that day.

He thought about calling Lucy to explain the wrongful arrest; to convince her that he hadn't anything to do with the murder of her ex-partner. After she'd ended the call to him that morning, he opted for the face-to-face approach, sending a short text to say he was on his way.

Brian, the receptionist at the Premier Inn, was standing at the door. He backed off in a hurried shuffle when he saw Danial walk through the car park. Peering over the desk, he had the look of a man who had just seen a ghost. Danial's car was still where he'd left it, and he hadn't received an overdue parking fine, much to his surprise.

Pulling off, he mumbled to himself, trying to find the right thing to say before he arrived. Everything he thought of could be taken as inappropriate, incongruous, or even insensitive, after what had happened.

Lucy's garden flat looked different today. The hedge had either been moved or had fallen. Either way, he had a clear view of the flat. He opened the gate, lifting it to lessen any noise, but not knowing why, as the metal steps would alert her to his presence. He braced himself, apprehensive to the response he might receive.

"Dan, what are you doing here?" The voice came from the side of the flat. His eyes widened. With shaking hands, he turned to face her.

"Er, sorry. I texted saying I was on my way, but—" His sentence cut short by Lucy's comforting embrace. Her long hair tickled his bare arm as he placed it on her.

"I'm so sorry, Dan. What was I supposed to think? It all happened so fast. Please forgive me for thinking—"

"I would have come to the same conclusion."

"Come on up; I'll put on the kettle."

Danial loved the way she called him Dan. He had never seen himself as a Dan, but he liked the shortened version.

Lucy brought down two mugs from the glass-fronted peninsula unit.

"How do you take yours?"

"Strong with two, please."

"Like me, then," she said, switching on the kettle. Her head remained over the kettle and Danial saw her hands clench tight. Standing, he walked toward her. As she turned, her face tightened. Danial watched as tears poured down her pale cheeks.

"Let me finish that." He walked her over to the kitchen table. Her elbows slid across the varnished pine surface, pushing her hands up to hide reddening eyes. Tortured, broken laughter filled the room, but it was clear to Dan that she wasn't laughing, and that her emotions ran rampant. He rubbed her back, trying to comfort her. Her bloodshot blue eyes looked up at him.

"I'll make the tea. Kettle's boiled," he said, regretting his flippantness.

"Thanks, Dan," she said, smiling up at him. "Strange how a cup of tea makes everything all right again, don't you think?"

"Sorry, I'm not too good with emotion. I didn't mean to trivialise… well, you know…"

Lucy's face wrinkled as crying turned into laughter. "No, I mean it! Tea for a tea drinker is like whiskey to an alcoholic. It makes you feel like you can get through whatever life throws at you."

Danial didn't think it prevalent to suggest adding whiskey to the tea, or the fact that he had done so regularly of late.

She smiled again after he asked where she kept the coasters. Both shrugged their shoulders as if connected within the moment. Caressing the mug with both hands, Lucy talked, and like an appointed therapist, Danial listened, giving reassurance where needed.

He was glad that she was opening up about her most personal experiences with her ex; her partner; the murder victim. She had somehow avoided even mentioning the murder. Maybe it hadn't sunken in yet, or maybe she was getting around to it? Maybe the details were too painful to explore so soon after the event. He listened, all the time wanting to cry himself. Never in his life had he been so low, yet so high in her presence. The catalogue of bizarre occurrences shadowed the beautiful, vulnerable women sitting opposite him. She was relying on his strength of character to see her through this trying time; a time she was unaware of him having. She had thanked him countless times, telling him that he was the only man who had ever confronted David without fear. Danial played it down, as neither of them took pleasure in David's life being taken away in such an extreme way, so close to home.

"Who could have done such a thing, Dan?"

They were back on the subject that had, earlier, reduced her to tears.

"Well, er..." he lowered his eyes to the empty cup.

Lucy stood and walked over to the sink, the cups clapping together as she lowered them into the bowl. Danial looked at his watch, as until now, he had avoided doing so. Half eight, and he hadn't made a hotel reservation. He didn't fancy staying at the Premier Inn after what had happened this morning.

"I need to make plans for tonight, so I'll pass, thanks."

"What do you mean, silly? Where do you live?"

Panicked by the simple question, he gave her a nervous smile and said, "Not far. Maybe I'll have another."

A jamboree of excuses flooded his mind. If he stayed, he would have to explain about his flat, the multiple murder, and the fact that the man who had been burned in his cell was the one who had done both. If the shoe were on the other foot, he would suspect her of the crimes, and label her a bunny-boiling psychopath. Why should she believe things that, if he'd not experienced, he wouldn't believe himself?

"There you go." Placing the tea on the table, she looked at him with concern. "Sorry I never offered you anything to eat. Great host, I am."

"No, I'm fine, honest." His words joined grumbling from the depths of his gut.

Lucy leaned across the table, held both of his hands, and looked into his eyes. He stared into hers, like opening windows to her soul. No more lies, no more running. She needed to know.

"Lucy, I need to tell you something, but I need you to stay calm, as it all sounds… wacky, but it's the truth."

"Nothing can come close to what we've been through, so go for it."

Taking a deep breath that staggered its way back out of his tightening throat, he started from the afternoon he'd seen the apparition. He told her about Len Happy and Ronny being Vetala. That he believed that after tormenting him, Vetala killed his neighbours and could have also killed David. That somehow, the suited men were involved, and were following Len, and had interviewed him after the police.

Lucy's mouth widened with every word. Fearing that she would ask him to leave, he took a breath in readiness for her response, stood up, and reached for his coat.

"You're scaring me, Dan. I don't believe it! Why is this happening to us?"

"I know it sounds weird, but the events are real enough. Len told me he would find someone who possesses pure consciousness, and that person would rid the spirit called Vetala."

Danial put his arms through the sleeves of his jacket. "I've been shit-scared the whole time. Thought I was losing the plot; going crazy after working at Woodrush for so long. But after the agents more or less confirmed Len's words, I knew it wasn't me that was crazy. I understand you don't need this—"

"Please don't go, Dan. I can make a bed for you on the floor or the settee. You might not be comfortable with your legs over the arms of the settee, but there's room next to it."

Danial was taken aback by her wanting him to stay over; her innocence and the fear of being alone was clear to see.

"The floor will do just fine, thanks."

A folded duvet made the makeshift mattress. Another folded neatly on top with a single pillow to one end completed his bed for the night.

Lucy handed him the TV remote and told him she would take a shower. Flicking through the channels, he turned over to the local news and weather, settling for that rather than Red Dwarf, as he didn't think she would like it, and although he wanted to watch something lighthearted, under the circumstances, it didn't feel right.

He could hear the shower running and had to stop himself from imagining her naked, thoughts of water dripping off her long blonde hair and her... the noise of the shower stopped, and the cubical door opened. He picked up the remote control and, in an attempt to hide his guilty thoughts, looked down at it in a rehearsed pose.

A breaking news story appeared midway through a story about how farmers were on the brink of bankruptcy. Just as it did, Lucy walked over to him, dressed in pink bunny pyjamas. Pressing just about every button on the remote to change the channel, the story of a dismembered body being found on a public pathway commenced. The news reporter hadn't said his name; it was only a matter of time before he announced that it was Dave.

"It's okay; you don't have to tread on eggshells around me. I cried for six hours straight before you came. I feel numb and afraid right now. Afraid of what might happen if Ronny is out there looking up at the window, waiting for an opportunity to strike."

"Please don't worry, you said yourself the police are keeping an eye on the flat, and you have me. I won't let anyone hurt you. I'll stay awake and keep watch until we can find somewhere for you to go for a while."

Lucy hated that she couldn't feel any remorse for Dave, and she kept trying to block the voice in her head from saying, *the bastard had it coming.* She was more upset that her life of solitude was shattered. Like the lush green hedge that once stood proudly in her little oasis, she felt amputated, her life force drained.

For Danial, it had been a long time... no. *Never* had he had a beautiful woman sitting next to him wearing only pyjamas. Lucy sat with crossed legs, her back nestled into the arm of the chair, trying not to listen to the TV.

"Red Dwarf's on, if you like that sort of thing," she said, forcing a smile.

Surprised that she had recommended the show he wanted to

watch, he flicked the channel. With so much to talk about and so many plans to make, they both took comfort in being in each other's company.

* * *

Charlie lowered the volume on his radio. There was a *bang* from within the cabin. Again, the same sound. He pulled into a lay-by and switched off the engine, sure that something had come loose, as it didn't sound mechanical.

The lay-by was a short stay, big enough for only three vehicles. He remembered it from a few years ago, when he'd pulled over for a nap on the hottest day of the year. Before he knew it, the police were knocking on his window, asking him if he was okay. Cameras everywhere nowadays. Long gone were the days where a truck could pull over for the night. An hour or two, and they would move you. Not that he did long haul nowadays; these short runs suited him fine.

He released the catch, and the door swung open. Hoisting himself up, he noticed that the wooden crates closest to the door had fallen. There was fish everywhere.

"Bloody hell." He pinched his nose tight as he moved passed the strapped-down containers.

The door slammed shut, plummeting him into complete darkness.

"Shit!" he yelled, for such a schoolboy error. He thought he'd fixed the door back on the latch, but he couldn't have. This had happened before, and he knew just where to find the internal handles. Patting his pockets for a torch or a lighter, he had neither. He'd not carried a lighter since giving up smoking a pipe when the price of tobacco went up, and the torch was in the glove compartment. Moving through the containers, the smell no longer a priority, he stopped. A noise came from the corner.

"Bloody rats. I hate bloody rats." Baffled how a rat could have entered, having stacked the pallets himself, he ignored the sound, slipped, but stayed upright. Blinking hard, a wave of sanity flew through him. He was nowhere near his destination.

The lay-by was on the way to the guest house, not the Chinese. Suddenly, he realised he'd headed in the complete opposite direction to the drop point. He panicked as he fumbled toward the doors, found the catch, and swung them open. Oncoming headlights were a welcome sight. He was out, but not where he should be.

Starting the engine, looking for a break in the traffic, he shuddered at the sight of a man peering behind a tree. With no vehicle in sight, he was out of place up there on the embankment. No time to play Good Samaritan. He was already late in delivering the now-damaged stock.

Chapter 17

Two reservations so soon after Len's departure, Margret was optimistic for the season ahead. School hadn't finished, and the holiday period was still another week away. This time two years ago, all the rooms had been filled. She'd always left the advertising to her husband. Any savings had gone to greedy solicitors and their ridiculous fees.

A cool breeze blew her dress wide, sending a chill through her body as she exhaled a cloud of smoke. With the door on its latch, she reached into the porch and placed two separate keys under the pot dog. Both had leather tags with room numbers embossed—one of her husband's better ideas.

Inhaling a lungful, she thought about the two men and how they'd sounded like a married couple—one butting in, stressing two rooms; the other giggling. Sure, they would end up sleeping together, but glad they'd paid for two rooms, she stubbed the cigarette into a metal sand bucket and closed the door behind her.

She'd learned not to stay awake. The last time saw her into the early morning. Margret took a last look around the hallway, popping her head into the dining room to make sure nothing was out of place, then used the ground floor WC, partly to check that all was in order and partly out of necessity to go after the cold had hit her legs.

Footsteps, muffled. A rattle and click, like that of the door closing. They hadn't arrived yet. Margret often heard noises and knocking sounds. Her husband called it "water hammer", whatever that meant.

On her way up the stairs, she doubled back, realising the door wasn't locked. She looked through the dining room window. The road was quiet; her guests could be stuck in traffic or lost. Either way, they knew where to find the keys.

Door locked, keys out, lights off, and time to continue reading the epic she'd started soon after her husband left her. It saw her through troubled times and took her to lands anew. She'd left it on a cliffhanger where the heroine faced death, and although she'd read the trilogy out of sequence and knew the character was in the book after, she wanted to see just how he'd gotten out alive.

Sitting up with the pillow curled around the arch of her back, book open, she snuggled down for the evening. The Tibetan rock salt lamp cast a warming glow on the book, setting the atmosphere for what would be a good read. Turning the page, half-expecting him to break free from the grips of his captor, she sped-read the page, unaware that she was not alone.

* * *

Not having a vantage point on the incident, and with no way of telling how far along the motorway it was, Roger and James waited. Judging by the number of emergency vehicles speeding along the hard shoulder and a helicopter flying low, they were in for a long wait.

"No guarantees my bladder will hold out."

James handed him the empty coffee cup from the holder.

"Here, use this."

"Yeah, right... then I'll throw it over that dickhead who's changed lanes four times in two minutes."

"Rog, chill out. Think of cold running water." James tapped his fingers on the steering wheel rhythmically.

"CHILL! You're spending far too much time with the geeks." Roger gripped his crotch. "Next, you'll be saying LOL and—"

James said just that, the "L" lingered for effect.

Now at a standstill, heads shook, and a few got out to talk to other drivers. An argument broke out between the idiot who had changed lanes several times and a car filled with hotheaded youths, the idiot being outnumbered five-to-one in a fierce verbal exchange.

James followed suit, turning off the engine. Roger inspected the side of the car while peeing on the wheel arch.

"Better?" James asked. "Here, wipe your hands."

Roger took a wet wipe from the handy pack without comment. He'd done the "man who carries wet wipes" joke to death, so it wouldn't have the same effect now. Instead, he asked about Len Happy.

"So, do you think he'll find it?"

"It's not like Len to not find things. He's got a knack for finding the unfindable."

"Yeah, you told me... the boat thing, right?"

"If he can't, then Ronny sure as hell won't. Either way, once I warn Len about the hit, then I'm out of here. Heading back to face the music."

"So, you know Len's going to be hit? I mean, you know for sure?"

"Why else would they let him go, bugged as they did?"

Scrunching his nose, Roger rubbed his chin before looking back over to James.

"What?" James asked.

"There's more to it. You want to know what this thing is, too. You think if you find Len, he will lead you to the powerful being. Am I right?"

"We don't know it's a *being* or its *powerful*, Rog. All we know is that Len and Ronny—I'll use your words—have a hard-on for it."

"Knew it!" Roger slapped his thigh, as if proven right.

James started the engine and moved the car forward, following the car in front for two feet. Three ambulances drove by on the other side of the motorway. The helicopter took off, headed in the same direction. Casualties were on board.

Still unable to see past the sea of cars in front, he turned off the engine once more.

"So, if we're all spirits living a human experience, how come there are so many arseholes around? Don't you think a spirit would know right from wrong?" Roger asked.

James frowned. The question was nonsensical, but he understood.

"Spirits are sent from the greater consciousness system to live a human existence. To experience everything possible within a human lifespan."

"For what reason?" Roger asked. "Why experience life when there's no recollection of past events? Even if you're reborn, all is forgotten. It becomes a pointless exercise."

"To evolve. That's what Len would say. To feed that experience back into the greater consciousness system, allowing *it* to evolve." James sneered. How could he not understand? "Like a cash machine; one filled with knowledge, and the customer draws knowledge from the machine."

"Using a spirit cash card?" Roger asked.

166

"A thought, Roger. People capture thoughts, inspiration, and ideas from a conscious evolving database of knowledge and experience."

"So, what about aliens? Is there a spirit living an alien experience, or is it only reserved for humans?" Roger almost regretted asking. He'd already asked Len. He explained how we only see reality through limited senses, and that if an alien was conscious, then it would have a spirit feeding information back to the greater consciousness system, thus allowing it to increase its frequency and expand by way of evolution.

"Yes," replied James.

Roger slapped his leg but didn't shout *Eureka!*

"I get it!"

"Good for you. Now, can we change the subject?"

"That's what he means by lowering entropy. He wants to lower entropy, as it's too high with all the evil, terrorism, corruption, and crime. After the one with pure consciousness sends Vetala back into the fiery pits of hell, it can bring about a consciousness shift in humans, thus bringing balance back to the world. That's why he said there were no wrongs or rights, just good and bad intentions. Good intentions increase the frequency, and bad ones lower vibrational frequency. Now I get it!"

James nodded his head in agreement with Roger's understanding of the conversation that had taken place between the three of them. He'd noted that Len had told them a paradigm shift would occur; increased conscious awareness and mass enlightenment. But he'd go along with the high-frequency thing if it got him to the guest house with no more questions.

Roger waited for congratulations to his newfound understanding of events, but none were forthcoming. James watched the car ahead jitter to a stop.

Roger broke the silence. "Well?"

"Well, what?"

"Happenings around the world, rumours that World War III is coming, the immigration crisis, terrorism… all of it could stop if we find what Len's looking for. I don't think you believe that, do you? I know I don't."

"I need to warn Len, nothing more."

"If he's half the mystic you say he is, he'll already know." Roger pushed James on the shoulder. James turned to face him.

"This isn't about Len, is it? It's about you."

James let out a long sigh. "Maybe. Maybe Len's not right about a lot of things, but he's correct in saying we have free will, and there's always a wildcard that even he can't see coming. I'm sick and tired playing the *yes* game with Mr Green, hiding in corners, afraid to say what needs saying."

"You're afraid?"

"Yes, Rog. I'm afraid that when it's my turn to leave this life, all I'll have contributed will be that I followed orders. Good or bad. Followed, Rog. I'm tired of following."

Roger didn't comment; he'd spent enough time with his friend over the years to know when he needed quiet time to get his head straight and ponder life. He'd always seen James as a leader rather than a follower. Even when he was his boss back in the day, he'd always taken charge of the situation. Strange, how an individual's opinion of themselves doesn't always reflect the opinion that others hold of them.

Rain pelted the window. Roger turned up the radio. James stared at the sea of taillights. Both listened to Bobby McFerrin singing, "Don't Worry, Be Happy."

* * *

168

With eyes fixed on the page, Margret fumbled for the glass of water. A brief glance to locate it was enough. She raised the glass, pulling it toward her in a sideways motion. Sheets slid down, exposing her thighs. A drop of water sat on the top sheet before vanishing, sucked up by thirsty fibres.

She placed the glass on the bedside table and tugged the sheet; it pulled back. She tugged again, a little harder this time, but it didn't budge.

She got out, a little too fast. Her head swayed, and tiny dots danced around her eyes, causing her to drop back down with a bounce. This didn't unnerve her. The doctor put it down to smoking, as he did with all her ailments.

Standing, slower this time, annoyed and somewhat curious as to how the sheet had become snagged, she grappled with it. She feared it would rip, so she moved alongside the bed frame, pulling.

Lowering herself onto her knees, she peered under the bed frame. The lamplight didn't allow her to see the cause of her frustration. She yanked at it, not caring if it ripped. Her disgruntlement gave her extra strength.

She pulled. It pulled back. Something gripped her ankles. The crunch of bone hadn't any time to register as she clawed at the carpet. Flailing arms lashed out, she pushed away, sliding backwards from the blackness. Cutting pain in her back sheltered her from the strangeness of it all. The bottom half of her body lay under the bed. She shook at the sight of the sheet vanishing under, licking her thighs, slithering, winding, tightening its grip. "Help!" she screeched, her cries weaker now, a mere gurgle. The top of her thighs swelled with the pressure of the sheet tightening, twisting. Her broken ankles burned, sending shooting shocks up her spine. Darkness beneath the bed protected her from seeing her missing toes.

"Help..."

Unable to move, she watched as the blackness under the bed shimmered.

"My God. SMOKE!" she cried, pulling at the tightening sheet.

There was no smell. She felt no heat. Climbing up her legs, it felt alive, like tongs tasting flesh; tasting her fear.

Laying powerless, arms weak, legs tied, her pain faded. Short, deliberate breaths, gasps slowing with each one taken. The blackness had left the bed, enveloping her mind as she passed out.

Dripping water and the recognisable squeak of the bath stirred her senses. Margret's eyes flickered open. The dryness of her mouth made her gag. The tip of her tongue hit the cloth that parted her lips. She tried to move, but torn sheets held her in place. Arms and legs spread, the frame of the bed rocked as she struggled.

She tried to guide her tears toward her dry, numb mouth.

The toilet door creaked open. A naked, hairless man stood before her. Inward screams went unheard as he walked toward the bed. She shook her head, fearing the worst. The more she struggled, the tighter the restraints became.

"You are not the one."

Her eyes widened upon seeing the scars and welts on his hairless body. Eyes with no whites and black bulging pupils stared back at her.

"You're not the one." Disappointment embodied him. His fists clenched. She froze. Eyes closed tight, expecting the unthinkable, her body trembled. Wishing, praying, pleading for the bed to swallow her body, she pressed her head into the pillow as his fingers touched her cheek.

"Drink."

Opening her eyes, she saw the glass of water approach. She yanked her arm trying to reach it; the sheet tightened around her wrist.

Unblocking her mouth, he edged the glass closer to her wrinkled, peeling lips. Wetness loosened the inner workings of her mouth; a flood of nature's lifeblood gave her hope.

Placing the empty glass down, he turned to face the sliding wardrobe, looked in, then opened the freestanding wooden one which still housed her husband's clothes. Margret thought he might come back for them. Then she wanted to burn them, but never had, deciding instead to give the lot to a charity shop she'd still not found. Out of sight, out of mind. Until now. She watched as he dressed in the only suit her husband had ever bought. Worn twice, once on their wedding day and again at his brother's funeral. The shirt hung over the half-mast trousers, revealing the full length of his black cotton socks. Throwing items from the base of the wardrobe, he found shoes—a perfect fit.

Shaking, she remained quiet, almost relieved that her captor was getting dressed; assurance that his intentions weren't sexual. He turned to face her dressed in her ex-husband's old suit, but looking nothing like he had. He'd been a bastard, but she wished he would walk through the door right now.

Her guests would arrive at any minute. Was this one of them?

"What did the man called Happy want with you?"

She tried to speak, but the intended words never surfaced.

"WHAT DID HE TELL YOU?" His voice bellowed, vibrating every hair on her body.

"I don't... I'm—"

"Speak now and tell me what he said to you!"

The word Happy. Her first guest's name. He must be talking about Len Happy.

"He stayed as a guest. Please, what are you going to do?" Avoiding eye contact, she thought of what he said, his jokes, the crazy story about being let free from a mental hospital, the tale about walking all the way to Church Knighton without reason.

Lowering his voice, he said, "Thank you."

He moved closer, his face fractions from her own. His breath smelled like death.

"What is Church Knighton?"

She moved her head in a helpless motion from left to right and back again.

"What else did he tell you?"

"He was going. Compelled to be there. Doesn't know why. What are you going to do?"

"I believe you. You know nothing more."

"Take everything. I have money. Please let me go. I have jewellery on the dressing table. The top drawer. There's money in a box—"

"Why do you offer me these things?" His voice was slow and calm.

"In exchange for my freedom. Please, I beg you—please let me go."

Her words were robotic, stilted, afraid.

Scattering jewellery across the dresser, her mother's ring fell onto the carpet. She tried not to look in its direction; it was her mother's, and sentimentally irreplaceable.

He staggered backwards; she thought he might have a heart attack as bony fingers gripped his chest. With one swift motion, he swiped the contents from the dresser. What if he died leaving her tied to the bed? Her mind raced. She was about to speak, to plead for her freedom once more. He stared at the carpet, at her Bible. Kicking it across the room, he turned to her.

"What... What are you going to do?" her trembling voice seemed to excite him.

"Are you happy?" His tone low and deep.

She shook her head, not sure what to say.

"Answer me!" His voice was assertive; gravel-like.

"NO! NO! NO!" She pulled the sheets, tightening them further, her hands numb and purple. "What are you going to do?!" she screamed. She kept screaming, in the hopes that someone would hear, the scream losing momentum, anger turned to pleading as any reserved energy seeped through the bed.

He shuffled over to her. An object—silver, she couldn't make out what—was hidden, pushed into his right jacket sleeve. She continued to wheeze. He knelt beside her and placed a finger on her lips. She tugged her head away, then stopped screaming as he clasped both hands together and prayed. No sound, only a slight movement of his thin lips.

Prising his hands apart, the look in his black eyes was one of remorseful anger, fighting his actions. He stood, spasming as if to clear away a force possessing him.

"I'll set you free now," he said, in a low, unthreatening manner. "You deserve better."

The flood of hope was overwhelming. She nodded in agreement, not wanting to risk any further words on this disturbed man. She smiled, thinking it might cement his decision to free her.

He stood over her, a silver letter opener clasped in his right hand. It was her late mother's. He'd found it buried among the mass of objects within the drawer.

"My God—no—please, you said I deserved better, you said—"

"I'll free you from your decaying body. You'll be happy and free."

As she looked into his black eyes, the room turned white as the silver point entered her neck.

He waited for her spirit to leave the body before admiring himself in the full-length mirror. The trilby hat matched the jacket and cast a shadow over his face, making him look... more human.

Chapter 18

James listened to footsteps striking timber from outside his room. He glanced at his phone before caressing a memory foam pillow and snuggling into the thick duvet.

The staircase squeaked. Roger rubbed his eyes. He'd agreed to an early start, but this was too early. Half-asleep, he hunched his knees up to suppress the tingling in his crotch. It was no use; nature called. Belt undone, shirt open from the chest up, Roger walked barefoot into the en-suite.

They'd agreed to meet for breakfast, but that wasn't for another two hours. Visions of James questioning the owner and the brightness of the room took him past the halfway point of wakefulness. There was little time to rest. They shouldn't be far behind. Len was travelling on foot.

"Rog, wake up, bud," James called through his door. "I'll be downstairs eating your breakfast... If you're lucky, I'll save you a round of toast."

"For fuck's sake, it's half-five. We agreed six-thirty," Roger said to the closed door. "Why tell me six thirty and then make it five thirty?"

Half-expecting to see the owner or staff preparing breakfast, they saw neither. The place was as silent as when they crept in last night after finding the keys under the pot dog. It was still early; breakfast wouldn't be served for another two hours.

Yawning, Roger sat with James at the table.

"Place is deserted, mate," James said.

"Could it have something to do with you getting up before the crow shits, while every normal person is still in the land of nod?" Roger asked, following James' lead in pouring a glass of orange juice.

* * *

Danial rubbed his leg, digging his fingers in until the cramp subsided. Lucy had her head on his waist with her lips apart. Eyes shut. Asleep. Danial smiled. He'd become her pillow.

A line of bright sun fell on the sofa. Blonde hair covered his right side. He mouthed the word, "Wow."

Lifting her head, Lucy had one eye closed. She forced a smile. "What's the time?"

Still half-asleep, Danial stroked his fingers through her hair, then snatched his hand away.

"Seven in the morning." He couldn't recall falling asleep with Lucy.

"Guess we were both tired out last night. I didn't even make it into bed," she said, rubbing her eyes and entering a long stretch.

Opening the cupboard, Lucy reached on tiptoes to the top shelf and brought down a fresh box of tea bags. Without asking if he wanted one (he did), she made them both a cup of tea.

"I'm sorry, I haven't been shopping, what with the garden and then—"

"I'll take you out for breakfast if you like," he said, rubbing the sleep from his eyes.

"Okay, I'll jump in the shower," she said, smiling. This took Danial by surprise. How could she be joyful after what had happened? She looked fresh, even after sleeping on the sofa.

Danial opened the passenger door and waited until she was in his car before going around to the driver's side.

He drove to Little Chef. The ten-minute drive felt like two as they engaged in conversation about Lucy's missing cat and laughed about the program they'd watched, trying to guess the end, as neither had stayed awake long enough.

Although he knew she couldn't be interested in him—not in *that* way—he imagined them being a couple, going for breakfast and maybe a morning stroll. All the time, pushing the events that had led up to this moment to the far reaches of his mind, not wanting to spoil the precious minutes he had with her right here and now.

The restaurant was quiet. One family left as they entered, and there was a man sitting on his own reading a newspaper. Danial followed Lucy to a table in the far corner overlooking the carpark.

"Not much of a view for our first date, but they cook a good breakfast." He couldn't believe he'd said *date*. A Freudian slip of the tongue. Lucy either didn't hear him or paid no attention to his comment as she smiled and took her place at the table, lifting the menu from the wooden stand. Studying it, she looked up at him. "What do you what, Dan?"

"Mine's an Olympic."

"Make that two, minus the black pudding."

Danial smiled.

"What?"

"I don't like the stuff. Black pudding, I mean."

A man took their order. An awkward silence followed.

"Sorry for falling asleep on you last night. With all that's happened... it's taken it out of me."

"I'm not surprised. Me too."

"Yes, you must have been through hell dealing with the police."

Danial thought she must think him insensitive. It was she who'd lost an ex-partner.

Lucy sensed his unease. "Dan, you know you don't have to tread on eggshells around me, don't you? I think you're a nice guy."

Danial waited, expecting a *but* to follow. It never came.

Had she understood what he'd told her? He'd told her every detail and hinted about it continuing until they were out of harm's way. He was going to show her the book, but couldn't risk it driving her crazy, as it had tried to do with him.

"Lucy… about last night… the things I said about my flat… Ronny and Len…" He bit his lip as two glasses of fresh orange juice joined them. Thanking the man, he waited until he was out of sight. "About last night," he said again.

"I believe you. We need to get away from this place, Dan, and I don't feel safe in the flat after what you told me. If you haven't anywhere to go, then we could get a temporary place, away from it all, and try to bring an end to the madness. What I mean is, I have to get away. You don't have to come, but I'd like you to." Lucy lowered her head and raised her eyes to Danial. "I'm too forward." Her cheeks reddened.

Danial's heart thumped upon being included in her plans.

"Relationships born from crises never last." Danial regretted the words as they left his mouth. He was rusty at the courting game; as rusty as a shipwreck. He felt like he was doing a good job of wrecking any plans she may have had for them.

Saved by the Olympic breakfast and small talk from the waiter, Danial downed half a glass of orange juice.

"Can I get you any sauce?"

"Brown, please," they both said. Looking at one other, they

laughed. Tucking into the breakfast as if neither of them had eaten for a week, they discussed where they should go and how much money they both had. Speaking to Lucy was like meeting up with an old friend—not that he had any old friends he would meet up with and talk to without judgement, but if he had, he imagined it would be like that.

* * *

James and Roger batted about ideas, covering a range of topics, for over two hours. Finishing the last dregs of fresh orange juice, Roger stood up. "So, it's past breakfast time, and we've seen nobody – if no one's down here in the next two minutes, then you're cooking breakfast."

"Why me?"

"Have you ever asked Kath about my cooking?" Roger asked, pacing up and down the fleur-de-lis printed carpet.

James walked out the dining room. "No. Have you asked Jackie about how I set fire to the toaster? It has a timer on it."

James flicked through the guest book; one guest entry was all he found. Lenard Happy—next to his name, the word WOW in brackets. Why would she add that next to his name?

"Rog, come and take a look at this." He called him again, but he didn't reply. "Roger!" James walked back into the dining room; he wasn't there.

"James… you better get up here quick."

Roger's voice came from the first floor.

James climbed the stairs and stopped when he saw the concern on his face. Roger bent down and held up his finger. James knew he wasn't fooling. He padded a dark, viscous substance with his thumb. "Blood," Roger said, smelling his finger.

James pounded the door. No response. The door wouldn't

open. James moved out of Roger's way as he kicked at the door. The first two attempts failed. The third broke a bottom panel. They both kicked at the crack that ran from its centre. The wooden panel split. One final kick sent wood flying inside the room.

Roger entered through the small opening. James gave warning not to touch anything as he followed behind, then shouted, "Fucking hell!"

An unrecognisable face had a small book pushed deep into her throat, exiting through the windpipe. The women's broken legs lay twisted. Toes pointed down on blood-soaked sheets.

James wafted away flies circling and landing on the corpse, propelling themselves back into the air, only to find a different place to land. Roger had experienced dead bodies, but never anything like this. He looked at James, who was already squeezing through the broken door.

James' retching made Roger's empty gut growl. He swallowed whatever was working its way up his windpipe and placed two fingers on her neck; there was no pulse. Not that he expected to find one. Using his phone, he recorded the room, saying what the time was, the suspected cause of death, and location. He backed away to the locked door. Careful not to touch splintered wood, he climbed back through and took a deep inward breath when his head was clear of the room.

Roger followed James down the stairs. Two men entered. Both wore shorts, and the larger of the two's campiness was as loud as his Hawaiian printed shirt. Roger bounced down the steps. Before the larger man could get a word out, Roger ushered them back to the door.

"How rude!" They said in unison.

"Didn't want to stay anyway, it's a shithole," the larger one said, as Roger manhandled them both out, closing the top bolt across, followed by the one placed next to the door handle.

James thanked him.

"Right, what's the plan, boss?" Roger expected James to spring into action, but he didn't. His eyes were glassy; his skin ashen. Roger took the lead. "I'll check for cameras, and you make... Call whoever you need to." Roger stood behind the main reception desk. "You didn't hire the best field agent in the business not to get on with it, did you?" Roger asked, forcing a smile.

James felt his legs wobble beneath him. Roger opened a door marked *Private*. And there it was, a monitor with eight small boxes divided across the screen. He could see James on the screen, still standing where he'd left him.

"Jim, I've found the monitor."

James entered. Roger took no pleasure in seeing his friend like this. He was observing a control freak turned weak.

"James, have you called anyone yet, or are we dealing with this?"

James held out his gun. It shook in time with his arm.

"James—mate, put it away, he's long gone."

Holstering his weapon, James asked Roger to rewind the tape, starting from the time he called to book the room. Roger rewound on extreme mode, to the time they made the call.

"Okay, got it." Roger played the recording on plus eight, the quickest visible mode.

"Stop!" James said. "There. No, go back."

They watched as a figure walked up the stairs. Margret left the toilet, and moments later, switched off the lights.

"Zoom in on him, Rog."

"Doubt this has a zoom." By selecting the single screen mode, he enlarged the small square, filling the screen.

"Ronny!" James said, turning a shade paler.

"You can't see his face on this thing, but we can get it analysed back at the lab," Roger said, studying James like a doctor would a patient.

James tried to compose himself by taking long, deep breaths, trying to push out of his mind the time when Jackie found him on the kitchen floor, shaking. He'd thought he was a goner that afternoon. That same feeling had returned.

Without speaking, Roger led James to the dining room and pulled out a chair. James sat. With palms face-down, he spread his arms out across the table. Roger thought about calling an ambulance, but within minutes, his breathing had stabilised.

"You gave me quite a scare."

"Must've got freaked out."

"Shall we get the uniforms in on this?" Roger took his phone out of his trouser pocket.

"No—they're not to know. I need to call Green for advice."

"Advice!" Roger raised his voice. "You need advice? It's a straight-up murder, and we have no place in keeping this quiet. Whoever did this needs stopping."

"You call Green, and they'll come running. At best, we'll be arrested for noncompliance. They'll hunt down Len Happy, being as he was the only guest apart from us. We slept in the next room to the murder victim. Ronny runs free while the spotty bastards back at the lab figure out if it was him on the CCTV. Back off! That's an order," James said, unlocking his phone.

There was a knock on the door. Roger knew it wasn't a knock from a holidaymaker. He went over to the window. Four men in suits stood by their cars.

"Leave it." James breathed the words.

"McMilan… open the door!"

They both fell silent. The door's stained-glass panels masked the person on the other side. Roger waved James over to the window. There were two silver Mercedes, both with the driver's doors open, and two suits standing watch. He read the number plate to James, knowing he would recognise it as one of theirs.

"Why would they be here?" Roger mouthed the words across the room.

Pushing his chest out, James opened the door. Four secret services personnel. One he recognised but couldn't think of his name. As they entered, Roger eyed them. James showed his ID, saying, "We have a situation."

Roger recognised one as the driver of the family estate he had seen circling the car park of the service station. The man went to shake hands. James didn't raise his.

"My name's Lance. We're taking over your duties as of now. You need debriefing back at HQ. I need to collect your weapons and ID." He took great pleasure in saying those words, unlike the others, who displayed a mixture of fear and embarrassment.

James replied in a monotone voice, "Under whose authority? I answer to one man, and that man isn't you."

"He'll be with us in the next twenty minutes, so it would help you both to do as I ask before he arrives."

The name of the youngest of the four came to James. He'd taught him in a class of twenty.

"Mr Mathews, are you going to tell me what this is about?" James looked past the tall, dark figure, and over to the man whom he hoped would remember him. The young man dropped his eyes. The man calling himself Lance spoke for him.

"Loose lips sink the boat, my friend. If you prefer, you can both wait for him to turn up, but I will tell him—"

Roger interrupted. "Tell him what? That we're following orders, waiting for the right person to relieve us of duty? And it's 'loose lips sink ships', you fucking retard."

The man lunged at Roger. James pulled Roger away, whispering, "Not yet, mate. Cool it."

Following James, Roger kept quiet about the body upstairs, half-expecting one of them to walk up, see the smashed door, and scream like a little girl. He would have liked that, but James had other plans.

"Come on, Rog; we have a job to do."

"You're going nowhere," Lance said, pointing his finger at Roger.

James told him that until they were relieved by Mr Green, he was free to carry out orders.

"So, you want to play cat-and-mouse. You've already lost your jobs. You want to lose your freedom, too?"

Two of the men searched downstairs. James and Roger picked up their jackets. A scream from the first floor brought a smile to Roger's face. Time to leave.

"I'm driving," Roger insisted.

Flailing arms blocked their path. Roger clipped the wing mirrors of the two parked cars. James looked back, relieved to see the agent standing.

"Wahoo!" Roger sped off, kicking gravel to dust. He swerved away from oncoming traffic, overtaking an open-top bus.

"Slow the damn car. Pull over." James pointed to The Old Thatch Inn. Two cars parked close to the entrance wearing magnetic signs advertised *Sunday Roasts*. Roger drove to the furthest space and parked between a play area and a storage shed. Low hanging trees scraped the roof, screeching like fingers resisting an inflated balloon. James winced.

James opened his door, making a call. Roger followed. Lowering the phone without a goodbye, James slid it into his pocket.

"Well?"

"Code blue. As I thought, we're closed for business. The office was full. None of them were our men. They're shutting us down. Debrief, and give us a long holiday in the hopes that we forget we ever worked there. If we're lucky."

"So, what about the subjects?"

"Did you not hear me? It's a goddamn code blue! They'll terminate them, and anyone with knowledge of this will be—"

"Be fucking what?"

"Given a long holiday, if we play along. Give them our full cooperation. Play the yes game, Rog."

"And are we?"

James stood still, pondering the situation, then walked over to a small wooded area. Stopping at one of the wooden benches, James raised his right leg onto the seat, resting his arm on his knee in a casual stance.

He was acting as he would at a Friday night card game. Roger stared.

"What's the plan, boss?"

"I'm no longer your boss, mate. My plan to find Len and warn him hasn't changed. Whatever that brings, it brings. Who knows? If I get to him in time, he can go public. It will buy him time. They'll back right down, wait until it's old news. I owe him that much."

"Is this the same company man I know so well, or a different person saying this? You've been acting strange since we found the body."

"Maybe like you, I'm just tired of taking bullshit orders from faceless bastards who don't even know the man. Life's short, you said it yourself, Rog. Life's short. Wait here; they'll arrive soon. Tell them I told you to. I'll commandeer a vehicle and get going."

Roger squeezed his shoulder. "Like hell, you will."

"Rog—back off, you're not going to stop me."

Roger shook his head, "Not without me, you're not."

"Rog, I haven't got time for this. You have Kate."

"And you think Jackie will speak again if she knows I let you play Billy the Kid on your own?"

James looked at him. "It's no game."

They'd be arriving any minute. Taking Roger's car would put them at further risk. Extending his hand, he shook Roger's with a firm grip. Roger knew from the shake that he was going along for the ride.

"That County Man will do. Unless we risk the purple Datsun Cherry?"

James smiled. "Can you get it started?"

Roger walked over to the green Land-Rover. James was first to spot the keys on the passenger seat. Roger opened the driver's door.

James shook his head in amusement. "If I were anywhere else other than out in the sticks, I'd swear this was a rigged vehicle, sitting ready for the police to jump out of the trees."

A bolt slid back on the entrance to the pub.

"Hope this thing starts. These country folks have guns and will use them," James said.

The pub door opened slamming the wall. A woman wearing a brown dressing jacket looked straight at them. The engine turned but didn't fire the first time. She ran back in, banging the door shut. The door opened again. A stocky man wearing jeans and black walking boots appeared, holding an old wartime 303 Rifle.

The Land-Rover's engine spluttered to life. Roger reversed at speed, ripping off the bumper that belonged to the purple car parked next to it.

Clear of the pub, Roger steadied his speed.

"Who do you think will catch us first?" Roger asked. "The uniforms for stealing the wagon, or the suits for doing our job?"

James hadn't thought that far ahead. He hadn't thought of the consequences at all. With the world caving in around him, the one thing he was sure of was warning Len Happy. It was because of something Roger said earlier about him wanting to find the thing that Len said would bring balance to an unbalanced world. James had to agree that had played a part. But life before profit, Len had to know.

Ignoring Roger's comment about who they might bump into first, he told him to head for the town nearest to where the trace had found Len.

"What if he's still in the field?" Roger asked.

"If he is, then we're already too late. They'll be there."

Roger searched his phone for the town nearest to the field.

"Abbott Town's closest. I'll head there. Finding him won't be easy."

Having always had his team, James hadn't thought about how he'd locate Len without their help. Turning to Roger, he said, "Just as well I have the best field agent on board." He held his thumb up to emphasise the point.

Chapter 19

He'd walked through the night, focusing on displaced granite rocks standing tall atop the hill. Len took shelter between crevices and waited for daylight to arrive. A light show from the heavens reached down to the artificial glow of street lamps beyond the hills. Banking on it being the village he sought, he took shelter from howling winds and hazardous, mossy stones underfoot. Climbing the hill in wellingtons proved challenging, and had toppled him twice on his way to higher ground.

Len had never seen wild ponies. As the sun broke through a haze of clouds, their small heads, large, wide-set eyes, and alert ears resembled the magical horses found in a child's fairy tale.

Well-worn tracks led to his resting place, suggesting it was a matter of time before he saw his first person. Then he did. A woman walking alongside her husband. A pinprick on the landscape, like two action figures, they looked the part, holding long walking poles. Both wore woollen hats, and their clothes matched, from green jackets to thick brown socks overlapping waterproof trousers.

The female swung her pole toward him. Len wasn't sure whether they were looking at him or admiring the granite rock formation. He made his way down, intending to ask directions to Church Knighton.

Rain-soaked ground oozed underfoot. Len was thankful for

the wellingtons he'd found at the farm. The trail leading down was as smooth as a velvet sheet. Using protruding rocks for grip, he clambered down.

They met near a stream that was running clear, rapid water through the twists and turns of the hillside. Len stepped on a rock that had been placed to cross—or nature had been kind by providing a way to the other side, he wasn't sure. Taking two strides, he was over and standing in front of the couple.

Both were seventy or eighty years old, dressed for whatever the weather could throw at them. The man's well-worn face showed that he'd lived or worked outside for most of his life. "All right, my luvver?" the man said without moving his lips. His strong West Country accent confirmed that these were not just passing tourists.

Len smiled and asked if they knew where he could find Church Knighton.

The woman's grating voice said something like "grockle", the sound directed at her husband.

"You know someone there, bauy?" The old man said.

Len found the lingo interesting. He bent his head towards words coming from nearly sealed lips; his mind wandered as he imagined the old boy's face set in plaster. If he were to move his lips, then his face would crack into a thousand pieces.

It was the women's turn to talk. "Follow down there, this road be arable mind. Through the first village, which we live, called Burton Tracy, then through country paths down to Church Knighton. They'm a bad lot, mind."

"Hark at he. Yours were from there," the man said, raising one eyebrow as he did.

Len thanked them and heard the word "diddy kai" muttered by the old lady. He stood watching them navigate the stream.

He could tell a lot about a person by their aura, and knew they'd walked those hills for many years. Most would say they loved walking, but not Len; he was aware that they had walked in search of something that neither of them would find externally. Now, they walked to stay alive.

Len looked to the sky and back to the couple, who were some distance away. Rubbing the crystal, he smiled as the man slid his hand into hers. She pulled away before offering her own. Their love for each other would grow from this moment onwards.

The winding, tarmacked road led him to a stone pillar. Chiselled words read *Burton Tracy, two miles*. An arrow pointed to the distant lights he'd seen from the granite rocks. Now fewer in number, outlines of roofs replaced their sparkle.

Len looked back toward his resting place, which had vanished under rolling clouds. The couple he'd spoken with earlier looked as small as two field mice entering cotton wool.

Distant streaks told him rain was coming. Len quickened his pace, determined to reach his destination, keeping faith in messages sent while in a higher state of consciousness. Would the enlightened one shake his hand and offer him a bed for the night, or was the jigsaw bigger? This destination, like the others, might be a piece forming the whole.

The first village resembled a small town. Two banks, sizable shops, butchers, and several charity shops littered the road. Len stopped outside a refurbished restaurant. A wall-mounted menu was encased in a silver frame. *The Grand.* Meals he couldn't pronounce were written in italics with no prices. A pub opposite in its original state looked as it must have over two hundred years ago. The pavement chalkboard advertised a full English breakfast for £5.50. The other side was boasting a Pig Roast for £5.95.

Patting pockets, his thoughts moved from food to Alex, and the money he'd forced through his window. Len carried on past a chip shop and a traditional barber. A funeral came to an end. The grieving relatives, along with the spiteful money grabbers, gathered for their goodbyes and "see you at the wake" conversations outside a medieval church standing proudly on the top of Devon Street.

Next to a wooden bus shelter, an information pole with three arrows pointed to their intended destinations. Church Knighton. One and a half miles to go, and not a clue what awaited.

The winding road didn't have pedestrian pavements. High hedges on either side parted, allowing tractors to enter surrounding fields. For a country road, traffic was fast flowing. Len quick-stepped down the road, brushing thicket, stopping anytime a clearing appeared.

"Welcome to Church Knighton," he said aloud, as he read the sign above the one that read *Neighbourhood Watch*.

He looked back toward the village and saw the granite rock formation that sat high upon the distant hill. Faint tracks ran from it; one of which he'd walked down over an hour ago. The sky cleared, blue with only a few wispy clouds breaking up an otherwise pleasant day. He wasn't sure how high the hill was, but the change in temperature was noticeable.

There were pockets of newly built houses to his left, a small school, play park, and a church once surrounded by open fields—a focus point for all to see. The place looked nice, having little-to-no litter and ample dog waste bins. Apart from passing traffic, the village seemed calm. Not at all like the couple or Margret had described. *Margret, my God, Margret.* He shook negative thoughts from his mind, putting his paranoia down to fatigue.

The village shop displayed hanging baskets and window boxes looking bright. The date marked in stone made it one of the oldest buildings in the village. Len staggered in; the thought that something terrible had happened to Margaret had brought on dizziness. If he didn't get a drink and rest soon, then he would collapse. His head throbbed; his mouth sawdust dry.

The shop was large enough for a small village, having everything anyone could want both in the food department and most everything else, from alcohol to needles and thread. Len's eyes lit up when he saw a random pair of boot socks hanging from a rack of cards. More so when the fridge buzzed, reminding him that he needed to drink.

A woman appeared from behind the door holding a broom. She greeted him with a welcoming smile. "Hello, good morning," she said, passing him to stand behind the counter. The woman either didn't have a southern accent or hid it well.

Len returned the greeting with a small nod. "Good morning to you, my dear, and what a lovely one we're having." Flicking his tongue, he looked toward the fridge and back to the woman. "Has someone lost a pound? Or at least, I think it's a pound," he said, bending to pick up the coin from a display of chocolate.

"You might have dropped it. Have it anyway or pop it in the Air Ambulance pot." She looked with concern as Len struggled to stand. "Visiting?"

"Passing through. May stay awhile. Can you recommend any bed and breakfasts? Any casual work? I'll do most anything."

"Sorry, no B&BS in the village. Just the shop, the hairdressers, and a pub. Used to be a local watering hole, loved by locals and holidaymakers." She shook her head and looked down at the counter. "Taken over by bikers."

"Bikers—I know a few."

"Not these. They're evil to the core. Poor landlord... I feel for him and his daughter, having to put up with them. We've called the police. Landlord covers for them. Them lot have got him over a barrel."

"Sorry, who has him over a barrel?" Len asked, confused by her rant.

"The bikers—Mrs. Perkins who lives next to the pub had a heart attack because of them. They caused her no end of stress. Everyone is scared to death."

Len listened to her babble about every customer complaint she'd received over the years. All pointed toward the biker gang. Could be village gossip, or a real problem in the community. Was this the reason he was compelled to be here? He hoped not. The shopkeeper seemed scared; kept looking out of the window as she whispered happenings over the years. Thanking her for her time, Len paid for a bottle of water and walked to the pub that was causing such misery to the residents.

The old stable door creaked as it opened. Hit with an atmosphere as thick as his head, he murmured, "So much trapped emotion."

Looking around, he saw a snug area, clad in cushions, with side walls providing privacy. There was a refurbished coal storage area, the iron shoot door still in its original place. The area reverberated evil. The frequency was dull, waiting to infect whoever should sit there. It wasn't an entity, that he was sure of. It came from the living. Someone had left a part of their blackened spirit behind, like a worker would unintentionally leave his muddy boot prints on clean carpet.

Stale beer hit his nostrils as he walked over to the unlit open fire. A pile of logs was positioned in readiness to come alive and warm the customers. There weren't any. Not even a barman.

He looked back to the snug. "You're right, my dear."

"Sorry to keep you waiting… what can I get you?"

Len turned. A man smiled behind the bar. He looked troubled, more so than the shopkeeper; his haggard face like that of a man lacking sleep. Wearing a dust-covered suit two sizes too big, he'd lost weight. His painted smile didn't fool Len. Why here? And at such a critical time?

"Good morning! I'll have tap water, please."

The barman looked at a clock hanging above the door, then back at Len with a confused gaze.

"Yes, good afternoon. No problem. Ice?" he asked, getting a straight glass from below the bar.

Len looked at the clock. Five past one. Tired, he needed a place to sleep.

"I'm looking for a place to rest for a while. I can work as payment," he said.

The barman eyed him up and down.

"Sorry, I didn't introduce myself. I'm Len Happy."

"Yeah, and I'm the landlord, Brian Pratt. You here for a reason?"

"No reason. Time off. Taking in the sights," Len said, lifting the glass. "Do you need any help? I'm a quick learner."

Brian took his empty glass, raised his eyebrows, and offered him another. Len accepted.

"Thing is, mate, this place gets really busy in the evening, and the customers are—well—demanding. Tell you what, the cellar needs sorting out and cleaning. As long as you're not seen this side of the bar—or at all, for that matter—you can stay upstairs in one of the rooms. It's basic. I've not been in it for years, but if you're desperate, then you can have it now and clear the cellar.

Shouldn't take longer than two days, and you can have the room rent-free for the work, and say, thirty quid on top."

Len couldn't believe his luck. A place to stay and money in his pocket.

"Here, have one on me." Brian pulled a pint. "I'll show you your room after you've finished."

Brian left via a door behind the bar. Len looked across an empty bar and out the window. He watched three birds walking back and forth atop a purpose-built feeder. Another two joined, sharing fruit placed on top of a handful of dried seed.

Birds took flight. Popping and the distinct roar of motorcycles broke the silence. Len counted five, switched off one after the other.

The stable door swung open. A leather-clad man with a face not too dissimilar from the biker's creased jacket walked through to the bar, stopping within Len's personal space. Combing his grey goatee beard, he looked down at Len.

"We don't have faggots in this pub, and you're in my seat."

"I didn't realise reservations were possible. I'll go sit over there," Len pointed, nowhere in particular.

"All these seats are mine. It's my pub."

Brian walked up to the bar and whispered, "I'll meet you around back if you're still interested."

Leaving, Len turned. Brian had his hands up, as if being held up at gunpoint. Running around the building as fast as his thick legs could take him, he opened the back door and tiptoed to the door leading to the bar. Getting as close as he could without being seen through the gap, he listened.

"Zak—mate, the pot's empty. I'll pay you double tonight, but your friends need to buy their drinks. I can't—"

"Listen, Cogs will be riding with us tonight, so make sure you put on a pig roast and a good bottle of whiskey. You've met him, right?"

"Er... yeah, once."

"No fuck-ups—stay sober!"

"Yes, all right."

Len watched as Brien stared at the side window. Engines popped and spat as the bikes left.

Len backed off down the hallway and waited. Brian opened the back door and let him inside, "Hi, sorry about him. As I said, this place gets a little hostile. They'll be back tonight. Better you don't show yourself and be in your room from seven on. Use the back door if you go out."

"If it's all right with you, I'd like to get sleep now and work through the night. My body clock's haywire at the moment."

"Stay out of the way. That's all I'm asking."

The room was basic. A single bed under a dirt-smeared window and a lopsided wardrobe leaning against the wall.

Brian rolled his eyes as he cringed through tight lips. "I haven't been in here for a long time."

Len smiled and touched his shoulder, reassuring him that the room was fit for his purpose. Making contact told him all he needed to know. The message clear. Brian was in real trouble.

* * *

Roger liked that James had confidence in his abilities to track down Len Happy. He would either have to be lucky and bump into him or rely on the old-school way of finding the new guy in town.

"Might have to do this Sherlock Homes-style, mate," Roger said. "Unless we run him over on the way."

"There can't be many larger-than-life, borderline insane

visitors passing through, Rog. We just need to hope he chose a town and not a remote woodland. Anything goes with that guy, but I'll be damned if I'm going to sit back and read about how he had an accident somewhere, found washed up on a beach. Not on my watch."

Avoiding the route past the field that was their last point of reference for him, they took the A38, mindful of local police cars and unmarked cars used by the constabulary, as the man whose car they were driving would have reported it stolen by now, or was probably giving the details to MI5's wrecking crew.

"You do know, James, that all hell will break loose when they find my car with its keys still in the ignition and a farmer with a gun ready to explain how he chased us from the carpark?"

"Yes, Rog. What's your point?"

Roger laughed while trying to speak. "My point is—you're as crazy as I am, mate."

James parked the car next to a pile of pallets at the rear of a row of retail outlets.

"So, we burning her or what?" Roger asked as he got out.

His comment was met with a stony, yet vacant expression. "Sometimes I worry about you, Rog—I really do."

They both agreed to walk the town asking people if they'd seen the missing Len Happy. The storyline was that they were his carers, and he was a patient who had wandered off without telling them where he was going. Seemed legit enough and would explain his strangeness.

* * *

Mr Mathews, the young trainee, was left in charge of keeping watch over Roger's car. For him, that was his biggest responsibility to date, apart from belonging to the elite team who were supposed to relieve two agents from their mission which hadn't gone to plan.

Lance and three high-ranking agents had the go-ahead to take out Len Happy, while the other two stayed at the guest house, in charge of the police.

Local police and media were contacted to detain Ronny. MI5 had a knack for involving the public sector to carry out dirty work on their behalf. The old rule of thumb was to take out a subject before it hit the public, and if the news reached the public domain, then back the fuck off until it became yesterday's chip paper.

Wheels of the silver Mercedes spun as it approached the dirt track leading to the field where Len was last traced. Lance turned to the agent sitting behind him.

"Agent Snow, you brought us here, so do your thing and tell me where to find him."

Agent Snow looked down at the handheld receiver, and Lance watched as his eyes widened. "He's still here at Apple Tree Farm, or so this is telling me, but I don't understand. We should be looking right at him."

Lance drew his weapon. Holding it out with both hands, he beckoned Agent Snow to get out.

"Take me to him, Snow."

Lance followed the unarmed agent over the wooden stile and into the muddy field, causing a squelching sound underfoot.

"What if he's in the barn? We will be sitting ducks," Snow said, watching his once-shiny shoes sink into the soft ground.

"Our man is unarmed and not considered dangerous. I've got your back. Is this the first action you've seen, Snow?"

Snow ran the words over in his head— *unarmed and not dangerous*—then glanced at the gun, confident that the reason for taking this man out must be justified. *The order is coming from the chief himself*; he thought as he continued through the field. He stopped as the flashing red dot covered his handheld receiver.

"Should be right here," Snow said, with a confused look on his face.

Lance looked down at the pile of manure and then back up to Snow. Kicking the dry, crusty top he revealed the chip.

The barn was all but empty, apart from a set of clothes hanging on a hook above a bale of hay. The small square chip inside the grimy shirt pocket confirmed they'd hit a dead end.

Chapter 20

Resting the cup of tea next to Lucy's laptop, Danial glanced at the screen once more. After returning from Little Chef, they had spent all morning sitting together in the same place that they had woken up in this morning. Danial understood that Lucy had pushed the shock of what had happened to the far reaches of her mind. Searching for a getaway place helped to distract her attention away from the murder of Lucy's former partner.

After a long discussion, they settled for a log cabin in a remote location somewhere in Dartmoor. It was a private advert stating that the cabin would suit a couple wanting to escape to a remote, quiet location, surrounded by natural wonders. They both laughed, as the advert promoted as many negatives as it did positives, emphasising that there were no local facilities. The nearest shop was miles away, and a phone signal or Internet connection was ad-hoc at best. It was supposedly the perfect retreat for people who enjoyed hiking and orienteering. It also stated that, due to its remote location, some cars might find the track leading up to the cabin a challenge.

"It's a wonder they ever get any customers with that advert," Danial remarked. "I mean, they may as well say, 'make sure you bring plenty of reading material, as there is nothing to do.'"

"We could take a tent and sleep under the stars," she said, smiling.

Danial had always fancied camping, but never had anyone to go with, and thought it a bit weird to go out in the wilderness on his own. He was going to question the link between camping and the log cabin, as they couldn't stay at two places at the same time, but thought better of it, as she probably wanted the security of a roof over her head and was thinking of pitching a tent in the garden. If it *had* a garden. The pictures on the screen showed hills and rocks as far as the eye could see, but surely, that didn't belong to the owners of the cabin.

"Earth to Dan. What's on your mind? We can always stay over at a hotel or something. I just need to get away until they catch that madman."

"No, no, it's a great idea. How did you know I was thinking?"

Lucy laughed. "Because you frown when you're thinking, that's how." Danial felt her hand on his leg, and it excited him. He wanted to grab her and pull her close but resisted. He didn't want to misinterpret her signals and was afraid to make the first move.

"Dan, can I ask you something?"

"Of course. Ask me anything you want."

"I just can't help but think that you came to my rescue by—well, by accident. It just seems like you were looking for me. But why?"

Danial tensed as the question was asked and thought: *What if she thinks I'm a stalker or a creep who looks through her window every night to watch her change out of her clothes? What if she thinks...*

"Dan, you're deep in thought again. I can see you frowning. I think you came looking for me because you like me. You know... like me as more than just someone at work. More than just a friend."

His lips quivered as he smiled back, and before words had a

chance to form, he felt the warmth of her soft lips touching his. Placing her hands on his chest, Lucy slid them to the side as she held him close in a tight embrace. Frustrating signals turned in a direction that held no confusion for either of them.

Danial wriggled free and stood up, pulling Lucy off the sofa to stand in front of him. Bending down, he kissed her and held her close. Lucy took him by the hand, and he followed her lead into a room that only in his dreams would he have ever have found himself entering.

Danial squinted at the room's brightness; sun bounced from a full-length mirror standing in the corner. Garments hung loosely atop the pine frame, masking his reflection.

Lucy pushed him away, and for a split second, he thought the worst—until he knew her intention. She snapped the curtains shut and swung back around into his arms. Danial stumbled, his head lightened as she showered him with intoxicating kisses. He wanted to take charge, but at the same time, was relieved when she took control. She fell onto the bed and took him with her.

Listening to the shower running and knowing every curve that the unsuspecting droplets would encounter, Danial turned on the kettle and congratulated himself, not in an egotistical way, but in a way that only love can make a man feel. The sound of the shower stopped as the water in the kettle bubbled to its climax.

Danial, in a spark of inspiration, opened the leaded glass wall unit and pulled out two champagne flutes. He stopped before pouring in hot water—at first because the tea bag wouldn't fit in, and then it struck him that boiling water and thin glass was a bad idea.

Lucy crept up behind him just as he was pouring the already-cooling tea from the two cups into the flutes.

"What do we have here?"

Danial handed one to her. With crossed arms, they drank tea from the champagne flutes, giggling like teenagers that were home alone.

Danial called and made the reservation with a farmer called, Benny who told him they were the first to call, and he would make sure that an ample wood supply would be stacked before they arrived. Visions of cooking marshmallows on the open fire and Lucy wrapped in a blanket filled his mind.

After packing a week's worth of clothes and whatever else Lucy deemed important, they stopped off at a supermarket, where Danial purchased the remaining essentials, two tops, a pair of jeans, a toothbrush, and other oddments. They were both surprised to see that they had sleeping bags and tents on offer. On the way to the counter, Lucy picked up a camping stove and a set of plastic knives and forks. Both agreed they'd find another supermarket or shop closer to their destination for perishable foodstuffs.

Over an hour into the drive, Danial remembered that he'd left his phone charging back at Lucy's flat.

"I've not brought mine, either. No need, if there's no signal there," Lucy said. "It'll be nice not to have to think about phones and computers for a while, don't you think?"

Danial agreed. "Yeah, it will. Reconnect with Mother Nature." He was looking forward to this as much as Lucy.

Taking the next left turn onto a country road, trees arched over either side, creating a tunnel effect as far as the eye could see.

"Well, Lucy, we're officially in the sticks, and still have an hour's drive ahead of us." Both bent their necks to look up at a bird of prey hovering with its big brown wings looking as still as a stretched kite. It swooped down into a field of sheep, and Danial turned his focus back to the road, which was becoming narrower with every passing second.

Stopping the car, Danial reversed into a slight incline. The driver of a big blue tractor waved and smiled as he heaved the bulk past his car. Neither of them had ever seen roads like these, which were more like poorly maintained garden paths, with potholes of various sizes appearing on either side of the patchy grass that grew in the centre.

Danial regretted taking his car, as it banged up and down the uneven lanes, but was secretly enjoying the adventure. With every bump and bang the car made, Lucy made a sound like an excited child would on a fairground ride.

Lucy got out first to look at a small brown sign nailed to an old oak tree. She beckoned Danial to get out. *Bird Farm* was painted on the aged wooden plank with moss covering part of the M, making it look like it was saying *Bird Fart*. Lucy's sense of humour was rubbing off on Danial, as he was the first to point it out. They both laughed and looked at the arrow pointing up to the top of a field; beneath, painted in fresh paint, were the words, *The Hide Out*, which was the name that had been given to the log cabin they had booked.

"I can't see us driving the rest of the way. No wonder it was free at short notice. I bet most would have just turned around at this point," Danial said, looking at the steep grass track leading up to what seemed like the clouds.

Lucy put her arm around his waist. "Are we on foot from here then, babes?"

Danial kissed her, knowing she was waiting for him to make the decision, to take charge of the situation, and be the man. A spontaneous wave of adventurousness washed over him as he said in his best movie star voice, "Get in. We're going for it."

Using tyre tracks previously made by a much larger vehicle, Danial pressed himself tight up against the steering wheel and rocked back and forth, willing the Vauxhall Astra up the steep hill. They nearly made it before the rear wheels spun, causing it to slide to the side. Danial put the car in reverse and let it roll backwards, turning the steering wheel so that the car came to rest on a precarious slant under a tree. Trying to support himself by holding onto the dashboard, he slid toward Lucy, who giggled. She turned to him. "You just can't resist me, can you? I've heard about blokes like you. But this has got to be the funniest advance I've ever seen." Danial was nearly on top of her when he reached for her door handle and opened it. She practically fell out, and he felt a moment of guilt before hearing her cries of laughter.

Danial helped her up, and they hugged. "Well, I think we are on foot from now on," he said, gathering as much as he could hold, staggering and slipping, his hands and arms full of bags. Lucy picked up the tent, and they both stumbled up the hill like two drunks rediscovering the force of gravity.

Deciding not to follow the wheel marks in the grass that would lead them around the woodland, they bashed their way through ferns and trees. Lucy discovered one of Danial's fears as he walked through a cobweb and screamed an inward shriek as he patted his face with his biceps.

After a ten-minute walk, the thickness of trees cleared, and they saw the wooden cabin, looking a lot smaller, but otherwise identical to the one they had seen on Lucy's computer.

Danial tried the door; it was unlocked. He dropped the bags on the balcony, scooped Lucy up from her legs, and carried her inside. She giggled and made a whooping sound as he set her down. Lucy felt giddy as she found her footing and looked straight into his eyes. "Wow! And that's before the proposal. Strong, brave, exciting, and romantic. What more could a girl want?"

Lucy unpacked as Danial walked back through the wood to get the shopping they'd bought from the service station. He thought about the man Lucy thought he was. He didn't see himself as any of those things and wondered just when she would see him for what he really was. Or maybe he was that man, and just never had a chance to prove it to anyone before. His thoughts were interrupted by the cracking of undergrowth. He stopped to see what had made the sound. A deer looked at him. As if frozen in time, he looked at it as it looked back at him. Its nose twitched, and the white spots covering its back became a blur as it sped silently through the trees.

About to close the boot, he stopped. The urge to open the book was overwhelming. Wrapped in a tartan blanket, its shape was undefinable, but it was still with him, still teasing his curiosity, tempting him to unravel it from its hiding place and set it free. He slammed the boot shut, then opened it again, fully intent on throwing the book into the dense woodland. What if someone found it, someone with bad intentions—or good ones, for that matter? What if it led them to their death, as it nearly did to him? He couldn't tell Lucy; she would think he had drawn the disturbing pictures and strange symbols. She'd recognise her flat, and Dave! No, he couldn't explain why he carried it everywhere if it meant so little to him. He should rip it into tiny pieces and scatter them; bury the pieces every time he had the chance to. Better still, burn the bloody thing.

He continued to ponder on his way back to the cabin, where a large mug of steaming hot tea and the sweetest smile from his newfound love welcomed him home. Grabbing him by the hand, she gave him the guided tour of the small cabin. He offered to help unpack, but Lucy was insistent that she wanted to make the place homely and suggested that he relax and have a read of the Kindle that he had brought along with him.

"How about I get a fire going?" It wasn't cold outside, but the cabin was cooler than Lucy's flat.

"Okay. I'll prep dinner after I've unpacked. Shouldn't take long."

Lucy watched as he gathered the wood that had been cut and stacked along the side of the cabin. *Looks like enough wood to last a year*, he thought, as he looked at the neat pile that was almost as high as the roof.

* * *

As Roger tucked into his all-day breakfast, he looked up at James, who was staring at his phone, then down to his untouched steak pie. "Come on, mate, you need to eat something. It's getting cold."

"I just thought I might have missed a call from the hotel."

"He would have checked in by now if he was here. We have been looking for him all day, and I'm telling you, he isn't here, and just about everyone has your number, and is concerned for our missing patient, including the only hotel in town." Roger took another mouthful. "How about after dinner, we check out the villages around here? There's two not far from here, and I reckon we can search them both before nightfall, and then, either way, we're going for a pint."

"Since when do you drink pints?" James asked, looking out the window of the cafe.

"I mean a pint of whiskey. God knows I need it after today."

Roger saw James crouching, sliding under the table. He thought he was having another attack until he pointed into the café. "Look."

Roger spun his head away from the window, but only saw the waitress serving an elderly couple their dinner. By the time he looked back, James was sitting upright.

"Our own have just driven by, so we haven't much time. No time to hire a car. Try calling a taxi. Tell them we need to go to Burton Tracy."

Roger nodded in agreement and watched as James slipped his phone into his jacket pocket.

"I think we'd be better off sitting tight and calling around the local village shops and businesses."

Chewing on a chunk of steak, James shook his head. "No time. We can make calls from Burton Tracy."

* * *

Ronny quivered with delight as the lorry driver jettisoned through the cabin and onto the mangled remains of a family hatchback. It bore a resemblance to the woman at the guest house. His recollection came from twisted legs and the throat agape, as if smiling. There were the burning remains of a van, its cargo of fruit dancing across the road with each passing vehicle. The bloody, grit-filled hole made it impossible to tell whether it was male or female. Ronny listened as a woman wiped the blood from his name badge and shouted his name. "Charlie!" she shouted. "His name's Charlie!"

The road was gridlocked. The sound of sirens and a helicopter overhead spurred him onto moving forward from the carnage he'd caused. The games he'd played during the night hadn't hindered his journey. To the contrary, they had helped pass the time.

Confident that everybody's attention was on his creation, Vetala rested, having pushed the body they called Ronny to its limits. Sitting under one of the many trees along the embankment, he looked on as flashing lights came together like vultures swarming in anticipation of death. The distraction was necessary for him to continue, albeit a drain on the body.

Pressing on through the line of trees, climbing the embankment, he came upon a disused railway line cutting across fields and farms. The old line was coved in grass, with the original sleepers now barely visible. Raised up on a mound of earth, the old railway line stretched across land and roads. With no way of telling how long it was or where it would lead, he followed the scent of Len Happy, as a police dog would cocaine.

Ronny stopped. A woman walking her dog was heading toward him. His natural instincts beckoned him to hide, not to be noticed, and to blend in with his surroundings. The problem was that there was nowhere to hide. Walking down the hill would lead him into a field of cows. Walking back would send him to the busy road. He took the only option, which was to continue past the obstacle. After all, he thought, removing the trilby and looking down at his newly-acquired clothes, *I look like a gent enjoying an afternoon stroll.*

Tipping the hat down over his forehead, a shadow cast over his face. He had no intention of playing with her, as she would undoubtedly be reported missing, making his journey more difficult than it needed to be. Cars crashing were a natural event, not connected to anyone, but here and now, he was exposed; vulnerable.

The dog growled as she neared.

"Ben, what has come over you?!" she shouted to the dog, struggling to hold it by her side.

"I'm sorry. He's usually very friendly."

The dog, a German Shepherd, snarled at him as he walked. With both hands wrapped around the leash, she pulled on it, holding it between her thighs while nodding apologetically toward Ronny.

"Where does this end?" Ronny asked, pointing along the disused rail line in the friendliest voice he could muster.

"Er—it goes all the way to the Moors, I think."

The dog's deep growl rumbled through him as he turned and knelt. He looked into the dog's eyes.

"He's not very friendly." She pulled the dog back from Ronny; its growl turned to a whimpering sigh as it focused on blackened eyes. Ronny stood. The woman gasped at the sight of his stare. Pulling the dog away from the stranger, she continued down the track without looking back.

Ronny continued forward. Slowing, he looked back when he heard her scream. Her once-gentle Ben had bit into her leg. She let out confused cries of pain as the dog ripped into her flesh, tearing chunks of her face away as she beat at it with fragile fists. She looked up and saw the tall stranger staring back at her, her cries for help meeting the tilt of his hat. More a touch than a tilt, as it never left his bald scalp.

The dog shook her limp body like a worn doll. Continuing to chew, it watched the body roll down the hill onto an incline, sloping down to a sharp vertical face. Once designed to prevent grazing livestock from being able to climb onto the rail lines, it now provided a shallow grave for the torn remains.

The dog turned its attention to the distant figure and ran towards him. Its wild eyes looked up at its new master. In a show of submissiveness, it lowered its head and walked slowly beside him. The woman's death was necessary; a human walking his dog along an old railway line would be considered normal.

Ronny was pleased with his progress; he'd covered good ground in the two hours of walking the tracks. Like his new companion, he had a heightened sense of smell, and in places, the scent of oil and diesel remained soaked up within the wooden sleepers.

Ronny tilted his head upon hearing a shriek and the laughter of children, but couldn't see anyone past the bend in the tracks which banked off through the thick woodland. He heard them again. Three voices. Two boys and a girl.

Following the sound, he rounded its source, continuing through the trees, stepping over several branches strewed across the rail lines. The brightness of the day gave way to shadows cast by overhanging branches.

The voices of children became louder with every step he made.

"Hey someone's coming," one of the boys said.

"Stub it out!"

Ronny stepped on the smouldering cigarette. Three teenagers stood aside to let him through. Tipping his hat, he walked past the trio. Ben followed his master with his head hung low. Nose twitching, he sniffed the ground, and a pair of used, tangled knickers.

Chapter 21

Lucy reached into her jeans pocket, forgetting that her mobile phone was still at the flat.

"It's okay, found it." Danial strapped on his wristwatch.

"Four o'clock. How far are you thinking of straying tonight?"

Lucy walked to the window, then back to the wooden table, where Danial was studying a map.

"Not sure I understand what all these blue squiggles mean."

"They're streams, I think. We could pitch the tent on high ground and watch the sunset."

As it was their first time camping, they both thought it a good idea to eat first, and make hot drinks and roast marshmallows on the campfire. The fire... the book... Lucy would never know, if he could get it there without her noticing.

Danial had a neat pile of camping stuff next to the door and started an inventory of things they needed to take.

"Well, I should add organised to your list of qualities, but I see you haven't included the tent."

"I know. It's there," he said, waving his hand in its direction.

Danial never checked the time before bolting the wooden door behind them, but reckoned it had to be around five-thirty.

With backpacks and a tent under his arm, they walked the gentle slopes heading in the direction of a mass of rocks. The handle wasn't centred on the cloth bag, making it tilt awkwardly.

The higher they got, the cooler it became. The little wooden cabin looked as small as a discarded matchbox.

Lucy slowed her pace, taking in the view of the towering hills and rock formations in the distance. There was no one around. A few lost sheep and two cows were the only life they had seen so far.

"I'm thinking another hour's trek if you want to reach those rocks," Lucy said reluctantly.

Danial pointed. "What about we set up just over there? It's flat. The rocks will look great with the sun setting behind."

Lucy nodded, relieved that he hadn't insisted on reaching their original goal.

Danial limbered up, readying himself for the task at hand. He placed the bags on one side, and with the side of his size ten boot, smoothed the ground of any small stones.

Lucy removed the tent from its cloth bag and searched inside for instructions. Within minutes of finding the one-page, three-step guide to the pop-up-style tent, it was up and pegged to the ground. Danial placed rocks atop of the pegs for extra security as Lucy laid out two sleeping bags. The remaining items squeezed into two corners and, having forgotten pillows; she stuffed what clothes they'd brought into each rucksack, positioning them at the head of the two sleeping bags.

"Are you all right? You don't look well," Lucy said.

"I'm good, just drained after the drive and the walk and, you know—everything."

How she hadn't noticed the book, he didn't know. Maybe she did, but hadn't questioned it, and why would she? After all, it looked like any other book.

Danial looked for a suitable place to start a fire as Lucy clambered inside. The tent fluttered, vibrating as the wind changed direction.

"Maybe we should've pitched it nearer to the rocks. It's windy here," Lucy said, peering through the small opening. "Come inside and check out my handiwork."

Snuggled up inside, Danial felt warm and secure, and for a moment, forgot there was only a thin piece of material separating them from the elements outside. He had a fleeting thought of a cow or a herd of sheep walking over the tent in the middle of the night; a thought he kept to himself.

A sense of adventure and dread flooded Danial as he fastened his coat in readiness to collect wood for the fire.

Lucy laughed. "How are you going to cut it? We didn't bring an axe or a saw."

"We need deadwood, and I have this," he said, holding up a Swiss army knife. Having watched countless survival programs, he portrayed unquestionable confidence.

Performing a poor impression of a cavewoman, Lucy said, "Okay, but if you don't mind, while the hunter-gatherer is out in the wild, I'll keep the cave warm and cosy for his return."

Beating his chest with both fists, Danial unzipped the tent, flung his rucksack over his shoulder, and walked toward the rock formation in the hopes that he'd find wood.

The only trees visible were almost as far as where they'd originally planned to pitch the tent. Searching the ground for anything burnable, he saw deer droppings and the occasional cow pat.

Unwilling to return empty-handed, he headed for the trees and stumbled across an abandoned wooden walking pole. His first piece of wood.

Dry kindling was abundant under the batch of trees. Danial gathered as much as his rucksack could hold. The book remained covered under the thin tartan blanket. He tucked branches under his arm and set off back to Lucy, all the time thinking about ridding himself of the golden pages beneath its soon-to-be pyre.

Tired, he let the pile of sticks roll from bruised arms before Lucy, as she greeted him with a hot chocolate and a kiss.

Rain poured down without warning. Lucy went to move the wood, but with nowhere to store the sticks, they took shelter within the tent. Blankets of rain clouds obscured the sun's rays, allowing a watery orange tint through the fabric of the tent. Beautiful panoramic views gave way to the quick change in weather. The wind had turned from a fresh breeze to a strong, forceful, confused state, as it blew the tent from all directions, subsiding, then coming back again with a vengeance. Thankful that the base of the tent was attached to its sides, their weight held it in place as the frame rattled.

A ghostly sound buzzed along the sides of the tent as Lucy held Danial's hand. He knew by the look on her face that she would rather be back at the cabin.

"Jesus Christ, Dan, should we just go?"

Danial sat with his back to the rucksack and made a quick pros and cons list in his head. They were both ready to drop from the walk earlier. The sun was setting, and they would have to find their way back in the dark. What comes quickly usually goes quickly, and it might just clear up during the night. He was prepared to ride it out and would be ready to leave if the worst happened and they found themselves without shelter.

"I think we'll stick it out. Might stop soon," he said, stroking the back of her hand. "It'll give us something to talk about when we do get back." He knew that any distraction was a welcome one if it took their minds off the real reason for their quick getaway holiday.

* * *

After paying the driver, James joined Roger at the ATM.

"Rog, use your card and you may as well stand in the middle of the road and tell the world you're wanted by Her Majesty's government."

Roger slipped the card back into his wallet, flicked through it, and saw a twenty-pound note tucked behind his driver's licence. Emergency money.

Burton Tracy had a lot of shops. Mainly charity shops, all spurring off an old pub with a modern restaurant opposite, looking as if it didn't belong.

They called into the pub using the same cover story as before, adding the word *unpredictable*, saying the patient was a danger to himself, and to call as soon as they saw him.

After walking a full loop of the village, excluding residential properties—mainly small cottages and the odd old building which, at some time or another, would have been the home of a landowner or a Londoner who desired a second home away from the hustle and bustle of the city—they fell lucky. The owner of The Grand saw a man fitting Len's description looking at the framed menu next to the main entrance door.

Like a sniffer dog, Roger had his first solid sent of the illusive Len Happy, albeit an eight-hour-old lead. He was confident that Len was around this location, probably resting up after travelling so far in such a short time.

James was quick to refuse the hospitality of Mr Lewis, the owner of The Grand, who offered them a free drink. Roger, on the other hand, was quick to take him up on the offer.

They sat at a table for two next to the window. Within seconds, a very attractive woman in her early twenties approached, holding a small black notepad.

"Good evening, sirs. Would you like the wine or cocktail menu?"

Roger ordered a lager. James shook his head. "Just a glass of water, please."

She handed them two menus; one full of different bottled beers and local ales, the other a water menu. James had never seen a menu dedicated to water before, and if he weren't in hiding, he would have found that amusing. But right now, he didn't want to be here, looking at a menu, ordering a drink he didn't want or need.

"We need to be moving on, Rog, not drinking beer. Free or otherwise."

"I'll start making calls," Roger said, tapping his phone. "He's got to be staying somewhere close. We have a perfect view from here, and this was the last place he was seen. He might return. That Lewis guy said he was checking the menu—why check a menu if you're not staying locally? Trust me on this one, taking a taxi to the next village, and the one after that isn't going to find your man." Roger raised the phone to his ear. After searching the internet for the next village over, he called the only shop in Church Knighton.

* * *

Ben walked beside his new master toward distant street lights. Looking back, the granite rock formation appeared smaller. Having no control over the body's cranial wiring, he played along with the illusion.

Ronny no longer required any help in finding Len, as his repulsive smell grew with each closing step, like a flame getting stronger after fuel has been added. He would reach into his mind and drag out information on the one sent to destroy him, and then he planned to extinguish the flame known as Happy.

The body required replenishing. It was tired and hungry, its legs weakening. Vetala had no way of buying food and couldn't risk anyone seeing the body. The temptation to walk into the establishment and eat the meal seen through the window was overwhelming. Instead, Ronny took shelter within a small storage shed at the back of a fancy restaurant.

Vetala was getting used to its demands for rest and nourishment. Every twitch or bleeding cut angered Vetala to the point of wanting to punish it for not obeying his commands. All too aware that this body was the vehicle aiding in the search for the enlightened one, it had to be protected.

Vetala had resided in many bodies. Some were small, others were large; all had one thing in common. Human limitations. Vetala would not risk another body and suffer as before. After destroying the one who meant him harm, freedom and power beyond anything ever witnessed would unleash.

The chimney bellowed an array of food smells. Ben sat, hungry but content by his master's side. Among the many different aromas fired through the mesh that covered the small cannon, a faint scent of Len Happy was apparent. He was getting close.

Chapter 22

Alex glanced over empty tables as Roger and James ordered food after deciding to use the restaurant as a base to make calls. Len might return, they had a good view of the street if he was still in the vicinity, and Roger needed feeding—again.

Alex had something to prove to Lizzy's father, to show him he was good enough for his little princess. It was his idea to take them out for dinner after finding an envelope stuffed with bank notes on the passenger seat of his Nissan. He'd told Lizzy about his good fortune but asked her not to mention it to her family.

Her Mum was nice, like most Mums; cautious, but accepted him, as long as her daughter did. He never expected wining and dining his long-term girlfriend's parents, so he hadn't brought a suit or any fancy clothes with him—not that he owned any or had the need to in his line of work. Computer programmers were casual in every sense of the word, but tonight, he wanted to portray a more mature, serious side, as her father would accept no less.

Her family looked the part, paying little attention to his attire, but he knew that her father, although not vocally, looked down on him and wanted to forget he was there.

Seated in the corner, far enough to not overhear the two suited men in conversation, but close enough to see them looking at phones and notepads, Alex shuddered. Maybe the place would fill up soon; maybe someone else would enter wearing jeans and a baggy top.

Alex understood why her Dad thought Lizzy Harris was out of his league. Him being from a council estate, her living in the family's five-bedroom detached house on what was, at the time, a newly-built executive estate.

He hoped that one day, by default, Sean would be his father-in-law, and tonight, his goal was to achieve his acceptance, knowing he'd never fully gain his approval.

"Well, Alex, this is a turn-up for the books—you being able to afford a meal out."

"Sean, leave the poor lad alone. He was kind enough to ask us along with Lizzy," her mother said. "I think it's lovely. I can remember when you were Alex's age and you took me for a meal."

Sean cleared his throat and looked away from her.

"I didn't mean anything was wrong. It's just not like you." He looked Alex straight in the eyes as he said it.

Excusing themselves from the table, Lizzy and her Mum went to what Sue, Lizzy's mum called the ladies' room, leaving Alex alone with Dad.

"I hope you're not going to ask my permission for her hand in marriage," he said, frowning.

"No, Mr Harris, if I were to do that, I would have taken her somewhere special," Alex replied, in a way that could have been taken as sarcastic.

Sean looked in the direction of the toilets before leaning over the table. "So, where did the money come from to pay for this—or are you expecting me to? You *do* know how expensive this place is?"

Alex cleared his throat, ran the story of how he had saved up over the past year through his mind, but couldn't bring himself to lie.

"Well… I gave this bloke a lift. It was raining and everything, so he offered me some money."

"And you took it?"

"No—well, I said not to bother, as I was already going that way. But he must have somehow left an envelope full of cash as a thank you, I suppose."

After reciting the truth, it sounded more like a lie than the lie would have. Alex knew he wasn't buying it, so he made an excuse to leave the table, telling him he needed the toilet, hoping that he wasn't following.

The gents' was on the other side of the restaurant, next to a rear exit. The door was ajar, and Alex needed a cigarette more than he'd ever needed one before. Stepping outside, he rolled one, standing with his back to the wall, the overhanging roof providing shelter from the rain. The last thing he wanted was to go back to the table rainsoaked, what with Liz telling her father that he'd stopped smoking.

The rear of the restaurant looked like an ordinary garden, apart from having bright yellow bins five times the size of a normal household bin. The path led down to a wooden gate. Next to it stood a garden shed with a cracked window. Taking another long drag, he looked down cross-eyed at the roach of his roll-up and took another drag before flicking it across the lawn.

Growling came from within the shed. The door creaked open. Eyes low down stared up at Alex. A shiver crossed his forehead. A faceless figure appeared from the shadows. Alex turned to enter the restaurant and went to close the door. A man's hand stopped it from fully closing. Alex apologised and swung the door open, allowing him to enter. He froze upon seeing a hairless man wearing an old-fashioned hat standing before him. Alex nodded. Instead of returning the gesture, the man stiffed the air around him. Unnerved, Alex zipped through the small hall and ran into Lizzy's father, Sean.

"Thought you wanted the toilet?" he asked, looking past Alex.

Alex spun around, thinking the strange man was still there. He wasn't. Sean was looking at a different figure; the one above the word *Gents*.

They walked back to the table without speaking. Alex put his nervousness down to meeting the parents and could only assume the man outside was the owner, disapproving of him smelling of cigarettes.

Sean returned to the table like a man of importance would enter a conference room. A girl called Monique took their orders. Alex told her that he would have the same as Sean, not quite understanding what he'd ordered. He just hoped that whatever he had ordered wasn't fish; he hated fish.

Roger smiled at Alex as their eyes met. "Bless him, trying to impress the girl's parents," Roger said to James.

"When you're done people-watching, the taxi's arrived."

The driver was the same person who had dropped them off earlier. "Have you boys found the patient yet?"

James stared back at her.

"What?"

Roger butted in, "No, not yet. Have you seen him on your travels?"

The penny dropped with James as Roger was talking, but the mood he was in didn't allow him to make small talk with the driver.

"Shop in Church Knighton," James said, without looking at

her. Shrugging her shoulders, the driver pulled off.

Arriving within minutes, James paid the fare and stood facing the Wall's Ice Cream *closed* sign.

"Shit!" Roger said.

The opening hours stated the shop was open for another hour, but with the lights switched off, the shop had closed earlier than the online directory alleged.

James watched Roger's eyes widen. Shock was plain to see as he pointed wide eyes past James and repeated the word, "Shit!"

James looked around; a Mercedes pulled up beside them. Lance got out, leaving one agent upfront and two in the backseat.

"You two are in trouble—real trouble."

For a moment, James thought Roger was going to make a run for it, as he turned his back to them. Instead, he stood between James and Lance.

"Look, fuckface. Whatever you want, just go ahead and do it. My friend here isn't feeling too well, or he would have wiped that smug grin off your face."

Raising one eyebrow, James turned to Roger and held his hand to his chest. Moving him to the side, he looked Lance in the eye and said, "Sorry about my partner, had a bad day. So, have you found your man yet?"

"Which one?" Lance asked, never taking his eyes off Roger.

"Len Happy, who else?"

Lance signalled the others to get out the car. As they did, Roger braced himself for a fight.

They were now surrounded by the very people they'd trained—and, up until their stay at the guest house, would have held rank over. Instead, they were under suspicion—even worse, they were about to be taken back to Mr Green.

"The bloodbath you forgot to tell us about at the guest house wasn't the work of Subject Two. Subject One is at large—slipped past half the damn force and replaced himself with a member of staff. It didn't help that the psycho prison's records checked out; showed all staff accounted for." Lance said in a low, monotone voice.

"And you think Ronny murdered the owner of the guest house?" James asked, watching Roger sway from foot to foot.

"As far as the police are concerned, you're as much suspects as Subject One," Lance said.

Roger stopped swaying and gave Lance a sharp stare.

"Cut the 'subject' shit. We're talking about the freak called Ronny, and you think we might be just like him?!"

Lance shook his head. "No, of course not. You're an asshole, not a psycho."

Roger advanced. The other agents surrounded Lance, their Black Knight.

"You guys split up and search. And be sure—"

All ducked as an ear-piercing whistle sounded. A crack, followed by an explosion, forced them down once more.

As if he'd been electrocuted, hairs that Roger was unaware of having stood on end. It was loud, but distant.

"What the fuck was that?!" Roger asked, turning to James.

Moments later, flashing lights and horns rang out between the scream of sirens. Two ambulances followed by three fire engines roared past the shop. People stood half-in and half-out of their front doors with a mixed look of shock and concern on their faces.

Lance flicked his earpiece out, pressed his mobile up against his face, and turned away from James and Roger. Turning back, he said, "The explosion was at a restaurant. The next village along. Burton Tracy, they said."

A look on Lance's face told James he knew more than he was letting on. Differences aside, Lance was a competent agent.

"Change of plan." Waving thick fingers at Roger and James, Lance continued, "You two have a chance to redeem yourselves. Search the village. Any sign of either of them, call me."

Two police cars and an unmarked car flashed by, forcing Lance back to the pavement. Dashing around the bonnet, he squeezed his bulk into the driver's seat. All but one of his team followed his lead, climbing into the backseat. Dropping the passenger window, Lance said, "Smithy, keep watch over these two. They so much as cross the road without telling you what they're doing, call me. Work as a team, search, and I'll send a good word to Green."

The Merc sped off down the road, following the fading sound of sirens. Smithy stood about six-two, having a chiselled look about him. Hours spent in the gym had tightened the skin around his naturally strong body. Looking down at them both, he told James and Roger his intentions, which were going door-to-door, starting at the shop looping around the village. The pub was the endpoint. Smithy denied Roger's suggestion of splitting up after checking the pub.

"With only one pub in the village, we should start with that!" Roger looked at James for confirmation. Smithy was having none of it.

Pulling out his phone and putting it back into his jacket pocket, Roger put an arm around Smithy's back in a friendly gesture. "Bloody flat battery," he said, stamping his foot on the ground. "Need to call the missus."

Smithy unlocked his phone and handed it to Roger. Roger thanked him and turned away. When he called his wife by a different name, James frowned in amusement as he saw the phone drop from his hand onto the curb, followed by a slide of his foot. It fell into the rain grate, and the plop confirmed that Smithy no longer had a mobile phone.

The road where the Grand once stood had been taped off; thin plastic enough to ward off growing crowds. The fire, now under control, had left the restaurant destroyed.

Lance watched the charred remains of a person being covered over by a uniformed officer, three stretchers being pushed across to waiting ambulances, and a member of the public crying and gasping at the scene unfolding before their eyes.

A smartly-dressed man tried to explain what happened. His body shook as adrenaline rushed through his veins. Police officers tried to calm him as the medic encouraged him to breathe deeply into a plastic face mask.

Lance and his team walked over to the officers. Holding out his ID card, he forced a handshake, telling the officer they were taking over the incident, and introduced himself as Agent Lance White.

After the initial shock that he was talking with the British secret service, Officer Mason said he would call in his request to the station and cooperate in their investigations.

"I want this village blocked. No way in, no way out," Lance said to Officer Mason.

The officer looked blankly back at him before replying, "The whole village?! There are four ways to get to this place. Six, if you count two farm entrances."

"Then get six cars and plug the holes," he replied sternly. "I'll need a bird, too. Get it to concentrate on the surrounding fields."

"Sir, I don't understand. It's under control, and you're asking for the whole force to be dispatched."

"You don't understand because I'm not at liberty to say. Don't worry, I have a team on the way to relieve yours, but time is of the essence, so let's do this!" Lance patted Officer Mason's back before turning to his team, who were already gathering intel.

"Sir, you might want to talk to this witness yourself," came a voice from the side of an ambulance. Lance walked over to the youth holding a girl. They both stood next to an older couple; Lance presumed they were their parents.

Lance's demeanour changed as he asked in a calm, relaxed tone, "Did you see what happened, son? Start from the beginning, if you can." He crouched down to look less intimidating.

Alex took a deep breath and started from the point at which he saw a strange man come out of the shed at the back of the restaurant.

"I thought it was weird. He sniffed me, and his dog was a wild, crazy fucking thing, snarling and everything!" Adrenaline had kicked in, and each word became faster and less coherent.

"Okay, slow down. Describe him and tell me what he did." Lance spoke calmly and slowly; his training used to its full effect.

Alex continued, but had to raise his voice above the commotion. "He started taking food out of the kitchen, I think. Not sure. I heard shouting, and the dog ran through, past our table, grabbing at food on peoples' plates, and then it bit a woman's leg."

"A dog?" Lance confirmed. "He had a dog?"

"Yes. Anyway, then he came in, and the fire started breaking out, but not in one place, *everywhere*—like near the doors and in random places. No one could get out, because when they moved, a fire would just pop up from nowhere. The bloke looked strange, like a crazy man. He was wearing a suit and a hat, but he had no eyebrows, and he had crazy eyes, sort of like he had no eyes at all."

Lizzy stood with her parents. Mrs Harris was stroking her hair and covering her face in an attempt to shield the view. Mr Harris walked over to Alex and Lance.

"Excuse me, my name is Mr Harris, and this is my... nearly son-in-law, Alex. He's the reason we are still alive, and the others standing over there are, too." He pointed in the direction of Officer Mason and Mr Lewis, the restaurant owner. "He's a real hero. You see, we had no way of getting out. The doors wouldn't open, and then the opening filled with flames from nowhere. The flames kept appearing. Alex took the fire extinguisher off me and threw it through the window and made sure everyone left before leaving himself. He had no concern for his safety. A real hero." After patting him on the back, he rubbed Alex on his shoulder and walked back over to Lizzy.

Lance paid no attention to Mr Harris and focused his attention back to Alex. "Where is he now, Alex? Where did you see him go?"

Alex looked back at the smouldering remains of the restaurant. "He never left. He was still in there when we all went through the window."

Lance handed a card to Alex and asked him to call anytime, day or night if he saw anything or remembered any further details.

Chapter 23

Len shuddered. Cold water tickled his earlobes as he broke from a deep meditative state. The chipped ceramic bath had a dirt tide mark and a thick layer of scum floating on the water's surface.

Len stood. Water drained from his body as he came to his senses. He'd meditated with the intention of finding out more about the pub, the reason for being here, and the hold that the bikers had over Brian, the pub landlord. Instead, his mind filled with answers about the enlightened one; the one who would send Vetala back to his realm and bring balance back to the world. The answer was as shocking as it was simple. There was no being that possessed pure consciousness. The clear message he received was that no man, no woman, or animal would be found anytime soon. But why? He found it hard to believe that the journey to Church Knighton was in vain. His logical mind was at work, and he knew better than to rely on that. He would need to meditate further, and deeper next time, he thought, stepping out onto the dirty bath mat.

Len sat on the edge of the bed and saw small droplets of water jump off stripped floorboards. Thudding, booming sounds penetrated his room; a reminder that he had work waiting in the cellar.

Halfway down the stairs, he stopped and looked out the side window overlooking the car park. It was half-full of motorbikes of all descriptions. They must have arrived when he was asleep, or when he was in the bath, as he hadn't heard them arrive.

On the way to the cellar, he stopped at the door leading to the rear of the bar and listened. He heard shouting and laughing in-between the screams of what they called music.

The door swung open, hitting his forehead.

"Sorry. Did I hit you?" Brian looked strained, gaunt, and under pressure to please the demanding crowd.

"Just heading down to the cellar to start work," Len said, rubbing his head.

"Is everything under control? Can I help in any way?"

"NO! Stay out of the way, please," Brien replied, grabbing an open pack of cigarettes from the bottom step before dashing back into the bar, leaving the door open just enough for Len to see what was going on in what should have been a quiet country pub.

Len peered over the bar and couldn't believe his eyes. Between the till and a row of pumps, he saw a tattooed topless girl wearing a tight leather miniskirt, performing for a fat old man occupying the nook. His bulk stretched over both sides of the corner chair. The girl continued to wind her body ceremoniously while Zak, whom he'd encountered earlier, poured whiskey into his glass.

"So, that must be Cogs!" Len said out loud, with no fear of being overheard.

Brian had his back to the door. A man approached wearing an Iron Maiden t-shirt. He pointed to the top shelf. Brian moved from view as the man leaned across the bar and helped himself to Brian's cigarettes.

Reading the man's lips, Len made out the words, *a pint of cider for the slut*, pointing over to the girl still dancing for the fat biker. He emptied a small bag of powder into the glass, stirring it with his finger, before carrying the drinks over to the corner.

After handing the whiskey to Cogs, he gave the pint glass to the girl, who took a sip, then missed the table as she tried to put the glass down, spilling half onto the floor before catching the glass and placing it back on the table. Zak appeared from nowhere, slapping the girl's face so hard that her body wobbled as she fell to her knees. The fat man's laughter sounded over the music. He beckoned Zak over, cupped his hands around his ear, and Zak nodded.

The girl, no older than twenty, tried to rise, as Zak tangled his fingers in her hair. With nose and mouth pressed tight against the wet floor, she was moved back and forth like a mop. She tried to fight back, protesting with her hands, but her fragile wrists were no match for the weight that held her in place.

Cogs' enjoyment was evident as he rubbed his crotch. No one in the bar paid any attention to what was unfolding in the corner of the room. Brian looked away, focusing on dirty glasses.

The girl was dragged over on her knees to Cogs, who now had a wild, hateful look on his face. Cogs' thick arms rose around her neck as he pressed her head between his flabby thighs, bracing it tightly while he fumbled with the zip on his jeans. An open-handed slap met her efforts to move.

Len suppressed his anger, closed his eyes, and rolled them back, blanking his mind. With closed eyes, mind as still as if he was in a deep sleep, he walked out into the bar, lifted the bar hatch, and walked over to Cogs. His head spun as something or someone hit the side of it. He stumbled and fell to the ground with a thud. Wetness penetrated his jeans, reminding him of the man at the service station. Wetness turned to a sharp pain as something pierced his flesh for the second time.

He opened his eyes; a gold tooth caught the light as the face it belonged to smiled down at him.

"Trouble standing?" Cogs looked at Zak, then down to Len. "Help him up so I can knock him back down."

Zak tried to lift him. Len's bulk, with the help of gravity, kept him grounded. Zak went to kick Len's head. Len moved aside, sending him tumbling over the tattooed girl.

The music stopped. A crowd started to gather around Len. Once again, Len closed his eyes, and mouthed the words, "Your mascot is coming to find you."

Pushing the girl aside, Cogs stood over Len and waved away the people kicking and punching him. The room fell silent.

"Who are you?" Cogs asked, zipping up his jeans.

A trickle of blood ran from Len's top lip as he stumbled to his feet, smiling.

"I know who I am, and you're about to find out who you are."

Cogs was taken aback by how calm and collected Len seemed after taking such a beating.

Like a snake charmer, Len tilted his head. Cogs followed the motion with his own.

"The little boy you owned—your mascot—has a new body and will arrive soon. May I suggest you apologise to him before he takes your life? You might stand a chance in the next realm if you acknowledge your wrongdoings."

Cogs swayed. Vomit rose before descending back into the pit of his stomach, not for the words being spoken, or the impossible threat being handed out by a beaten man, but by the way he'd penetrated his mind. Pictures of the boy mascot flashed through his head. A picture of the boy dying and coming back to life to seek his revenge flicked through his mind. Like a film playing out, he saw his own death; could feel his bowels loosen as they lost control. He could see the crowd around him. Looks of disdain on their faces as he begged for forgiveness. It was as real as if it was happening to him right here and now.

"You can run and hide like the coward you are—"

Zak raised his fist towards Len, only to see Cogs shake his head. He lowered it, confused by his reaction. "—Or you can face your demise with what little honour you have left." Leather-clad bikers moved closer. "The choice is yours."

Len walked through the bar, picked a box of matches off the floor, and brushed past Brian, who stood open-mouthed in anticipation. Cogs' eyes welled, reddening before releasing two single tears. Never before had any of the gang members seen their leader in such a state of despair. Zak placed an arm out to comfort him while the others watched Len close the door behind him. Then they turned back to Cogs, some with a look of disbelief, others grinning at the weakness of the man they followed without question or thought.

Pushing Zak's arm away, Cogs lashed out, knocking glasses from tables. A pint glass emptied onto his foot. Cogs exploded in a fit of rage; throwing, punching and kicking anyone close. Their fear of him discouraged any form of retaliation. After punching a female biker square in the jaw, they held him down. The ones doing the restraining were soon overpowered by Zak and the others still showing allegiance to their leader.

Brian could only watch his bar being torn apart by a pack of animals that ran with the motto, *blood brothers*.

The stable door opened. Roger entered. "Fuck!" was the only word he got out before being pushed back into James. Knocking over a bird feeder, they fell onto hard patio slabs.

Roger extended an arm, helping James stand. Dazed, Smithy joined them, unaware of what was happening.

"What's going on?" His first thought was that there had been a fight between the two.

"A fucking riot, that's what. The place is full of bikers," Roger said, patting himself down.

"I need to call this in. Did you see our subject?" Smithy asked, looking at James.

A helicopter flew overhead, its searchlight sweeping the ground. Smithy's wave went unnoticed as it continued to the next village.

"Give me your phone. That's an order, McMilan," Smithy demanded.

"Right now, I'm giving the orders," James said. "The police will handle them. I'm here to find Len Happy."

Roger dialled the police. Turning to Smithy, he said, "Must have recharged itself."

Smithy walked off as Roger and James stood at the roadside waiting for the local constabulary.

"What did you see, Rog?"

"I told you!" Roger took a deep breath, "Shitloads of bikers kicking the shit out of each other. I only got a glance, then ended up on top of you."

"Rog, where's Smithy?" James asked, looking up and down the road, "Let's go sort out the rednecks and ask a few questions."

Roger waved his hand in a gesture for James to take the lead.

Smithy ran breathlessly toward them.

"You clowns are in the wrong village. Eyewitness reports put Ronny at the Grand Restaurant; we have our man cornered."

"We're coming with you!" Roger shouted back as he turned to leave.

"No room in the car," was his reply.

Roger and James looked on as Smithy got into the backseat of a patrol car. It sped off in the direction of Burton Tracy. Roger bit his bottom lip, shaking his head as James slammed the palm of his hand to his forehead. "Damn, could have been us in there, Rog. Ronny must have turned up as we left. Or he was watching us," James said between gritted teeth.

"He arrived after. Otherwise, we'd be dead already," Roger said. "At least he's being dealt with, and that'll keep the team and local police busy. Which still leaves Len Happy, unless you think he's there, too."

"Could be hiding in the pub, for all we know," James said, as glass flew through a closed window, smashing it.

"We're running out of options, Rog. Either we get over to the Grand and risk being handcuffed and sent back to HQ, or we go in and take control."

Roger stood in the road waving his arms. A car skidded to a stop. The driver got out. Roger showed his ID before flashing his gun. The driver was in his eighties. James looked at Roger in disgust before apologising to the owner of the car, handing him a card, and taking his details, assuring him they'd return the car.

Roger drove. James hissed, "Just get us to the restaurant, and I'll look out for Len on the way."

Roger slowed upon seeing the road blocked. Two patrol cars were nose-to-nose, with two blues standing behind at a safe distance. A uniformed officer approached the car. James got out.

"No need to get out, sir. Road's closed. Head back down the road."

"McMilan—specials branch. We're en route to the incident, so back up and let us through, please," James said, waving at the other officer who was approaching the car.

The first officer pulled out a card and dialled a number on his mobile. Using his mobile and not his radio could mean only one thing: He was calling Lance. The first officer walked back over to his car. The other told them both to wait.

James got back in, and Roger started to perform a three-sixty, struggling to turn the estate car on the narrow country road.

"I said to wait there!" the uniformed officer shouted.

James rolled down the passenger-side window. "Turning around and heading back, as you said!" He shouted back at him.

"Hurry up, Rog." James saw the one with the business card running toward the car.

Rear wheels spun, leaving the police officer chewing road grit and coughing on a mixture of car fumes and wet mud.

"It's just like the Dukes of Hazzard."

"The Dukes of what? Dukes?" James asked, confused.

"You're so uncultured," Roger said, screeching the long body of the estate around the corner.

"Rog, slow down!" Pressing his head up against the window, James looked around to the rear window.

"I think I saw him." James pointed to an empty field.

Roger slowed the car to a crawling pace.

"It's dark. How'd you know it's him?" Roger asked, struggling to see anything.

"Here—Park up here." James pointed to a farm entrance.

There was a chill in the smoke-filled air. James tasted bitter sulphur, reminding him of bonfire night last year, when Roger got very drunk and spent the night in his bathroom.

"Len!" James shouted. "Len Happy!"

The figure in the distance turned. They'd found him.

Chapter 24

Danial peeked through the tent's opening. Once the howling wind had calmed, the torrential downpour turned into a fine shower. If it was cold outside, then neither of them noticed as they huddled together, confined within the two-person tent.

Making love for the second time in the open, where anyone out walking could stumble on their moment of joy and listen to their moans of pleasure, gave Danial the rush of his life. Like before, he hadn't instigated it—or, in truth, even wanted it; he'd been content reading a book in the company of his new-found love. Lucy, however, made up for lost time, christening the tent before he had time to mark the page he'd read.

"Okay babes, it's up to you. We can pack up and head back to the cabin now that the rain's slowed, or see what tomorrow brings," Danial said pouring tea from the thermos.

"I'm enjoying myself. Aren't you?" Lucy shuffled back, giving Danial room to set the cups down. "Plus, it's getting late, and you've taken all the energy I had out of me, you mischievous man," she said, rolling her lips inwards. Danial lost count as to how many cute traits she possessed. To him, she was perfect in every way.

"Let me think about it. I tell you what. We can stay, but on the condition that we make love again."

"Agreed!"

His smile widened. "Outside."

"You are wicked! Agreed," she snapped. "But on one condition."

"What?"

"You make the tea afterwards."

They both laughed. Danial sipped from the plastic cup, burning his lips in the process.

* * *

Patches of dense fog appeared over the vaporous farmer's field. James shouted again. Len had vanished. Restraining his calls in fear that the sound would alert the officers further up the road, James climbed the wooden gate, slipping on green moss covering the bottom plank.

"Carefully does it," Roger said, helping him over.

"You stay with the car, Rog. Lights off, engine running."

"Yes, sir!" Roger saluted, relieved that he wouldn't be joining him in the cow-pat infused field.

Within seconds, a thick fog enveloped James, leaving only muffled calls. Roger climbed back into the family estate, turned the heater to level four, and turned the flow of heat to his body in an attempt to dry his shirt. He couldn't hear James from inside, so he lowered his window enough to listen, but not so far down as to let in misty rain.

Len approached James. "McMilan!"

"Jesus Christ!" He almost slipped. "Len, you scared the shit out of me."

"If you want me to accompany you to your vehicle, you will be endangering innocent people." Len placed his hand on his knees and tilted his head up to James. "I feel the strong presence of evil."

"Len, I'm here to help. Please trust me."

Len had no reason to trust him or anyone from the agency. They had exploited his abilities and bullied him for fanatical gains and tyranny against nations.

He closed in on James, invading any personal space between them. James stepped back. Len moved forward again, so close that James felt the warmth of his breath.

"I trust you."

"You do?" James asked, taken aback.

"I feel your intentions; you mean no harm. You came to tell me about your colleagues."

Dark clouds parted. A sliver of moonlight illuminated Len enough for James to notice the extent of his injuries.

"You're hurt. What happened?"

"Better me than an unsuspecting bystander."

"There you go again, thinking of everyone but yourself. Come with me, and I'll take you somewhere safe. I've gone through so much today; I'm not leaving without you."

"Mr McMilan."

"Please, call me James."

"James, I am the protector, unsure of who or what I'm supposed to be protecting. I've been guided to this place for a reason, and I need to do what I need to do. Please understand. Like you, I follow orders."

James scratched his head. How could he explain Len's execution order?

"If you don't know who you're protecting—" James shuddered. "They want you dead, Len. You've served your purpose. You were our experiment; a subject file."

"Vetala is gaining strength; should it kill the enlightened one, it will be all-powerful. I can't let that happen."

"I don't understand. You can tell the future. You would know if there were such a being, wouldn't you?"

"There is always an unpredictable wild card."

"Did you not hear me? They are going to kill you, Len."

"There's little time to explain the human ego, or the arrogance of people who believe that killing a body destroys its spirit. My spirit will transfer to another being or remain within the ether until required." Len looked past him, aware of subtle environmental changes. Cocooned within a blanket of fog, Len noticed the ground turn custard yellow.

"So, you don't care if they kill you? Is that what you're telling me?" James argued.

"The short-term inconvenience would be unpleasant. Not for me, but you and anyone within a hundred miles of Vetala. Long-term will spell humanity's demise. Let me go. If you want to help, then tell the men with guns that you haven't seen me." Len sighed and looked up, as if thinking of what to say next. "You asked for my trust. I'm now asking for yours, my friend."

James watched Len part a curtain of fog as he hobbled away. Yellow-tinged miasma filled the space that his bulk had left.

"Let me drive you. Len, you need to go to the hospital."

"I am heading for the hills. Your car won't get me there. If you encounter Vetala—"

"You do mean Ronny, right?" James questioned.

"Yes, Ronny. Let him go. He will follow me, and I'll make sure I'm away from people and property."

"I can't—" James hesitated. "—Promise that, Len." James looked down at his feet. He couldn't see them. "Take care, Mr Happy. Take care!" he shouted.

Following a low rumble and ticking of the engine, James approached the family estate car.

Roger jumped. "Bloody hell, you scared me shitless."

"He's injured, travelling on foot. Doesn't want our help," James said solemnly.

"Well, isn't that just great. We've sacrificed everything. Lost our jobs. We're unemployable—or worse; we could be arrested, and for what? For nothing. Told you not to waste time on loony Len. Now what? Sit here, wait to be carted off and thrown in prison? Thanks, mate."

James turned to Roger. "Our department was shut down before any of this, and as far as wasting time, what choice did we have?" A moment of silence filled the car. "Well, I suppose we could have stayed at the guest house and took it up the arse. Is that what we should have done, Rog?"

"Well... the thought of big Lance up ya bum," Roger said, smiling.

"Piss off. If anything, you're the pretty boy."

They both sighed after one of their normal two-way spats.

"I could be having a nice hot bath, pint in hand, and be looking forward to a night of passion," Roger said, looking up at the roof's faded cloth.

"I'm going to follow him," James said, nodding his head. "You can go get your bath, even though you always take a shower. Have that pint that I've never seen you drink, and as for the passion, well, no comment on that one."

"I do have a bath—sometimes," Roger said, still looking up at the car roof. "Where did he say he was going?"

"To the rocky hill," James said.

"He's on foot—limping, you said. I reckon it'll take him over an hour on foot, if he makes it at all. How about we drive up as far as the roads take us and keep an eye open for him?"

James agreed. Roger turned on the headlights; light bounced back from a wall of fog. Creeping the car forward, they headed toward where they thought the hill stood.

* * *

"Well at least it isn't raining, and the winds dropped," Lucy said, caressing the hot mug as she looked up to the sky.

"Still no stars, though, and look down there. It's like we're floating on a cloud. Where'd that fog come from?" Danial asked, pointing while wiggling tent pegs into the ground. "Why don't you rest a little? I'll get a fire going."

Pulling out tinder from his backpack, Danial built a tepee-style structure around gold pages.

"Dan, you don't think that's going to light, do you?" she smirked.

"Not sure, but I guess I'm going to have fun trying," he said, lighting the instruction manual from the tent bag. Lucy laughed as the paper smouldered and shrivelled up before going out.

"Here, let me try," Lucy said, rummaging in her bag, pulling out a tub of Vaseline.

"Here, pass the tub." Stretching his arm, Dan took the Vaseline and delved through twigs and tinder until he felt the book. Smearing it over the book's cover, he lit a scrap of paper, and the fire started. Confident the fire would burn long enough for him to get more wood, he pecked Lucy on the cheek. "I'll go get some more wood."

"It's foggy and dark, Dan. What if you fall?"

"I'm just going to check base camp's perimeter and find supplies, ma'am," he said, saluting and quick-turning on the spot.

Taking a small but powerful torch from the tent bag, Danial walked off, leaving Lucy's head exposed to the elements, the rest of her snug within the tent.

Swallowed by a foggy haze, the beam from his torch danced a vapourish dance, looking to Lucy as if it was taking itself for a walk. She thought about the film *Invisible Man* that she'd watched the day she moved in with Dave. Shaking her head as if to clear any thoughts of him, she walked around the tent to clear her mind. Thoughts of Dave and guilty relief for him no longer being a part of her life troubled her. After three laps around the tent, she stopped to look in Dan's direction.

The popping and cracking of smouldering wood brought back memories of Woodrush and the fire that could have taken her life. Looking into the distance, she considered shouting Dan back to the tent.

Sensing danger, her protector was nowhere in sight. Negativity ran through her, and the thought of approaching danger forced her back inside the tent. She zipped the door flap closed and sat holding the Brocken walking pole.

Trying to reason away emotions, she sat huddled up, knees touching cheeks. Everything in her life had changed. New job up in flames, an escaped convict on the loose, and after the fight, she no longer wanted to live in the flat. Sitting back with eyes clamped shut, she thought about what good had come out of her ordeal. She'd met the man of her dreams, and Dave was gone for good. She quivered for thinking of Dave's death as a benefit.

Danial found two thick branches and a broken deer antler. The fog was thickening at a rapid rate. He could no longer see the tent, and any light from the torch didn't penetrate the yellow substance; a similar substance to that seen in the flat. Shaking off the thought and not wanting to press on any further, he turned to head back.

He froze.

Growling rumbled in the distance. A threatening fierce snarl, like a guard dog warning a trespasser. His instant thought was of a farmer rounding up sheep. No one would be out walking this time of night in such a remote place. The growl turned to a death gurgle.

"Hello, is anyone there?" No reply. He flashed his torch on and off. "Hello!" he called again. Still no reply.

Growling intensified; became fiercer as the unseen animal neared.

Dropping the deer antler—then, for some reason, picking it back up again—he started back in the opposite direction to whatever was out there. His vivid imagination didn't help as he envisioned a beast roaming the moors, its two heads homing in on him.

Quickening his pace didn't deter the approaching animal. Still unseen, he swore he heard it pant. Dropping wood, he started jogging. Ferns parted. Danial clawed outstretched antlers toward the sound. His own animal instinct told him to get away as fast as possible. He ran. Glowing eyes drew closer. Slipping, Danial landed on his side. The antlers, still firmly gripped, were held upright. Lifting the torch startled the German Shepherd. A mouth full of serrated teeth widened as it growled back at him.

Dazzled, the dog stopped and stared. Covering his face, Danial crawled back into the thicket. Snapping at thin air, the dog arched its back in readiness to pounce. Grounded, Danial pushed himself back, holding the antlers at arms-length.

"Stop right there!" A voice came from the side of him. The dog pounced. Pushed away mid-flight, it let out a screeching yelp.

"I'm growing tired of your trickery. Face me in your bodily form."

The dog ran, absorbed within a yellowing mass.

Blinded by torchlight, Len covered his eyes and limped over

to Danial.

"I'd help you up, but I'm afraid I might drop you."

"Len!" Danial gasped. "Why—what was—how did you find me?"

Danial stood and held shaking antlers toward Len.

"It was a dog, Danial," Len said.

"You better start explaining."

"I sent it back to Vetala."

Danial gulped. "Ronny sent it? Why are you here?"

He looked at Len's stained trouser leg and saw the rip from which the blood stain originated.

"I'm as surprised to see you, as you are to see me." Len held his hand against the small tear in his trouser leg. "It was a spy, sent to find you."

"Bullshit, Len. That's bullshit." Lowing the antlers, he continued, "You can sense who a dog belongs to, but you didn't sense me?"

"My abilities cannot tell who is around every corner, Danial. The dog's a scout, sent by Vetala. He's not far from here… Maybe."

"Maybe?!" Danial cried.

"There's always a wildcard where free will is concerned, Danial."

Danial shook his head in disbelief. "Why would he come here? He couldn't know. *We* didn't know until—"

"We?" Len asked.

"Me and Lucy."

Len bent over before regaining his posture. Taking two deep breaths, he put his hand up to his eyes. Danial lowered the torch.

"For the same reason, I was compelled to come. To find the enlightened one before ending my life," Len said, lowering his hand from his face down to his leg.

"If what you are saying is true—"

"It's true, and you need to leave—no hesitating, just leave," Len insisted.

"Okay. Follow me back to the tent. Lucy has a first aid kit. She knows how to wrap a bandage. Did a good job with my hand."

Len looked back as if someone was approaching, turned, and waved his arm to hurry him along. Danial set off with Len in tow.

Five minutes passed with neither of them saying a word. Danial had a thousand questions and worried about just what Lucy would say when he turned up with Len Happy. He couldn't leave him to bleed, not having saved his life for the second time.

Danial broke the silence. "Thanks anyway, for the dog thing. How did you make it do a backflip and run without touching it?" He thought the best way to get to the bottom of this was to start slowly.

"I was in its head, and through its eyes, it saw a lion. You were the lion, Danial. It decided to backflip and run—well, more instinct than a decision, I suppose. As I was in its head, so was Vetala."

"This isn't crazy talk now. This is happening, isn't it?" Danial slowed, allowing Len time to catch up, his leg dragging behind him. Danial didn't know if he'd make it to the tent.

"I will never misguide you or tell you untruths. What I say may not be believable, but it will always be true." Danial nodded back in agreement. "Now, how about we sing a song to cheer ourselves up and lighten the mood?" Len asked, as he started to hum "The Sound of Music".

Danial looked back in disbelief.

"He feeds off negativity, Danial. A positive vibration will do more to slow him than any fighting could ever do."

Danial continued his pace, stopping every few yards, until Len joined him. Len almost looked as if he was enjoying the experience; singing, humming, and whistling whatever song played in his head.

The outline of flapping fabric and the glow of fire appeared ghost-like in the distance. Thinking it better to warn Lucy, Danial hurried off, leaving Len following.

"Lucy!" There was no reply.

The tent appeared zipped tight; he knew she wasn't inside.

"Lucy!" he called out.

No answer.

Len limped up to him. "Could she have gone back to your vehicle?"

"No. We walked from the lodge. It's over an hour's walk, and the fog—Lucy!" Louder this time, his voice quivered.

"Please be quiet—shush," Len whispered, closing his eyes. "Over there." Len pointed. "Quick, now. She's frightened."

Danial ran, calling her name. "Lucy, it's me! Are you okay?"

The fog thickened the further he ran. His only point of reference was the faint sound of crying, along with Len making his way down after him.

She came into view just before he ran into her.

"Lucy, what's wrong?" He held her tight. Looking around, he saw nothing.

"Dan, thank God it's you." She squeezed air from his lungs. Lucy moved as Len approached, coming into view, walking sideways down stony grass.

Trembling, Lucy pointed. "He's come to hurt me. He wants revenge."

A sudden cold sweat hit Danial; sure she was talking about

Ronny.

"Where is he?"

"It disappeared, Dan. I hit it, and it turned back into the fog. I can still hear him in my head."

"Who, Lucy?"

"Dave. Dave's ghost. The fog changed into him; he came after me. I had to run, Dan. It changed back to vapour. It's out there, Dan." She held him tighter. "He said it was my fault, and he'll make me suffer."

Len held his hands together, palms flat, fingers pointing skyward.

"It's an illusion, Lucy."

Lucy screeched at the sound of Len's voice. Danial pulled away from the ear-piercing scream. Her eyes widened at the sight of Len Happy. "What—He—I—" Her words a jumbled, she loosened her grip on Dan's arm. Flickering eyes rolled back before her body jellified and fell before him.

"How long have I been—What's happening, Dan?"

"A few seconds. You fainted," Danial said, helping her to her feet.

"What is he doing here?" she mumbled, still dazed.

"He's here to help, Lucy."

"I don't need his help." Lucy shrugged away from Danial. "Or yours, or *anyone's*. I'm not a wilting flower that needs watering. I know what I saw, Dan, and *he*–" She pushed Len in the back. "–is the one who needs help. Don't you see, Dan? Whenever he shows up offering help, everything turns to shit. And where the fuck have you been? Did you know he was coming?"

Danial gulped; his dry throat sponged away any spittle and any words before they could form.

Len's head darted around, as if aware someone was approaching.

"Come now. Hurry. I'm sorry I startled you. Danial, go back to the cabin."

"Yes," Danial replied.

"Go now. Don't turn back. I'll catch up. I remember you made a good cup of tea. I'll follow you both while you brew the drinks."

"Forget about the goddamn tea. Dave is out there," Lucy said.

"There is no Dave. No ghosts. Only your fears, Lucy. He will use them in any way he can. Just know that whatever you see on your way back is an illusion. Now, go."

Grabbing the bag containing personal belongings, leaving the tent and the fire still burning, they made their way back to the cabin.

Near-zero visibility made for an uneasy journey. Looking back, Len was nowhere to be seen. Danial knew he was on the right track, and at the halfway point, when he saw what he thought was a snake winding past his foot, he stopped, and Lucy clung to his arm. "What is it, Dan?"

"I don't know," he said, before screaming. Snakes piled high, slithering as they surrounded them. One rose from the heap, its mouth wide, tongue flicking and bending.

"Dan, what is it?"

Standing paralysed where he stood, Danial's mouth fused shut.

Lucy pulled him by his arm. Wading through a torrent of scales, Danial watched as they immersed into a fleshy ooze.

"You scared me, Dan. What did you see?" she asked.

Len's words rang in his ears; he'd met his fear. Lucy not seeing anything proved Len correct. It dawned on him that Len had no idea where the cabin was as they trudged on through what felt like deep water. Reaching the slope leading down to the cabin, relieved, they ran the rest of the way.

A rush of cold air hit Dan as he opened the door to the cabin. Lucy slammed it closed, bolted it, and flicked every light in the place on while drawing the curtains closed.

Glad that he'd prepared a fire, Danial lit it and turned to Lucy.

"Dan, it's happening again, isn't it?" Lucy said, looking up at him.

"Everything's going to be all right, Lucy."

They both looked towards the door seconds before someone knocked on it.

Lucy gripped his arm. "Don't answer it, Dan. I don't trust him."

Len bellowed through the door, "Hello!"

Against Lucy's protests to ignore him, Danial opened the door and saw Len crouching, about to drop. A golden book was pressed under his armpit. Upon seeing him, Lucy helped Danial guide Len into the cabin. Danial bolted the door as Lucy pushed the book aside and sat Len at the table.

"Can you get the first aid box?" she asked, pointing at the kitchen cupboard.

Grabbing tea towels and the first aid kit, Danial slid the green box across the table while covering the book with a tea towel, nudging it out of Lucy's view.

"A bowl of clean water and another towel, too."

Danial filled the kettle and prepared the cups to make a hot drink. *How did he find the book? Why has he brought it back here?*

Len winced with pain as Lucy cleaned around the open wound. Dan kept his focus on the boiling kettle as Lucy went to work on Len's leg. He vaguely remembered her saying that as a requirement for working at Woodrush, she'd had to pass a first aid course.

Lucy leaned forward across Len and dragged the bowl closer

to her. She jumped as he placed the palm of his hand on her stomach.

"Dan!" she shouted.

Danial turned. Lucy backed away from Len with a look on her face which told him that Len had said or done something to offend her.

"It all makes sense," Len said, with a wide smile.

"He touched me, Dan."

"What makes sense, Len?" Danial asked.

"The enlightened one is but a seed within you, Lucy. You are carrying the one we both seek. The one who will bring balance to the world, the universe, and—"

He stood, and for a moment, Danial thought Len was going to shout *Eureka!*

"You're crazy," Lucy said. "After I've bandaged you, I'll be asking you to leave us both alone. Deal?" Lucy looked at Dan for confirmation. "Now, please sit down and let me finish what I've started," she insisted.

Len bounced on his good leg. "No time!" He looked at them both with panic on his face. "The timing is all wrong; the escape should never have happened. You both need to leave. Don't tell me or anyone else where you are going. The seed needs to mature. It will not reach its full potential for some years and will be helpless until the birth. You both need to protect the baby."

Lucy looked at Dan. He looked at her stomach.

"You have the beginnings of the most powerful being growing inside you, Lucy."

Danial tittered in disbelief. Lucy ignored the remarks and continued to unwrap the bandage.

"Len, stop talking. You're scaring Lucy," Danial said.

"I'm not scared. Being scared would validate his ridiculous

claims. I can't be pregnant unless I'm the Virgin Mary."

Lucy was on the pill. Danial saw her take it daily. Could it have failed? How could Len know, anyway?

"I will never misguide you or tell you untruths, Lucy. What I say may not be believable, but it will always be true," Len said, looking at Lucy, and then at Danial.

Danial was told that very thing on the way back to the tent and couldn't deny that everything Len had professed as true ended up happening.

Len tried to talk. Lucy tightened the bandage, making him wince while explaining that he needed stitches and explaining that she'd slowed the bleeding long enough to find a hospital.

"I will protect you and the child until it reaches enlightenment. Vetala will try and kill you. Or worse—manipulate the child when it arrives," Len said.

"Like hell. You're here to protect my child? I'm not even pregnant," Lucy said, watching Danial turn ashen. "What is it, Dan?"

Danial's body quaked upon seeing a bright yellow substance seep under the door. Twisting, pulsating forms slithered. Their shape was unfathomable, but alive. Materialising before his eyes, some were thin and long, others slug-like. All had faces; little shrunken heads. One rose, its face a miniature of Bill's. Kicking one from his ankle, Danial smashed his toe on the table leg. His sock dampened.

"Whatever you're seeing isn't there, Danial," Len said, "Clear your mind. Breathe deeply and think happy thoughts."

"Bill… they're smiling… snakes—For God's sake, Lucy, can't you see them?!" Danial cried, slapping his body down with the flats of his hands.

"I can see fog, Dan, that's weird enough. There's nothing else.

Honest, babes. Nothing."

Len placed both hands together and closed his eyes. A wash of positivity cloaked Danial. Eyes drug-heavy, Danial wore a smile that he was aware of, but had no control over.

"What's happening?!" Lucy cried.

Obnoxious miniature heads retreated, their faces pleading and desperate as snake-like bodies withdrew into the cold night air.

Snapped from his trance, Danial studied the back of his hand. Smearing a trickle of blood before it had a chance to drip, he looked at Len.

"How did this happen?"

"You did it to yourself. Has it gone?"

"They have. Hundreds of..." Shuddering, Danial continued, "I don't know what they were. One looked like an old friend."

"They left, taking your fear with them, Danial." Len's eyes flicked between Lucy and Danial. "I helped a little by changing your mood. The rest you did yourself."

"Don't forget this," Lucy said, holding up the golden book. "We need to get you to the hospital."

"It should stay with you." Len turned to Danial. "Keep it away from others until such a time as it is needed."

Danial threw a look of bemusement toward Lucy and put the book into his holdall.

Chapter 25

The small, winding road came to an abrupt end in front of a rocky embankment.

Roger's eyebrows raised. "We could cut across the hills."

"Do I need to remind you that you're not driving Big Black, and I doubt this family estate has 4x4? Wait here, I'll take a look," James said, pointing to the rocks.

Guilt fell over Roger as he watched James slip-slide his way to the top.

"Rog! I see something. Switch the engine off."

Roger got out into unknown territory. "Adders and cowpats, mate. Shitty snakes and more shit, and if you're lucky, a cow or three," Roger muttered, buttoning up his jacket.

Roger joined James atop what was, in essence, a pile of rocks. "You're afraid of snakes? Never knew that," James said.

"There's a lot you don't know about me."

"I know that when I say you should sit tight in the car while I check out that fire, you're going to come with me, and piss and moan on the way," James said, combing an imaginary beard.

"Smart-arse," Roger replied. "Anyway, so what? Someone's out camping, probably making out, and you're going to show them your gun. Is that the plan?"

James was already walking off. "Yeah, that's the plan."

By the time they reached the fire, the flames had turned to

smouldering embers.

"Who'd leave a tent wide open?" James asked. "Look, the sleeping bags are soaked."

"Smells like women," Roger said, sniffing the interior of the tent.

James widened the beam of his touch before narrowing it to look into the distance. "The fog's so thick I can't see my feet, Rog."

"Maybe the fog monster got them," Roger joked.

"Yeah, or adders!"

"That's not funny. Look, I've found a footprint. Two, three sets of them leading off in this direction."

"Stay close," Roger said.

"Why? You scared?" James replied.

"No, I'm serious. We're near-zero visibility, and anything could happen, and no fucker would find us for days." Roger fed the fire with a broken walking pole.

"Why are you building a fire? Planning on stopping?"

"It's a two-man tent. Three separate sets of footprints, so someone didn't have an invite. Probably your Len Happy. The fire's a reference point if the worse happens."

"Okay, Rog, you're right. Maybe I have spent too much time in the office," James said.

James watched Roger in action. Not following a blip on a screen—*in action*, doing what he did best. Neither of them could have stopped the department from closing. Playing the yes game would have secured a top-ranking office job for James, and Roger would have been assigned a new mission. Instead, they chose to follow blind leads in the hopes of saving Len.

Roger gave James a concerned look. "What's wrong, mate? Not saying much."

"Nothing much. Feel bad for dragging you into this wild goose chase, Rog."

"If you call stopping an innocent man from being deleted—albeit a crazy bastard—from getting killed a 'wild goose chase', then what I'm doing is the right thing. And it's my choice; not even you could force me into something that isn't right, mate," Roger said, smiling at James.

James returned his smile. "Thanks."

James was in awe, watching Roger track down three unknown people in the hopes of finding Len. If anyone could conclude this crazy mission, it was Roger.

James knew that MI5 was interested in more than Len's psychic abilities. He knew about their project involving consciousness, or as top scientists called it, "the hard problem". Having gained what they needed, it was time to kill the source; conceal their knowledge. After warning Len, there was little he could do, apart from exposing Len's oppressors, be there when the proverbial shit hit the fan, and learn the truth.

"One of the three followed some distance behind the other two. Re-joined the track at this point," Roger said, pointing to the ground.

James couldn't see the ground, let alone a footprint. He looked back and shuddered. Cocooned in a shroud of mist, the fire was no longer visible. His chest tightened. Breathing deeply, he put faith in his friend and partner.

"Who do you think the other two are, Rog? And are we close to finding them?" James thought of another question, but held back, awaiting answers.

"Male and female. Probably lovers cheating on their partners. And one with a bad leg, which ties in nicely with being your Mr Happy. Can't say how close, as we don't know where they're heading, but we shouldn't be more than forty minutes behind. The woman has green eyes and small ears."

James wasn't expecting such a thorough answer. "Okay, explain to me how you know so much from seeing a footprint, Rog."

"Well, you said he has a bad leg. Cut, you said. The footprint shows a leg dragging behind and the other foot taking most of his weight. That, coupled with the fact that he was seen heading in this direction, and—"

"Yes, I get that, but what about the rest?" James asked, hurrying him along.

"Must be lovers. We know one's female from the footprints and body deodorant. It's too cosy in that tent for brother and sister, and who the fuck would want to be so close to their wife? So, I reckon lovers," Roger explained.

"So, how do you know the colour of her eyes and that she has small ears?" James persisted.

"That bit I made up," Roger said, laughing. "Could be true."

Footprints faded halfway up a steep hill. James asked Roger to stop. Disoriented, they headed for a clump of trees, unsure which direction to take next.

James rested his back on a tree; legs bent in a crouching position. Roger walked around the trees, looking for any obvious sign of recent damage, broken branches, or upturned rocks. Any directional hint. Sighing, he joined James.

* * *

"There's no time left. No time. Find your vehicle and drive as far away as you can," Len stressed.

"I'm done running. We came here to get away from this madness, and it keeps following us. *You* keep following us."

Danial looked at Lucy. She nodded in agreement.

"He will end your natural life if you stay, Danial. He won't stop until he kills your unborn child. There's only so much I can do to protect you."

"Then we stay and fight!" Danial shouted. Lucy held his arm tightly as she looked into her hero's eyes.

"This isn't a game, Danial."

"Life's a game, Len, you've said it yourself. This time, we're not leaving the poker table."

Len closed his eyes. Danial thought he was performing mind tricks. "You're right, Danial. It's not clear, but your intent is strong. The timing is all wrong. If Ronny is killed, then Vetala will return; stronger, within another form. Our only option is to detain him and restrain his uprising until such a time that your child becomes enlightened," Len said, before turning to Lucy. "I'll go instead. I'll face him before he has a chance."

"Not with that leg, you won't. You won't last five minutes," Lucy protested.

Len smiled back. "There will be no bar fight, Lucy. It's not who has the biggest muscles; more who has the strongest intent. Stay true to yourselves. You can't harm him with anger." Len picked up his coat but failed to catch the arm. "Has someone sewn my coat together?"

Lucy helped feed his arms through and went to fasten the buttons, unaware that the jacket didn't reach around his stomach.

"Laughter is its greatest enemy, Danial. Load your gun with laughter bullets." Len chuckled, held an imaginary gun, and pretended to fire. "*Ha-ha* instead of *bang-bang*, Danial."

"Please stay?" Danial asked as Len hobbled out the door. Without acknowledging, Len vanished into a blanket of fog.

"I've got a bad feeling about this, Lucy. Maybe it's best if we do leave. He could be right about Ronny. Maybe we should pack up and go."

Lucy kissed his cheek. "We only have the word of a madman to go off of, and as for being pregnant, that's just wrong. He's bonkers and should be in care."

"How else can we explain what's happened? The thing with the snakes? That was real. Well, not the snakes, but the experience, Lucy. That happened."

"Maybe he did it somehow. Maybe he drugged your drink or gassed you. But his claims are ridiculous; you must know that," she insisted.

Was this their first argument? Danial tried to compromise by explaining away his fighting talk as no more than bravado. He gulped as he handed her the golden book.

"Here, what do you make of this? Go on. Flick through. You wanted to know how I knew where you lived? Open it."

Turning away, Danial screwed his eyes shut as Lucy flicked through the book.

"Looks old," she said.

"Do you believe me now?"

"I never disbelieved you, Dan. I've lived alone for so long that I've only had to think about myself. We'll cut the trip short and leave first thing in the morning." Danial was already packing and managed to convince her to leave tonight.

"Okay darling, tonight," she said, squeezing his bicep.

Lucy handed over the book. Danial's face dropped when he saw the cabin. Shooting stars leapt from its roof, forcing him to blink. Stick-like people, more than he could count, littered the page, and his car stood under trees. He slapped it shut and hurled it across the room.

"Wow, good shot."

The book landed inside his backpack, a nearly impossible target from where he stood.

"That proves he's unhinged, Dan."

Sweat specked Danial's forehead. Wiping it with his sleeve, he said, "I had to show you."

Lucy huffed. "A blank book." Her smile confirmed that she hadn't seen anything.

The book chose you, Danial; I only sold it to you. Len's voice echoed through his mind.

* * *

Lance approached Officer Mason. "Why are the roads still open?" The officer shook his head and started to speak, only to be interrupted again. "I told you to block all ways into and out of the village, yet I can see a pizza delivery van turning around. Explain."

Officer Mason bit his lip. Flushed, he said, "I can't do it. The fog's grounded the search helicopter, and I have four cars circling the area. The weather—"

"I'm not interested in excuses. Get it done!" Lance shouted back.

"Agent White—it's for you." Lance snatched a mobile phone from one of his agents.

Lance paced alongside the blue police tape as he heard that backup wouldn't arrive anytime soon due to zero visibility. Two helicopters, unable to find their destination, laid idle in a field. Vehicles were stranded while officers tried to gain their bearings and get a directional fix.

Looking at the empty shell of a once-modern restaurant, Lance ended the call.

"Harris! I need a body count. Is everyone accounted for?"

"Yes. And before you ask, no, we haven't located a man fitting the suspect's description, and no dogs. I spoke to the fire department a minute ago, and they confirmed staff and customers only. Ask them yourself. The good taxpayers of this borough pay my wage, not you. Do your own dirty work," Harris stated.

Heads turned skyward as a low bass tone radiated. A crack and a squeal, rising into an ear-piercing screech, rang out before jagged lightning spat down onto the restaurant's burnt skeleton. The second bolt of lightning struck the same spot moments after the first. Muted silence hung heavily, giving charred timbers a voice.

"What the hell was that?!" Harris shouted.

Lance, his team, and the fire brigade looked up open-mouthed.

"Lightning this time of year, with fog like this, impossible," one of the firemen said.

Dumbfounded, people gathered in awe as blinding stars flickered above like a soundless firework gaining in momentum, expanding through the night's sky.

The light show ended as quickly as it had started. No thunder followed. The crowd didn't cheer. The atmosphere was foreboding, triggering the crowd's primordial instincts to run and hide. Their sense of duty and confused states of mind held them in place, in anticipation of what would follow.

Crack! Another bolt, fiercer than the two previous, hit the road. Debris erupted as tarmac turned molten, dripping gloop into a smoke-filled hole. Two onlookers fell to the ground before running, heads down, into the distance.

Harris dodged a surge of electricity from high above as it stabbed the ground on either side of him. He scrambled into the patrol car, slamming the door shut on his foot. Strikes of lightning came every five seconds, each time fiercer than the last. Lance ran toward the car where his agents gathered.

"Get in!" were the last words to leave his mouth. His body jolted as forked lightning pinned him to the road, his entrails followed black tar down a smoky abyss.

The door to one of the three waiting ambulances swung open. The medic ran to Lance, stopping short as lightning struck the corpse again.

Harris opened his car door, ducking as another bolt of lightning hit the medic and agent standing next to Lance's lifeless body. Another hit the fire truck. A man taking cover crawled out. Staggering, he turned as it burst into flames.

Cupping his ears, blinded by the flash, Smithy fell back over the curb. His body felt the force of the second explosion. A white mist swam under his eyelids. "I can't see—hear—who's there?"

Feeling his way, Smithy kicked something soft. His fingers sunk into the flesh of a body; next to it was another. Regaining vision, he gagged upon seeing his friend's battered bodies.

Harris guided Smithy toward his car. "Get inside, quick." Once inside, he looked out at the burning fire engine, the empty car that Lance and his team had arrived in, and an ambulance devoid of drivers. Bodies littered the road; any spectators were either dead or scattered, lost within a vaporous chasm.

Harris shuddered. His knees and lower legs rattled in spasms as he reached for the radio. It was dead. He pulled his phone from his high-vis. That was dead, too. The car wouldn't start. Not a chug or flash of light on the dash.

Screeching, Harris sat bolt upright, banging the locks down with his elbow, automatically triggering the rest. "What the hell is that?!"

Smithy squinted through dazed eyes.

"What is it?"

"I—I don't..."

Smithy covered his face as something crashed onto the bonnet. Harris lunged forward, the downward motion sending his face into the steering wheel.

A black oily mass crushed the window. Streaks marked the inward bulge of the window screen as it was dragged down, revealing hair, cheekbone, and ripped burnt clothing. Shards of flesh and dirt smeared the glass as Smithy and Harris pressed themselves back into their seats.

The car rocked, and the bonnet popped from the weight of the figure as he threw Lance's limp remains aside.

Wedged between his and Smithy's seat, Harris pushed with his legs, trying to gain distance.

Smithy patted the concave glass in a futile attempt to push it into place, trying not to look at the figure.

The car rose; a scrape on the surface of the road. Smithy couldn't see the figure but heard him grunt as he hurled Lance's lifeless remains through the damaged window screen.

Harris unlocked the driver side, simultaneously unlocking Smithy's door.

Through wailing cries, Harris opened his. Smithy followed and ran around the car's rear to help; to fight. He froze at the sight of Harris pinned to the ground. A dog swung its head from side to side. Something—he didn't know what—lashed out with the strength of ten men, knocking Smithy sideways into a wall.

Smithy's eyes flitted open. He forced a cough, breaking the silence, confirming that he could still hear. His body trembled as he stood with his back to the wall, squinting, bringing his finger to his eye, poking it in an attempt to see. Blackness. Total blackness enveloped him. No foggy haze or light. No stars or glint of moonlight, house or street lamps. All were absent, rendering him blind. Scrambling, he found a lighter inside his jacket pocket and cried as a single flame appeared. He followed the shadowy figure, keeping enough distance to remain unseen. Ears compensating for his eyes, the smell of rotten fish and sweeping hands served as his only guide.

Chapter 26

"James, I'm blind. I can't see my hand. Those explosions came from over there." Roger pointed an unseen arm toward the sound.

"The torch has died. Shit, Rog, I can't see."

James ran his fingers across rough bark. "Bloody hell."

"What's wrong?" Roger feared James was having an attack. "I can't see you."

"Splinter. Where are you?" Their hands touched. "Rog, what's happening?"

"Wait." Raising his right ear, Roger listened. Rustling, something moved ahead of them. Ferns snapped. "Can you hear that?" Roger whispered.

James' hand signalled Roger forward. Unable to see, the click of his gun spurred Roger to draw his.

Aware that they had the high ground, they'd chosen to rest before heading down, in the hopes of regaining the trail of footprints. Whoever was out there was below them.

Guns out, crouched, years of training came flooding to the forefront of their minds. Still working blind, between their intakes of breath, they heard whistling in the distance. If only they had night vision glasses a standard issued item that neither had ever needed until now.

The sound of a foot slipping alerted them to the location of the unseen person.

"Stop, or I'll shoot!" Roger shouted, followed almost simultaneously by James shouting, "Armed officers! Identify yourself!"

"My name is Len. H.A.P.P.Y. Len H.A.P.P.Y." Len sang his name; his deep bellowing voice was unmistakable.

"Len, stop. We're moving toward you. Keep talking so we can find you," James said, holstering his firearm.

Roger raised his gun, pointing it at the sound. Their arms bashed together as he did.

"Rog, put it away." Patting his way up to Roger's arm, he palmed the top of the gun, forcing it down. "It's Len. Put it away," he said again.

"Warm, warmer. Hot." Len said, as they approached.

"Len, can you see us? Everything's black."

"I see you fine—through the fog, that is. Here, this will help." Striking a match from the box he'd found behind the bar earlier that day, he was met with a childlike joy from both Roger and James.

"I don't understand," James said.

Len threw a flinching smile. Pain-stricken, his head trembled.

"He's switched off the lights; isolated you, and others, no doubt. They're still there; I can vouch that the universe still blesses us with a moon and stars."

"Where are they? What have you done with them?" Roger asked.

"Pardon? Who do you seek?"

"Cut the shit, Len. Who else is with you?"

"Who else?" Len looked artificially surprised by the question.

"We know there are two others. Stop fucking around and tell me who they are."

James put his arm in front of Roger. "Steady on, Rog."

Len looked past them, through the thick fog. "You've come alone?"

Neither James nor Roger answered his question.

"He's coming." The match went out. Len struck another. "He wants the unborn child."

"What child?!" Roger snapped.

"Over there in the cabin. A lovely couple. Very kind people. She was fertilised and has within her the seed of hope. Ronny is drawing power from it."

"Wait a goddamn minute. Are you saying Ronny wants to kill a pregnant woman?" James asked.

Len tilted his head, then looked up and back down, his eyes meeting James.

"Too soon to tell. I would imagine he doesn't know. After all, I've only just found out myself. One thing I *do* know is that they need protecting, and that's why I'm here. They are very stubborn. Won't leave. I tried to warn them."

"Crazy bastard!" Roger hissed. "I'll check the cabin."

"I'll come with you," James said.

"What about him? Could have done them in, for all we know."

"I'm coming. Len, wait here."

Placing the box of matches in James' palm, Len walked away, vanishing as if a black curtain had been drawn between them.

James and Roger walked aimlessly until they saw a distant light flicker.

"There."

They tried to run but couldn't manage more than a trot. Blackness as thick as stone threatened to down them if they argued against it. Hands outstretched, they followed the flickering light like zombie moths attracted to the only light left on Earth.

"Last match, Rog."

"Save it."

"There." Roger pointed toward the outline of a window. James couldn't see Roger, but he did see what Roger had seen.

The empty cabin was unlocked. James entered first, swinging his gun to the left. Roger covered centre and top right. Both swung their guns toward the fire as a log popped, sending sparks upward through the ornate-looking chimney.

Blinking, James and Roger waited for their eyesight to adjust.

James fingered a hot cup of tea. "Whoever they are, they haven't been gone long."

"They probably never left. Can't you see? That crazy bastard has more to do with this than meets the eye. I'm not buying the power-baby story. And you just let him go. *Again.* I say we get him in here now and make him tell us what he's done with them."

James stood at the stable wooden door; a thick, foggy cloud drifted through.

"Len, come down here right now."

Roger shook his head in disbelief.

"Len, we're in the cabin. Come down right now," he repeated.

As Roger was going to explain that potential killers rarely came running back, Len stepped into the cabin.

He looked around. "Where are they?"

"We were going to ask you that same question," Roger said, raising one eyebrow.

With both mobiles out of charge, they were alone, tangled in a cobweb of madness.

Len leaned on the table; his good leg bore his weight.

"They've taken my advice. Gone as far away as possible."

James swished his head toward the window. *THUD.* The sound

came again, this time with clawing and snarling. James drew his gun. Roger followed.

"It's a dog. The same dog that attacked Danial. He's coming."

"Danial? Enough. Tell me where the two others are right now." Roger pointed his gun at Len. "This loon has been playing us from the start. I'll ask again. For the last time, where are they?"

Unperturbed by the gun pointed at his chest, Len counted down from three, moving aside as the door swung open.

Roger moved back, his gun still aimed at Len. James dropped to his knees, pointing his weapon at the black void the open door presented.

"Armed officers. Identify yourself."

"It's me. Don't shoot." Firelight yellowed his face. "What are you doing?"

"Danial Morris?"

"Yes. What are you doing here? Len, what's happening? We went blind. The car's dead. The moon... There's no light."

Len rubbed Danial's shoulder. "Calm yourself, and remember, stay positive."

"It's safe, Lucy," Danial said, opening the door for Lucy, who stormed in and over to the fire.

"For a remote location, it sure seems busy in here," she said, rubbing her eyes. "This man needs help." Lucy aimed a gaze toward Len. "You're police, right?"

Fatigued, Roger flashed long, snapping blinks, unable to adjust or understand that there was no light apart from that provided by dying flames.

"If seeing is the issue, then stock the fire and light torches. He will try anything to isolate us." Arching his back and lowing his head, Len looked at the gathered few within the cabin. "Danial, take Lucy somewhere safe. Hide, and I will rid Ronny of his inhibitor and find you. I am prepared to kill Ronny if forced to, thus releasing the spirit within. Remember, trickery can't hurt you or your baby."

Frantic, garbled words filled the cabin. Roger's voice rose above the others. "There, got you! You've been preaching that he can't be killed. You said he would reincarnate and grow stronger. Now you're saying he has to die. Which is it, Len Happy?"

"I have never said Vetala's form cannot be killed! Ronny is flesh and blood, not immortal. Vetala will return stronger and continue its mission to increase entropy; to enslave the human race and destroy the enlightened one."

"Where is this enlightened being you speak of, Len?" James added.

Len looked at Lucy, then back to James. "Part-baked. Won't be ready for some years."

Lucy stomped over to Len. "*You're* part-baked." Patience running thin, she turned to James. "I want to see your identification."

Ignoring her request, James bolted the door. "We have nowhere to go. Power's out. We have no communications or transport. I suggest we all sit tight and wait for daybreak, and if trouble finds us, then I need you all," a sweeping hand covered Danial, Lucy, and Len, "to leave it to myself and Roger. We're trained government agents."

"Daybreak happened long ago; you are where you are and see what you do because he wants it that way. Killing him is our last option. Give me the chance to end this once and for all."

"How, Len? If what you're saying is true, then how can you destroy the spirit that you say resides in Ronny? I want to believe you, but physics, God himself, and even you know that isn't possible."

"You don't want to believe because—"

"Don't you fucking dare. Do you know what this man has given up for you?"

"Rog, don't."

"His career, maybe his freedom, not to mention risking his life because he *does* believe in you and your crazy nonsense."

"And you," Len turned to Roger. "Do you believe I can release the spirit and set it free?"

All heard Rogers's teeth grinding. "I think you're a lunatic. I'm here to make sure no harm comes to my friend. One false move, and I swear I'll take you out and sleep easy."

"Rog."

"No, James. You think what you want, and you're not off the hook, either," he said, pointing at Danial. "Heading up country to visit your brother, are you? Just happened to be in the same place as the man you let back into Woodrush before it burnt to the ground."

"Rog." James cupped his ear before pointing at the door.

Roger pulled his gun. Waving the piece at Len, he waved his free hand at Danial and Lucy, ushering them into the bathroom.

James crouched, moving over to the opposite side of the door, mirroring Roger's actions.

Without speaking, James waved his arm in an up-and-down motion, telling them to get lower. Ignoring Roger's bathroom request, Lucy and Danial hid under the table, leaving Len standing between them and the door.

"Your guns will not bring this to an end. Move out of the way." Len hobbled toward the door, "He has arrived," Len said, reaching for the handle.

"Get back, or I'll shoot," Roger said, without looking at him. "Into the bathroom."

Swinging the door inward toppled Roger and a wooden coat stand. Len hauled his leg forward and walked outside, vanishing into the inky blackness.

James mouthed "Thank you," to Roger, whose face turned radish red. "I'm going out. No promises," Roger whispered.

James knew that statement meant he'd shoot Len, if warranted.

Looking back to the fire, James broke the legs off the coat stand, snatched tea towels from the side of the table, and tied them tight around the varnished wood.

Under the table, Danial held Lucy and watched as the room brightened from fiery torches. Jolting her head from his chest the moment the door slammed, she turned to him. "Dan, bolt the door."

As he did, he parted the curtains, but saw nothing more than his reflection.

"Lucy, we're safe. You can come out from under the table."

The table crashed onto its side. Danial flinched, having not seen Lucy push it over.

"I need your muscles for this one," she said, forcing her weight down onto the leg of the table.

Joining her, Danial unbolted the leg from inside the frame, aware of her intentions.

Unable to see the person he was chasing, Roger slowed his pace, and James ran into him. The flame brushed his jacket. Its dim orange flicker couldn't penetrate the density of the fog, giving little comfort. With the cabin no longer visible, vulnerability washed over them.

Breath held, they stood silent, waiting for a hint, a sound, and the fishy odour to return. The beating of hearts and stilted release of breath were amplified, as if cocooned in a glass jar. There was not a bird nor a brush of wind; deadly silence both friend and foe. Roger disappeared along with the flame. Hopping turned to jumping as he broke audial cover. "Argh!" Bending, he patted his legs, headbutting James as he lowered.

"What? Rog!" James dipped the flaming torch. Fire licked the wood, serpentine-like, up to his wrist before he threw it to the ground. The lights were out once more. Roger wailed and lashed, causing James to back away.

"Rats! All over me! Rats! ARGH!"

Lunging forward, James grabbed at Roger's jacket. Roger hit the ground with a padded thud. Screaming and cursing made way to panting murmurs.

"I'm right here… Rog, there's no rats." James palmed Roger's juddering body, spread his figures, and swept his surroundings.

"He can't hear you." Len's voice thundered down on them. James gasped. His chest tightened. "Fear has a hold of him. In his mind, he is being eaten. Eaten by what he fears most."

"Len, save him, I beg you… Please." James shook Len, stopping when his leg gave way. "He saw rats, but I can't—"

"They're bunny rabbits. Little white ones. Look, I'll show you."

Blackness faded to grey-white. He could see. "I see him—you—I can see."

"You always could. Help me lift him."

James watched as Len scooped thin air from Roger's chest and commenced a stroking action. Roger smiled with teary eyes. Sanity had returned, leaving Roger deflated and bewildered.

"What happened? I can stand."

James flicked his gaze away from Roger's blood-soaked trousers. He'd torn a nail. His fingers were tacky and stained from clawing at his flesh.

Shaking off the tightness rising through his chest, James hobbled with Roger toward the cabin. The return of Roger's vision had motivated a deflated man into motion.

Looking back, James made out two figures; one stooped to the side, the other bowing, as he took off a hat like a stage performer shrouded in an opaque theatrical cloud.

Chapter 27

A yellow tinge of light flooded the cabin. Somewhere out there, through thickening vapour, daylight had found a way. Checking sockets, flicking light switches, all were out.

Danial grabbed Lucy back as she jogged toward the door. Shrugging, she helped James and Roger over to the sofa.

"What happened?" Danial knelt, looking at Roger's torn trousers.

"Someone's out there with Len."

"Ronny?"

"I couldn't—argh!" James held his chest.

Snatching the cloth-wrapped table leg and a poker from the inglenook, Danial went for the door. He stopped short as the door moved and pulsated. He lunged for the handle, burning his hand in the process. He turned to Lucy. Pockets of flames appeared on the wall behind her.

"Lucy."

She swung her head and backed away from the sofa.

"We have to get out." Lucy tried pulling Roger from the sofa. "Dan, behind you!"

Orange flames layered the bottom of the door; blue tongues licked timber as it climbed. Something fell from above, sticking Roger, knocking him into the upturned table.

Lucy held Roger upright, snatched a bucket from under the

sink, and started filling it.

Danial and James pounded the door, distancing themselves as the flames intensified. Closing his eyes, Danial recalled Len's words, *He will use mind tricks, and the things you see are not real.* The wind whistled through the door as he opened it wide.

Lucy screamed and ran to him. Leaving Roger propped up by the sink, she threw water and followed him out, padding his body.

"Fire! Roll on the ground!"

James hurled Roger out. Both fell to the floor, gasping.

"Lucy, I'm not on fire—please, listen!"

He moved closer. Lucy backed away, flapping a tea towel at his legs. He looked down, smoothing his hands down his body, trying to convince her that he was not alight.

"Close your eyes. Trust me. Do it."

She did.

Danial wrapped his arms around her, encasing her with his body. Whispering reassurance, her body slackened.

A limpid realisation hit him. Len was correct. Illusions. Nothing more than cheap circus tricks. His confidence grew, along with anger he never knew existed.

"You are injured, brother." Ronny looked down at Len's leg. "The people you protect hurt you; imprison you. Still, you serve them."

"Let me help you," Len said, wincing. "I can free you from this realm; from your misery. They won't stop until they kill you."

"This body no longer serves me. I will reincarnate. Grow stronger." Ronny's demeanour changed, his face twisting tight. "Take me to the enlightened being."

"You know as well as I do; no such being ever existed."

Sensing movement nearing, Len closed his eyes. His mind

told Danial to stay back, protect Lucy. Silent words deafened Ronny into speaking.

"Why do you protect the girl? She means nothing."

"Armed officers." Roger's gun shook as James shouted, "On the ground!" to the voices ahead.

Their demands were met with Ronny's laughter as he turned to Len.

"Tell me where the enlightened being is, and I'll spare their lives."

Looking skyward, Len rubbed his neck chain.

"I can't do that."

"Very well."

James and Roger looked up and watched the fog part above their heads, groaning and swishing before an almighty *thud* as a motorbike hit the ground. Its frame was twisted and mangled. Fluid gushed from its split engine. Another fell closer, forcing them back.

"Stop this and let me help you."

Time was running out. Ronny's abilities were evolving. He drew power from the beginnings of the one he sought.

More bikes rained down.

"Back inside!" Danial led Lucy to the cabin. She pulled away. "No!"

"This way!" James turned away from what he saw as the building's burning remains.

"It's not on fire. Vetala's making you think it is. Fight your fears; it's the only way. Believe it isn't on fire and—"

A body, leather-clad, fell from the sky, crushing Rogers's legs. He didn't scream, cry, or push the body aside.

By the time Danial got to him, James had rolled the remains of Cogs to one side.

"He's still breathing," James said.

"Don't move him." Lucy had her hands either side of Roger's face.

"Stop this now!" Len lunged at Ronny.

"I'll ask one more time," Ronny said, through broken teeth.

"I can't tell you where she is, but I will take you to her."

"Her?"

"Hold my hands, brother. Leave these people alone. They're meaningless and serve no purpose. Let me guide you," Len said, holding out his hands, palms flat.

"You know her. I believe you. Take me and reign with me for eternity."

Vetala knew Len had made contact with the enlightened one. He was telling the truth, and Vetala could sense the one he sought was close. Trusting Len Happy to guide him to her, and to save the humans Len was so fond of would backfire on the weak-minded fool, as all would be at the mercy of Vetala after he returned from the kill. Tilting his hat, he agreed.

Unbeknownst to Len, the wild card–the random, unpredictable wild card played by a power higher than him, higher even than *Vetala*–was fast approaching.

Gripping Len's hands, Ronny inhaled the thick vapour. Fog gathered and swirled as it entered his body, clearing the area completely.

The true extent of the littered machinery revealed itself as the mist cleared.

Danial watched Len stagger away from Ronny, who, at first glance, looked twice as tall. Hypnotised by the spectacle, Danial didn't notice Smithy vaulting down the hill toward them. A faint, yet distinct image of a man hovered above Ronny, floating skyward, a green umbilical cord anchoring the spirit from its host.

Danial turned as a dog pounded toward Lucy.

Lifting the fire poker, spear-like, he ran toward Lucy, shouting her name. Snarling, the dog pounced. Danial thrust the poker into its side, rolling with it until its head flopped and its back legs twitched their last.

Looking from his blood-soaked hands into Lucy's eyes, he saw alarmed revulsion turn to concern as she flung her arms around him, moving his hair, pressing hard against his ear.

Gunshots spat in the distance like fireworks before the bang. Snatching the gun from James, Danial ran toward Len. Standing spread-legged, Smithy fired again, propelling Ronny backwards. Elated, Smithy fired again before turning the gun on Len.

"No! Stop!" His words were stilted as he ran toward them. "Don't shoot."

Len's leg buckled as Smithy fired. Desperate, Danial pulled the trigger. No bullet left the chamber. Pressing, flicking around the base of the gun, Danial aimed and fired, sending Smithy flying backwards.

"Len!" he called as he approached. "Len, are you—"

"I'm alive. I don't think he shot me. Danial, what have you done? Lucy, you need to pro..."

Len turned pallid; his eyes flickered before rolling back.

"Len."

He was out cold; blood loss and the energy Ronny had drawn from him had weakened his earthly body.

"Len." Danial turned to Smithy. Blood trickling from his mouth sealed his worst fear.

"My God, what have I done?"

He checked for a pulse as bile entered his throat. A name badge, in blue, read Agent Smith. His head swayed like a feather, his

279

chest pressed heavily on a swooshing gut. Len's words invaded his empty skull. *Be careful what you wish for.*

Short breaths left his lungs. Strained, yet powerful, he shouted, "Agent down. Suspect down." Tears pooled before showering his cheeks. "Len." Audible only to himself. "Len down."

"Dan." Lucy embraced his back, lifting him to his feet. "Dan, is that him?"

"Lucy, I've killed." Adrenaline-fuelled gasps stopped his words. "I'm sorry."

Blinded by Danial ending their nightmares, killing the person responsible for slaying his neighbours, murdering Dave and saving them from certain death, she didn't mentally connect him with the murder of Agent Smith.

Lucy started to check Smithy's vitals.

"He's dead, Lucy; I killed him." Danial's nostrils flared.

Blank-faced, she walked over to Len, joined two fingers together, and moved his collar aside. Danial stared down at the grass in anticipation.

"Glad to see you're unharmed," Len blurted.

Lucy flinched. "I thought you were—"

"Just fine, I think. Is the leg still there? I can't feel it."

Helicopters, not yet in view, advanced. Mechanical rotary blades slicing through the air were both distinct and welcoming.

James approached with his mobile pressed to his ear in stern conversation.

"Agents down, one unconscious and stable, one fatality." Pressing a finger to his mouth, silencing the others, he continued. "Subject One terminated." He looked at Len. Hesitating, he said, "Vaporised." He shrugged his shoulders. "I tell you, he vanished. No remains. I'm alone with my partner. That noise I hear better be the air ambulance." Ending the call, he turned to Danial.

"Morris, get yourselves gone and take him with you." He turned to Len. "Len, disappear. If you're spotted, I can't guarantee your safety."

"The car wouldn't start," Lucy said. "What do we say if the police ask questions? Dan shot..."

"My mobile started working and lights are back on in the cabin, so fingers crossed, it does start. Leave the police to me. You left two days ago; cut your trip short when the fog came." James looked back at Roger, then to Danial. "Put this behind you. I won't name you in my report," he said, running back to Roger.

Arm around Danial's back, Len made it to the car.

When they arrived at the hospital, Len insisted on walking into the A and E department alone, saying he felt better already. Lucy walked into the all-night chemist, leaving them to say their goodbyes. Peering through the chemist's door, she watched as Danial hugged him.

"So, this is it. It's over. Will we see you again?"

"Has anything I've said sunk into that brain of yours?"

"Er, which bit, Len? You've said a lot."

"He will return. Look after your daughter; she will be different than her peers, and for a good reason. I will know when Vetala returns, and whether in this form or another, I will find you. Take care, my friend. One more thing: Bury the book in consecrated ground, away from people, away from evil. You do believe in good and evil, don't you, Danial?"

Len hobbled away, neither wanting nor expecting a reply.

Chapter 28

Danial noticed Lucy tense as he rounded the corner that led to her flat.

"We could stay at a hotel."

"I've told you, Dan, I'm fine. Sorry, didn't mean to snap. I just need a shower and…"

"A cuppa tea?"

Lucy smiled as they pulled up next to the broken hedge. A lack of sustenance had turned the evergreen a shade of yellow-brown. A pot moved under the steel steps leading to the front door; a bedraggled looking grey cat stretched and meowed pitifully.

"Smokey!" Lucy ran to it; her demeanour changed to one of joyful glee as she scooped the cat up into her arms. "Dan, meet the other man in my life."

Danial's head thumped as he climbed the steps to the front door. Controlling his body to an inward tremble, he led Lucy through the flat. Sighs of relief left them as they embraced. The events leading to them being together, alone, were so implausible that thoughts of any kind hit a steel plate lodged somewhere in his mind.

After feeding Smokey, Lucy pressed the TV remote as Danial filled the kettle, rolling his eyes as there wasn't any milk, but choosing to continue regardless.

"Dan, they're there."

"Who?"

Dan turned and saw the cabin, intact, on the TV. Squeezing Lucy's hand, they flopped back on the sofa; traumatised, yet compelled to watch.

"We're now going over to Trever Haze to explain the unfolding developments at Bird Farm, Devon."

"Yes Moira, through the police cordon, police are starting to cover what is believed to be two fatalities. One male is currently being airlifted to the nearby Royal Hospital; his condition at this point is unknown. There are several motorbikes scattered, in pieces, across the field, leading to a single purpose-built cabin. I managed to speak to an officer, who has informed me that the police are investigating two further instances close to the farm. It's yet to be confirmed whether these are related. There have been reports of an altercation at an otherwise peaceful public house—The Clay Pitt Arms, situated in the village of Church Knighton—where a fight broke out between rival biker gangs. A number of bikes were seen fleeing the area to the nearby village of Burton Tracy, where a restaurant was set alight, and at this time, we are unsure as to the cause of the fire. We are told there have been three fatalities yet to be identified."

"Trever, can you shed light on the sudden loss of power hindering police efforts and the unusual and sudden change in weather conditions reported by residents in the Southwest?"

"Meteorologists from around the globe have described the unusually severe weather conditions as unnatural. Theories range from human-induced global warming and solar flares to a toxic spillage, similar to the one spotted off the coast of Dover. The strange phenomena have baffled scientist and experts from all fields, some suggesting mass hypnosis in the case of objects bursting into flames and the total blindness of what seems to be residents as far down as Cornwall."

"Are there any witnesses or survivors at the Farm? Have any arrests been made?"

"As you can see behind me, a large gathering of uniformed officers and medical teams are present and unable to comment on this. Moira, I believe we have someone waiting to talk to us."

Danial and Lucy watched as James came into view, straightening his tie, looking nothing like the man they'd seen hours before.

"My God, he hasn't gone with Roger. I thought I saw him get into the helicopter," Danial said, biting his nails in anticipation of what he'd tell the waiting reporter.

"No doubt he's in charge of the police, the only one who knows..."

"Yeah, he knows I killed his friend, the other agent. Maybe I should hand myself in; take what's coming."

There was a commercial break, and someone selling insurance appeared on the screen. Lucy flicked through other news channels. None had live news on the event, but all were commenting on the happenings at the farm. She changed the channel back, and they watched endless adverts without talking.

The same newswomen appeared, announcing breaking news. The view turned from her to the same man, who now stood in a different location. His backdrop was a large transit van advertising their channel.

"I have with me Agent James McMilan." Trever held the mic in front of him; the camera highlighting scratches and a bruise under James' left eye. The anorak he'd acquired covered what would have been a torn, dirty suit.

"I can confirm, and was witness to, two separate, unrelated events at Bird Farm. During the pursuit of an escapee and murder suspect from a detention hospital, an agent lost his life. We have informed the family, and our heartfelt condolences are with the family and friends of the deceased. As one of three agents, I confirm the escapee was shot and killed. I can confirm, no other persons were present at the farm during this time. We have eliminated the owner of the farm and guests residing at the farm before the event from our inquiries. Our inquiries will continue, in the hope to establish the separate event relating to what we believe at this time were two rival gangs congregating at the farm shortly after the altercation leading to the death of the murder suspect and acting Agent."

"Can I ask what you are an agent of? Can you explain the strange occurrences…"

Danial and Lucy watched James walk over to the waiting officers, looking up as the helicopter took off with Roger on-board.

"He mentioned guests staying at the cabin."

"He also said they were eliminated from further inquires, Dan. Don't beat yourself up. You saved Len, saved me, who knows what that agent was going to do and whether he was in his own state of mind? James has come through, done what he said he would, and if he were in any doubt, he would have arrested you. He said to put it behind you. It'll take time, but you have to."

"You gonna be all right if I go out for a while? I need to clear my head, and we're out of milk."

"Take your time, babes, and bring back a bottle. I could do with a drink."

"Yeah, me too. Will red do?"

"White. Can't stand red."

"Should know; I feel like we've been together years and should know these things."

"All in good time. See you later."

Moments later, Lucy ran from the bathroom waving a slim white plastic tube. A car door slammed, drawing her to the window. She watched as Danial pulled off before looking down at the colour displayed on the tip of the tube.

* * *

The double iron gates to the graveyard clattered, held closed by a huge padlock next to a sign pointing to the gate alongside. Danial pulled up under a bank of low-hanging trees. He felt the book through the towel wrapped tight around it, like a present waiting to be torn open. Only he knew that this was no present. An omen maybe; a thing possessed.

Guilt rose in his throat as he approached Jim Osborn's graveside. Years had passed. The blue vase once containing flowers was still where he'd placed it next to the headstone bearing Jim's name and dates of birth and death. He hadn't thought how he was going to bury the book after Len said *holy ground*. He knew the only friend he had ever confided in wouldn't mind. Spots of rain fell wide, not reaching him until he saw them hit the slab of marble. Coloured gravel lay atop, no more than two inches deep. Spreading it, he felt cloth before soil.

Jim, I need your help again, mate. Sorry, but I need you to keep this safe, out of harm's way. I promise to visit more, now that it's over. Rain soaked his hair, disguising his tears. *I got the bastard, Jim, like I promised. Met a girl, too. You'd like her; she's a keeper.*

Danial looked around at the formal gravesides; he noticed a tin bucket stuffed with gardening tools. Sitting next to it, a grave in bloom.

Thanks, Jim. Keep this one between us, buddy. Our secret.

Danial dug down six inches under the cloth. Satisfied there'd never be a cause to disturb the grave, he took the book out of its cover and… Wait, no. He wrapped the towel back around it, wiping sweat from his forehead. Like the alcoholic he could have become, he was compelled to open it, spread its pages, and feel it for the last time. He didn't recall removing the towel, nor opening the book as he stared down. Leading from the spine was an outline of a woman, her hair flowing past naked breasts and onto a swollen stomach. Hands clawed their way up from the bottom of the page, fingers pulling a drawing of a book downward. Closing the book with a slap, Danial threw into the hole, covering it with consecrated earth.

The book that had warned Danial of things to come, its pages *healing* Lucy's burns after Len rubbed them over her skin, out of view of the surgeons. The book that Len had asked to be buried in hallowed ground, *away from people*, was now out of sight, if not out of mind.

Danial wanted to pray, to make peace with Jim, but could no longer fight the urge to leave; something deep inside told him that Lucy needed him now more than ever before.